The
Parts
We Share

The
Parts
We Share

A Saga of Family, Humor & Health

written by
Marty Monical

When the fourth-grade teacher of acclaimed author Marty Monical asked her students to write a list of their top five favorite things, he surprised her by including "A blank page" on his list. No surprise he published his first news article at fifteen, his first book at twenty-two, and has been asked to write commercials, screenplays, books, articles, newsletters, marketing pieces and even songs ever since.

Marty honed his craft at the University of Illinois, completed and sold his first screenplay, and co-won the People's Choice award at the Black Earth film festival. He thrived in a corporate marketing career but always maintained one foot in the creative sphere.

When his brother announced he had stage four kidney disease and needed an organ donor, life changed. Marty left his lucrative management job, joined the crusade to bring attention to the growing need for living organ donation, and committed to write pieces that he can powerfully entertain while making a positive impact. _The Parts We Share_ is based on a true story, inspired by the journey of a beloved man's desperate need for medical help.

To see more from this author, please read _Seventeen Little Miricals_, a fun, whimsical autobiographical account of growing up with sixteen siblings (and no, that's not a typo).

Dedication

To my brother Greg for his bravery,

my family for their relentless support, and

living donors everywhere for their sacrifice.

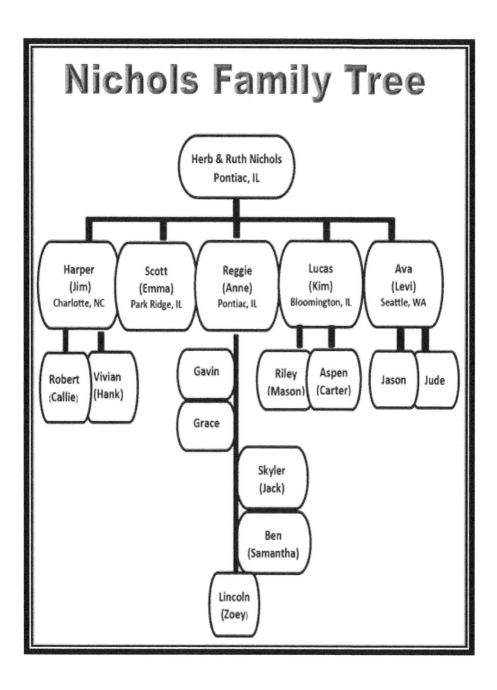

CHAPTER 1

Twisted It

Though it was written in the company handbook not to cut breaks or lunches short, employees knew that when deadlines loomed, it was expected. Several months had gone by since Reggie Nichols had to cheat into his break – score one for his expertise. He checked the clock. If he worked through his entire shift, he should be able to complete the job in time.

Through the years, Reggie had operated the tippers, magna strippers, and flat cutters but the Stima poly bagger was *usually* his favorite. He gripped his wrench in frustration and whacked the dirty metal contraption. The client had expected 20,000 pieces to be mailed *last* night, which is why Reggie was quickly put on the job. Typically the most problem-free machine of all, the poly bagger seemed to notice his angst and chose this long and frustrating day to be temperamental, mocking him with every tweak. Nervous from the pressure of a late deadline, sweat beaded down his face. He had already used half his toolbox today to make adjustments.

Trying to ignore the predictable stabbing pains to his body, he grabbed his largest wrench and yanked hard on a bolt for yet another adjustment. He reached for his Nova rolling walker to wheel himself to the bright green button. He smacked it with his palm. Finally! The machine hummed smoothly and the poly film perfectly covered the business magazines that came whirring down the line.

Reggie used his walker to move around the machine, inspecting the mechanics. The adjustment seemed to hold, leading to a much needed, deep breath. He felt like half his time at Drucker's was spent anticipating what would break next.

He patted his walker as if it were a trustworthy stallion. He admired his walker. The new design had a pouch to store things, brakes, rugged all-terrain wheels, and it doubled as a chair. He spun it around and sat, giving his weary legs a break.

From birth, a condition called vertical talus prevented Reggie's left leg from fully developing, wreaking havoc all the way up through his hips. His left foot looked twisted, sticking out at an angle as if he were about to kick a soccer ball. He walked with a severe limp that appeared as if one foot were always stepping in a hole. Instantly recognized around town by his unusual gait, those around him could sense pain when he moved despite his attempts to conceal it. His childhood sentence was to walk with a severe limp. In his late thirties, he began to use a cane and at forty-eight, he purchased his first walker. Now fifty-six, the walker was mandatory, and moving twenty yards could deliver excruciating pain from his feet all the way up to the middle of his back.

His supervisor waddled up. Co-workers had given Angelo the nickname Jelly Man years ago. If ever a man jiggled when he walked, it was this round and jolly fellow who embraced and embodied his nickname wholeheartedly.

"Hey Reggie, gittin' caught up?"

"Sort of. Don't worry about it. I'll get it done before I leave."

Jelly Man knew there was no room for error -- it was crucial this job got mailed out today. That's why he had put his best employee on it. He waited for a wise crack, something funny or witty from Reggie. Nothing came. He must *really* be stressed about hitting the deadline, he thought, as he nodded and waddled off.

Reggie glanced at that jiggling stomach. His own personal rule was to never poke fun at physical attributes. Given his own handicap, he was sensitive about respecting peoples' appearances and various body types. Now, making fun of their *behaviors* -- that's where he found comedy gold. Jelly Man was the one exception – so confident in his own skin, he encouraged the world to poke fun at his blubbery belly.

Reggie thought he should inspect the machine again but felt too tired to move. After twenty-six years, he knew the equipment better than his managers, heck, even the techs. This was physical, hard labor, even for an able-bodied person. He found the job more taxing each month, but where else could he go? In the quiet town of Pontiac, he had so few job opportunities. He probably should have trained for an office job long ago but now he felt it was too late.

As he scanned the twenty-eight machines in the plant he had to admit that he enjoyed working here. He made it fun, leaving notes on his timecard for the office staff to find and doling out treats for the secretaries. He couldn't afford to give constant cards, gifts or flowers, so he drew cartoons instead and sneaked them to the ladies who had anniversaries, birthdays, and kid's weddings. Reggie had never once been called popular to his face but he felt respected for his honest work and *attempts* to be charming.

With his toolbox ready, he turned his attention back to the machine, anticipating more problems and making expert tweaks as the job progressed. He worked straight through his break and as promised, completed the job five minutes before his shift ended. As Reggie wheeled off the plant floor, Jelly Man gave him a big thumbs up. He was forever amazed at Reggie's efficiency with the clunky old contraption.

Reggie slid his timecard into the slot. As it produced the familiar, loud "ka-chunk" noise, he closed his eyes and thought to himself, *I am lucky to have a job,* a ritual he had performed since his first day at Drucker's. After each shift, he also rated his own pain on a scale of 1 to 100. Today he put it around 76. At least he had a few hours to rest before the big gathering tonight.

He was excited to celebrate with his family. Gavin, his stepson, had signed to buy his first house. Three years ago Reggie had worked closely with Gavin to create a plan to help him manage finances. He was so proud of Gavin for finally saving enough for a down payment.

Reggie, a softie, relished every moment he could get with his wife and "five children."

He wheeled through the foyer to the employee entrance. A popular second-shift co-worker, Willow, sat on a bench attempting to adjust a knee brace. He had heard rumors her husband was diagnosed with some type of cancer, that they had lost their house and were raising twin boys in a trailer. Grumbling in pain, she yanked on the Velcro straps causing a loud *rriiiipp* that echoed through the foyer.

Reggie reached the door but stopped and glanced back at her. She stood up, holding onto the wall, testing her ability to walk. She squirmed in pain, sat back down and fumbled further with the knee brace. Reggie looked at the door in front of him. He was tired. He hurt. Rest and a wonderful night with family awaited. He turned and walked back to the bench.

"Hey, Willow. Tonya Harding pay you a visit?"

She grunted, a short break from her exasperation.

"It doesn't help at all! Stupid brace – it's useless!" Reggie saw the knee brace packaging on the bench. She had obviously just purchased it.

She ripped the brace off her knee and shoved it in her backpack. She tried to hide her anguish.

"You're not thinking of trying to pull a shift like *that*, are you? What happened?"

"Stupid laundromat on Main... Everyone carries a big ol' pile of laundry leaving that place. Who puts a big step right out the front door!? I twisted it."

She tried to stand again and winced in agony, forcing her back down.

"Happened an hour ago. No time to find a sub – ain't nobody answer their damn phone no more! They'll fire me Reggie. I already got checks against me."

"You can't work if you can't even stand up. Let me take your shift."

She looked at his walker, then at him. He looked tired. She was astonished he would offer after just clocking out.

4

"No. I can't let you. Besides..."

She let two employees pass and reach the door so they wouldn't hear. Then she looked at the floor, embarrassed.

She whispered. "I need the hours. Tony... he done got sick."

The rumors must be true. He sat on his walker directly in front of her.

"Here's what we're gonna do. I'm your sub. Go home and alternate ice and heat on your knee. If you text me your address, my wife Anne will come over tomorrow and wrap it for you. She used to be a nurse."

She looked at him with pure gratitude, but he could sense it didn't solve all her problems. He continued.

"Now this next piece is all part of the deal. Non-negotiable. You might not like it, but here it is. When my paycheck comes in, I give you the money for this shift. Pay me back if you can. If not, no big deal."

Purposely giving her no time to respond, he stood and headed back towards the time clock.

She yelled, "Reggie! That ain't right!"

Reggie turned. She tried to stand yet again but winced and fell to the bench.

"What would be right? Let you work on one leg? You're in pain."

She shrugged and pointed at his legs as if he were missing the obvious.

"But Reggie... you're always in pain."

He took a deep breath. It was hard for him to admit it.

"Yes – but I've had fifty years to get used to it."

Without looking back, he dragged himself to the timeclock.

He texted his wife: "Sorry -- will miss party. Picking up a shift. Love you."

He wondered if he could even handle a double shift. For years, his body had given him signs – little hints that something wasn't... well... that something was a bit off.

He slid his timecard into the slot and closed his eyes.

"Ka-chunk."

CHAPTER 2

Step, Step, Hold

Exhausted from the double shift and a short night's sleep, Reggie held the coffee mug up to his nose and breathed in the deep aroma of roasted vanilla coffee beans. Holding the mug in his right hand, he leaned on his walker and inched off the sidewalk just outside his back door. When his wheels hit the wet grass, the walker lurched forward. His body tilted and his left arm flailed. He tried to stop the walker with his wrist, but that just pushed it further away. Off balance, he fell hard to the earth, the hot coffee searing his arm. He lay on his side in the dewy grass clutching the mug, feeling ridiculous. He breathed in the chilly, fresh May air and prepared for the pain ahead.

"Idiot!" He chided himself aloud, though no one could hear. *So much for "all terrain" wheels!* He had used the walker countless times from his back door to the picnic table to enjoy his morning coffee; this visit to the dirt was a first.

He pulled himself up, managing to keep a couple ounces of coffee in the mug while he completed the trek. Sitting at the weathered picnic table and holding what was left of the coffee for warmth, he winced and inspected his arm. Only slightly red from the coffee spray. He decided he was alright and would not let the fall ruin his day.

To distract himself from the pain, he focused on his glorious hibiscus plant. Too painful for him to do yardwork these days, he asked a friend each year to plant one in that corner of his yard. With its braided trunk, emerald leaves, and brilliant red, tropical flowers, it looked like a special valentine against the neighbor's white fence. It had no business even growing in Illinois. The blooms made Reggie feel like he was vacationing in paradise, easing the disappointment that he couldn't afford those trips.

He twisted his shoulders and felt the effects of working a double shift. Aging sucked. Lately, he would get *winded* just walking across the house, his skin itched more than ever, and his pain was ever present. He needed to use the bathroom three times a night but fought it because it was painful to get there. He knew there must be something *else* wrong with his body. At least twice a week he asked himself just how much time he had left, and sometimes didn't care if the answer was, "probably not much."

He took the last sip, knowing that meant it was time to get back in the house to eat breakfast with Anne. He braced himself for the piercing stabs that had become part of his lifestyle. He stood, using his arms to lift much of his weight, when his cell phone rang. He didn't recognize the number, probably a telemarketer, but it would delay the pain of crossing the yard.

"Hello, this is Reggie."

"Reggie Nichols! Hi! This is David Carvell – from Central Elementary."

Reggie didn't believe the caller at first. No way would Mr. Carvell, his eighth-grade teacher, be calling. They hadn't spoken since he graduated from Central over forty years ago.

"Mr. Carvell? Great to hear from you. How've you been? Did I forget to turn in a paper?"

"Ha! Right? My goodness, you sound exactly the same! I'm doing well, thanks. Retired, now living in Iowa. I'm calling to see if you'd help me plan a get-together. You probably don't remember this but your class at Central was my first year teaching. I gotta say, it was also my favorite class. I was hoping to plan a reunion of sorts, even if it's just meeting for coffee with as many students as can make it. Would you be up for helping me organize this?"

A chance to connect with old friends? With one of his favorite all-time teachers? What a thrill. He was tight with his family but felt short on time for friends. Too much of his social experience, like everyone else's, was pushing buttons on a phone.

"Absolutely. I am so glad you reached out. Have you called anyone else?"

"Not yet. *You* were my favorite student."

"How could that be? I got all B's and C's."

"Who cares about *that?* You were my definite favorite. I found you on Facebook but thought I'd call before I sent a friend request. Can we connect and get to work on this?"

This was wild. Reggie had flipped through the yearbook a few years back, the last time he had even thought of David Carvell, and remembered rumors that his wife Minnie died from a widowmaker heart attack in her early fifties. This had prompted Reggie to research widowmakers: a ninety percent mortality rate if the patient goes into shock -- the most severe of all cardiac issues. It terrified Reggie so much that it became one of those irrational fears for him. Thinking of Anne, just the word "widow" now gave him chills.

Reggie replied, "You bet. Let's make it happen."

He hung up. Some fleeting thoughts of eighth grade flashed in Reggie's mind: getting elected the basketball team's manager, singing a *Yankee Doodle Dandy* solo at the annual Silver Tea concert, and getting in trouble for forgetting, before a rainy weekend, to take down the U.S. flag that flew in front of the school.

With his mood softer, the pain was slightly more tolerable. He stood to go in the house and focused on the dingy gravel in front of him. Only a month ago, they had taken down the children's swing set and playground. Almost a hundred youngsters giggled and played here over the years, learning, laughing, screaming with delight and whimsy. Anne stopped running a home daycare four years ago and they finally had the rotting wood removed. Reggie was surprised he had outlived the swing set, sometimes feeling he was rotting alongside it – a thought he never shared with family.

He rolled to the house with his walker and pushed it aside. He opened the door and clutched the railing to help drag himself up the four steps to the first floor. Anne kissed him before delivering bad news.

"Lincoln's manager is sending him home – not enough work. I'll go get him. Breakfast is ready."

She grabbed car keys off the peg on the wall.

Reggie offered, "I can get him. You drove him out there."

"You need to rest. After breakfast, I'll run to Willow's and wrap up her knee. Sound good?"

She kissed him again and was gone.

Crap. This was the third time this month their eighteen-year-old son had to be driven home from work early. A respectful boy, teachers and friends often complimented Reggie on Lincoln's personality -- but he had already been in three minor car accidents. Anne concluded he was easily distracted, his driving too hazardous, and she insisted they drive him to and from work.

Reggie felt he had failed Lincoln, and not just as the father who taught him to drive. His last year of high school, Lincoln fizzled out, barely graduating after losing focus -- typical senioritis. Repeating the path his Dad had taken, Lincoln was choosing to spend most his time with a girlfriend instead of on schoolwork and planning for his future.

Reggie never knew whether to be hard or lenient on Lincoln who had inherited the same vertical talus that Reggie suffered from – but in *both* feet. Lincoln had already endured numerous surgeries. He even used the same style rolling walker as his Dad. When they walked down the street together using their walkers, traffic often slowed as if the drivers were mesmerized by a roadside car accident.

Reggie used the counters to hold himself up as he moved through the small kitchen. The aroma itself helped lift him. Blueberry pancakes, maple syrup, twice baked hash browns, fried bacon and fresh orange juice. A self-taught gourmet cook, Anne used double the ingredients you might expect in any dish, creatively blending unexpected flavors from the food palate. Recipes handed down for generations combined with a relentless pursuit of all things she'd ever tasted, and loved, had turned her into the town Top Chef. Reggie took one bite of bacon which he knew had been sizzled up with five types of sugars and spices. Though he'd tasted it dozens of times, he still closed his eyes to fully enjoy the smokey nirvana.

With just a few bites left, Reggie heard the mailman shove today's offering into the slot. He grabbed it off the front porch and moved back to the kitchen, tossing several ads for products they could never afford into the recycle bin. He opened the credit card statement.

How can this be? Did we really eat at Logan's Roadhouse twice this month?

This can't be right. 149 dollars? We never... oh, right, that was to fix the dishwasher.

$6.99? Honestly? Is that for one iced latte?

Reggie tossed the bills into the "to do" pile and eyed their old harvest gold refrigerator. It would need to be replaced any day now – a miracle it still worked. Another thousand bucks they didn't have. They called it their "honeymoon fridge" because they purchased the used appliance the day after they got married in lieu of a real honeymoon trip. Reggie sometimes superstitiously worried the day the refrigerator died, something in the marriage would die with it.

Feeling tired again, he stretched. He wished his few sips of coffee would have given him more of a boost. It was rarely a "yawning" kind of tired that attacked him, just an overall fatigue that made him want to sit on a couch rather than do... anything. He wished he could be more helpful with chores. Last month during a spat, Anne screamed, "I have to do everything around this house!" Reggie made a deal with her. "I'll do one small task at a time."

Reggie felt blessed. Fights like this with Anne were rare. That was the beauty of both of them coming from failed marriages – a strong appreciation for each other and softer communication. Deep down, he knew they loved each other very much.

Determined to get "one small task" done, he remembered the humidifier in the bedroom needed water. He would fill that. He stacked his dirty dishes as best he could. With much effort, he moved to the stairs, looming like a mountain before him. Family pictures lined the stairwell. He grabbed the railing. Following a pattern he had worked out the last few years, he started up the stairs.

Deep breath, step, step hold. Only two stairs, but it felt harder than normal. He paused, focusing on photos of Anne and Lincoln, really looking at them for the first time in months. What a sweet kid. What a love story. What a history. OK, he was ready for the next round.

Deep breath, step, step hold. He paused again and looked intently at a photo of strong and rebellious Ben, now 24, a son from his first marriage that he later learned was *not* his biological son. And then a photo of sweet Skylar, now 26, Ben's half-sister. He noted much complexity in their smiles.

Deep breath, step, step hold. More photos – Grace and Gavin, 28 and 26, Anne's children from her previous marriage. Beautiful. How hard he had worked to try to be a father figure to all five of these children. How he anguished over them when things didn't go their way or when he missed a chance, like last night, to celebrate with them. Though he could never give them fancy clothes, vacations, that magical gift-filled Christmas, or *any* material advantages, he had tried his best. And now? With his energy zapped and his body fading? How could he continue to be a father? What could he possibly give or do for them as they worked through their early adult years? He felt flush and overwhelmed. *Was it the climb?* A hearty breakfast usually made this easier.

Only two more stairs to reach the landing. He paused again, longer than before. And finally, step... step... hold. He had made it to the landing, though it wiped him out. His chest was heavy, his legs wobbly. He glanced out the window at the view of the sky and the old walnut tree. The light coming in seemed to grow, getting brighter, more intense. Suddenly, no sky, no tree, just white light flooding in and encompassing him.

A wave of fatigue clouded his eyes and plugged his ears. He felt dizzy, falling, grasping for the railing, a lifeline, anything, just as his back, shoulders and head pounded into the stairs.

And then – blackness.

CHAPTER 3

Chugga Chugga Chant

Anne drove the Buick Enclave through the aging neighborhoods to pick up Lincoln. She had passed these older, small ranch homes so many times they were a blur. *The Johnsons re-did their porch? The Smith's put in a new driveway?* She would never notice. She felt hypocritical sometimes, constantly wishing her own home had the "wow" factor. What if Reggie could be the type of husband to build a picket fence? Or create a dazzling array of tulips or daylilies in the front yard? What if he could fix the crumbling front porch? She no longer noticed anyone else's home – would anyone even notice if Reggie provided her a dreamy landscape?

She pulled up to Kemp's and saw Lincoln already coming out the door. Like every vehicle they had ever owned, the Enclave had over eighty-thousand miles on it, but the muffler was never quite right. The vehicle sputtered along to its own special cadence that was easy to recognize from a block away. Lincoln had critically dubbed it the *Chugga-Chugga Chant* and often made fun of it, but there were times it was convenient. He had heard the labored tune twenty seconds ago, alerting him that his Mom was arriving.

Anne purposefully stopped several parking spaces away from the front door so she could watch her son's walk to the SUV. She hit the button to open the lift gate and closely observed Lincoln in the rearview mirror. As he moved to the SUV, he leaned on his walker like Reggie did, and now more than usual. His right leg dragged rather than stepped. She could tell he was in pain, but she had to see for herself because he certainly wouldn't say a word about it. He struggled to fold his rolling walker and hoist it into the back. She used to help him but she was trying to let him do things for himself.

Lincoln climbed into the passenger seat. She noticed he had one shoestring untied, a small spot on his shirt where he may have spilled a drink, and his hair needed combing. Being a mother was tiring, no question. Being Anne Nichols, with two grown children from a former marriage, a mother with Alzheimer's in a nursing home, and a son and husband with mobility issues was a twenty-four-hour siege of worry, compassion, tension, and love.

"Hey, what happened?"

Lincoln was annoyed. Though arguably the most polite and grateful kid his age in the country, he was just eighteen. Questions from his mother still felt like an attack.

"One of our credit card clients merged with a new bank, so we lost the account."

Anne had babysat the Kemp's two boys years ago. From her talks with Mrs. Kemp, she knew the credit card clients were their big accounts. They required a lot of data entry, what Lincoln was hired to do.

"That's a drag. Do you know when they'll need you back?"

"They said they'd call me."

More money issues. Anne gritted her teeth and thought of Lincoln's career to date. Terrible timing with employers. Soon after Farm & Yard hired him, a new feisty manager came through trying to make a name for herself. With his walker, he wasn't fast enough and was fired for "talking too much" even though his co-workers supported him. He landed an office job at Westminster Retirement, but they closed two months later. Finally, he landed a non-physical job with some benefits at Kemp's, but consistent work now looked sketchy at best. She drove off towards home.

"We need to talk about setting your next appointment."

Lincoln took a long breath and stared out his passenger window. Six surgeries already. His feet. His legs. His hips. Breaking bones so they would heal differently. Metal pins and plates. Casts. Medicines. Infections – one that forced a twenty-five-day stay at the hospital. Missing school. Missing friends. On spring break, they vacationed while he travelled to Chicago for check-ups. On this next appointment, doctors would remove the latest metal plate in his hip. The surgeon seemed ecstatic explaining to Lincoln he would use titanium plates this time instead of the stainless-steel used in the past. Lincoln didn't care, but the doctor acted like he was offering Lincoln strawberry ice cream after years of vanilla.

"Well, doubt I'll be working, so... anytime is fine. Can Zoey come with us?"

Lincoln looked at his Mom for her reaction to his bold request to bring his girlfriend.

"It's an overnight stay, Lincoln. We'd have to get a second hotel room."

"Why can't she stay with you and Dad? I looked it up. A lot of hotels have a rollaway cart at no charge, or you could just get two queen beds." He studied her, hopeful. He wasn't prepared for...

"No! No! Noooo!!!!" Anne slammed on the brakes. A plump squirrel had darted in front of the black pick-up truck ahead of them. Despite wearing his seat belt, Lincoln flew forward, catching himself on the dash. The truck drove on without even braking as the Enclave came to a halt. Luckily, there were no cars behind them.

The red splotch on the pavement horrified Anne. She closed her eyes but could still see it and tears welled up. Pain or death, in any form, made her weak. She had seen so much of it during her twelve-year career as a nurse. She transferred from the birthing unit when a young Hispanic lady lost her first born, left pediatrics after an infection killed a five-year-old deaf girl and quit the cardiac ward after just one week. She had cried herself to sleep worrying about her patients, especially in the years she worked second shift. She had learned to *hate* hospitals. Anne had the perfect, warm heart to be a nurse, but it took a dozen years for her to admit she did not have the emotional stomach for it.

Lucky for her, Reggie and Lincoln had "consoling her" down to a science. Lincoln put his hand on her arm to comfort her. He knew there would be no more words exchanged until Mom could overcome this unsettling moment. Usually, it took a half hour. Thank God they were only ten minutes from home.

Anne wiped her eyes and avoided looking at the squirrel or at Lincoln. She pulled away slowly, embarrassed that this weakness was so evident. She was trying so hard to be a rock, a role model, a vision of strength and grit for her son, yet one dead squirrel reduced her to a bawling idiot. At least it was a good excuse to avoid talking about Zoey. There was no compelling reason *not* to bring her for the removal of the titanium, but she didn't want her there. She wasn't ready to share Lincoln with the world because... because he wasn't ready. Even as she said this to herself, she knew it was a classic case of dear old Mom refusing to let go. *She* was not ready.

They pulled into the driveway and the familiar Chugga-Chugga Chant reverberated through the backyard and then through the garage. It was so loud it woke Reggie inside the house, lying at the base of the stairs. He lifted his head and looked around, confused. His back ached terribly, his legs were numb, and he was bleeding from his left temple. *Had he fallen down the stairs?* Nothing like this had ever happened before. He dragged himself up and held onto the railing, wondering how he might explain this to Anne.

Lincoln and Anne came in quietly. Anne went straight to the kitchen, cleaned up Reggie's dishes and served herself pancakes and bacon. Lincoln found his Dad by the stairs. They shared a silent look. Each raised a single finger to their lips, agreeing to keep quiet. Lincoln would not say a word about the blood on his temple.

"It was a squirrel," Lincoln explained. "Mom's calming down." Reggie understood. What a huge relief. Reggie could make it up the stairs and avoid having to explain anything to Anne, except maybe a bandage on his temple. Had she come home and found him on the

16

floor, questions, worry, and probably panic would have let loose. Number one on his priority list was to make sure Anne didn't have anything *more* to worry about. He genuinely felt it made him a thoughtful husband.

Reggie repeated his "step, step, hold" pattern and made it up to the bedroom. His plan was to wash up in the master bathroom, but it suddenly dawned on him... he had fallen *twice* this morning. He changed plans and sat on the bed, reached into his nightstand, and found the Drucker's *Health Benefits* packet. He was grateful to have any insurance at all, but it was well-known their health plan sucked. Reggie chose to pay the smallest premium he could, making his deductible outrageous. And the co-pays? Eighty dollars just to talk to a doctor? What a rip-off! He had avoided all things medical for himself for years because he needed that money for so many other things.

He called the number, expecting to leave a message on a Saturday, but a service picked up.

"Drucker's Medical Employee Line, how can I help you?"

"Hi, this is Reggie Nichols. Employee number 101562. I'd like to schedule a general physical."

Reggie felt a tickle on his cheek. He twisted his shoulders to glance at the mirror and noticed his bleeding temple was much worse than he thought. A strong trail of blood ran down the entire left side of his face. He winced as he reached for a tissue to mop up the blood.

"Just a moment, Mr. Nichols. Let me pull up your file... I see you're with Dr. Basson. And your last appointment was... oh my, is this right? Has it been six years?"

Reggie glared at the mirror, lifted his shirt, and saw a massive purple bruise on his side. He twisted further to see his back – two more bruises, larger than the first. He looked beaten. He felt beaten.

And with a wave of guilt, as if admitting to a kindergarten teacher that he had cheated on a test, he came clean:

"Yes... it's been six years."

CHAPTER 4

Harry

Reggie still ached mightily from his tumble down the stairs and worried he was too bruised to make it through the workday. Sweat dripped down the side of his face, the oversized bandage on his temple making matters worse. His doctor appointment at 4pm, right after his shift, kept gnawing at him and the poly bagger seemed to have it in for him for the second time this month. It gave him fits, as if daring him to schedule anything immediately after work ever again.

Jelly Man appeared with a big grin on his face. Productivity in the plant was up slightly and the hiring freeze was over.

"Morning Reggie. I have a new trainee. He's with HR now, payroll next, then security. I'm going to have you train him on the floor this afternoon. I'll introduce you at lunch."

Reggie had trained several poly baggers over his career and secretly enjoyed it. On several occasions, he had asked for bonus money or vacation days, *any* perks for being a trainer, but three different ownership groups had turned him down. At this moment only one other worker on all three shifts could run the machine efficiently. Job security. At least he could tell they trusted him and hopefully found him valuable.

"Sure. See you at lunch."

Trying to make Reggie laugh, Jelly Man raised his fist and cheered, "Lean on the green!" – referring to the numerous green "Start" buttons on the machinery. Nothing. He eyed Reggie, concerned again about his stoic demeanor. Anyone paying attention would sense Reggie had something weighing on him.

After a painful hour, Reggie headed to lunch, passing a handful of employees waiting in line for the quarterly blood drive. In high school, he was thrilled to donate when he turned sixteen. It gave him a real sense of anonymous giving and was something altruistic his body could handle. But a few years ago, the Red Cross booted him out three times in a row, alerting him that his blood pressure was too high to donate. After that, he stopped trying.

He was gobbling a ham and cheese sandwich and Pringles, still edgy about his doctor appointment, when Jelly Man and the trainee entered the lunchroom. The trainee, late twenties Reggie thought, was unlike any man he had ever seen. He had to be a few inches over six feet with cheeks puffed out and rounded to his overly pinkish nose. His two front teeth stuck out squarely from the rest of his mouth. He looked like a rabbit.

Reggie grinned. Growing up, Reggie's Dad had purchased a Beta VCR, just before the world decided VHS would be the industry standard. His Dad had recorded four Beta tapes with "quality" programming, and it was all he allowed the family to watch. The movie *Harvey* was on tape #3. They watched it so many times the family had it practically memorized. For the first time in his life, Reggie had a solid image of what Harvey, the imaginary six-foot rabbit, might look like in real life. He felt ashamed of it, but he giggled at the sight of this man's face.

"Reggie, I'd like you to meet our newest member of the team. This is Harry Schott."

Harry? All Reggie heard was "Hare-ee." So close to "Harvey." And "Schott?" It sounded like "Shoot." His mind flooded with images of Elmer Fudd singing, *Shoot the wa-a-a-bit! Shoot the wa-a-a-bit!* Reggie stifled a powerful urge to laugh, wondering what was *wrong* with himself today. *Get it together!* he thought. He stood politely to shake Harry's hand.

"Nice to meet you, welcome aboard."

"I hear you're the best. I'm so happy you'll be training me."

"I'll leave you to it." Jelly Man smiled, nodded, and jiggled out of the lunchroom.

Reggie sat back down and tried to compose himself. The rabbit-face seemed to twitch slightly so he avoided looking at it. Sitting opposite him, Harry unpacked his sack lunch.

"Sorry if I complain about my lunch. My wife and I are now *vegetarian.*"

Reggie snorted with laughter. *All rabbits are vegetarian!* He still avoided eye contact. He watched Harry pull out a can of Coke and a large Tupperware container. Reggie's eyes teared up thinking what it contained. He thought to himself, *No... don't do it... don't let it be, please don't let it be.*

Harry opened it and there it was. Next to a macaroni dish sat a huge pile - of sliced *carrots.* Reggie burst out laughing.

"What's so funny?" Harry asked.

Reggie glanced around the room, finding a poster of a cartoon octopus with eight hands and gangly, oily fingers. It read: "Please wash hands after operating equipment!" He pointed it out to Harry.

"I never noticed that before."

Harry turned to look at it and shrugged. Obviously not worth a laugh. Then Harry got serious.

"Reggie, is it OK if we talk about... that."

He pointed at Reggie's walker. Reggie nodded.

"I want to say how impressed I am that you're working a physical job like this. And that you don't use your limitations as an excuse not to work. How people talk about you around here - it's inspiring. I hope it's OK to say that."

Reggie looked him in the eyes and the rabbit face was no longer evident. Very few people had the guts to go right to the "handicap conversation," and even fewer could do it politely. This man was genuine, with a real heart. Reggie could tell he would enjoy working with him.

"Thanks for that. Most people are afraid to bring it up. But Harry, please try your best to treat me like you'd treat anyone else."

And that turned the day around. Harry proved to be an intent listener, a dedicated worker, and picked up the machine's quirks quickly. With Harry's help, Reggie finished the job early and found himself driving out of the pot-holed parking lot with plenty of time to get to Dr. Basson's office.

While driving, Reggie usually enjoyed Chicago talk radio – WGN, WLS, or WBBM. He was a button pusher and knew he drove Anne batty when they travelled together as he searched for the topic that most interested him. But, on edge, he turned the radio off. He wasn't even sure why. Did he feel like he didn't deserve entertainment? Or perhaps, he needed to focus on what might happen next?

Given how he felt every day, he had no excuse for waiting six years, except being stubborn and overly cautious with every penny. He had the highest respect for Dr. Basson. Six years ago, spring temperatures had gone from twenty-five to seventy-five degrees in two days, and the blooms exploded overnight, causing allergy issues. Reggie took Claritin – the wrong choice. It caused his stuffy nose and ears to dry up, clog his sinuses, and resulted in infection, fever, and four days of misery. Dr. Basson gave him a prescription for pseudoephedrine, a strong decongestant, but added, "I'm not sure if this will work for you. Try this, and if you don't see improvement in four days, call us and we'll devise another treatment plan."

Who does that?! The medication worked, but Reggie never forgot the first time a doctor spoke to him, not in a condescending, all-knowing manner, but as if they were teammates trying to solve his medical issues together. Because Reggie was about to turn fifty at the time, Dr. Basson also recommended a colonoscopy. Reggie conveniently forgot to schedule one.

The last thing Dr. Basson told Reggie: "You know what's really going on with your body better than I do. Listen to it carefully." He was right. Reggie listened. He had heard the messages for years. But he had chosen to disregard them.

Once at the office, Reggie checked in, updated his medical profile, and waited. Doctor offices always looked the same to him -- the exact mix of sick people, healthy people getting labs, and hypochondriacs needing to hear they were healthy. They called his name and a plucky nurse named Sandra got the ball rolling. Weight. Height. Blood pressure. A dozen questions. He was led to the lab area where they drew blood, then moved him to the back-hallway bathroom for a urine sample. Finally, back to the waiting area.

He sat for a long time, growing more nervous by the minute. When the waiting room was nearly empty, Sandra finally announced his name and led him back to the examination rooms.

Dr. Basson was ready. Reggie thought "NFL Linebacker" when they had first met. Thick. Solid. Like he could walk right through the wall if he wanted. He had some ethnic mix to him, but Reggie always felt rude asking for someone's cultural or racial background. Reggie's chart was pulled up and a dozen file folders sat ominously near the computer. Sandra moved Reggie's walker to the corner and helped him walk to the observation bench. She immediately left without even looking at him or Dr. Basson. *That can't be a good sign.*

Dr. Basson was all business. He checked eyes, ears, lungs. He tested reflexes and muscles. He did the "bend over and cough" to check his prostate. He was dialed in as if trying to find the source of a major problem. After a thorough exam, the doctor spoke more sternly than Reggie remembered.

"Do we need to talk about that?"

He pointed at the bandage on Reggie's temple, which Reggie had completely forgotten about. He shook his head, and suddenly remembered his bruises. Dr. Basson had listened to his breathing through the shirt, but never did ask him to remove it.

"Reggie, why did you schedule a physical for today?"

"Well, I figured it'd been a while since I've seen a doctor."

Dr. Basson knew better. Patients withheld information - it was all part of the gig.

"Could it be because you've been very fatigued lately? Are you going to the bathroom several times a night? Are you often itchy?"

Busted. *Dr. Basson is smarter than I am.* Reggie nodded.

"Reggie, I have one thing to yell at you for and some news to share with you. First, let's pretend a mad terrorist has placed bombs in houses all over Pontiac. So, Pontiac has, what, ten thousand residents, the U.S. averages 2.2 persons per household, so let's say there are forty-five hundred homes in town."

Reggie was highly impressed with people that could do math quickly in their heads. He could *do* the math but needed time to think it through – sometimes pen and paper. He would often get flustered figuring the proper tip to leave at a restaurant.

"Now, let's say the police tell us that four percent of homes in town have a bomb, so two hundred homes contain a deadly explosive. And the bombs are not hidden behind walls or anything, they are easy to spot. Don't you think you'd check your house to see if it was safe?"

"I would. Definitely." Reggie was confused, not sure where this was going.

"Well, four percent of people your age have a ticking time bomb inside their colon. We won't know if you're one of them unless we look. Colon cancer is our third-largest cancer killer, but a colonoscopy will tell us if you have a bomb inside you. We call them polyps. If we find any, we'll eliminate them. Can I count on you to schedule one?"

Reggie felt foolish. Of course, he'd heard stories, mostly funny or embarrassing, about colonoscopies, but he'd blown it off for six years already. It was time to be a grown up.

"Yes. I'll schedule one."

Dr. Basson handed Reggie a referral on a slip of paper.

"Next, your blood pressure is much higher than it was on your last visit. I don't think diuretics are safe in this case so I'm writing you a prescription for Zestril, an ACE inhibitor. This will dilate the blood vessels which should help reduce blood pressure. Let's try this for a month. After that, I want you to check your blood pressure three times in one week at one of the local drugstores. Call my nurse to let her know the readings. Sound good?"

Reggie nodded and took a second piece of paper from Dr. Basson. *Why did I wait six years? This wasn't so bad.*

"Now for the last, and most important part of our discussion. I'm concerned. You have elevated levels of protein in your urine and your creatinine levels are high. These are signs of failing kidneys which may be the cause of your fatigue and itchiness. I'm recommending you see a nephrologist for more testing as soon as possible. Any questions on that?"

He handed Reggie a third slip of paper. *A nephrologist?* Reggie didn't know what that was, but it sounded like "*specialist,*" which sounded pricey.

"Is that serious?"

"Yes. It's important you make this appointment and be sure to follow up with us."

Dr. Basson waited but Reggie had no more questions. Over the years, this trait infuriated Anne. Reggie would return from a doctor appointment, she'd ask him a dozen questions, but Reggie wouldn't have any answers. She started going with him whenever possible, which was just one more reason it had been six years between visits. Anne was unaware Reggie was seeing his doctor today.

Dr. Basson left the room. Reggie let it all sink in. How much would bad kidneys cost him? He had a little retirement savings through work but he didn't want to blow it all on high deductibles. He already struggled mightily just moving around. Would this add to his suffering? Was it really *urgent?*

Reggie made his way to his walker and headed toward the exit, his back and leg pain intensifying with each step. The reception and waiting rooms were empty, adding to the overpowering feeling of aloneness that swept over him. He was surprised the front door was still unlocked.

As he walked to his handicapped parking spot, he noticed a tall garbage can a couple yards from his Enclave. He looked at his slips of paper. In six years, he'd done just fine on his own, and he didn't like making doctors *rich*. Perhaps the nefro... the nephra... the *whatever specialist* could wait, and he could just focus on the colonoscopy. After all, we can't have a bomb going off in the house. He had promised Dr. Basson he'd make *that* appointment

He crumpled up the nephrologist note but held the wad of paper in his hand for several seconds, contemplating what this meant: Lying to Anne and his family, gambling on his health, and walking around with a massive question mark on his back. *Would anyone miss him if he were to check out anyway? Would it take anyone much time to get over his funeral?* He pictured himself falling down the stairs again.

Well... if he didn't say anything, Anne wouldn't have to worry about it.

And with a guilty, tortured mindset, he tossed the crumpled referral into the garbage.

CHAPTER 5

Snapping Turtle

Lucas parked his company Ford Escape in the empty parking lot next to his Springfield office at exactly at 7:01am. He reviewed his crazy routine: the alarm buzzes at 4:30am, he and his wife Kim run five miles, then he hops in the shower. He dresses, then mindlessly consumes a healthy breakfast on the hour-long drive from Bloomington.

He yawned. Not ready to rush into his office, he took in the amazing scenery. Of all the MediaCast offices, his was certainly one of the most dilapidated and in desperate need of a remodel, but it had a spectacular view. The developer built two retention ponds in the center of the complex. Because the office stood a couple miles from the edge of Springfield, the gorgeous vista seemed to invite every deer, fox, coyote, rabbit, and hard-to-find bird within miles. His team had watched egrets, herons, robins, ducks, cranes, and geese swoop in and navigate their way around the oasis. Last year, two bald eagles nested there for a week.

Lucas spotted a family of goslings in the water, then two beautiful, familiar swans passing in front of the office door. He decided to wait for them to move out of his way. These massive birds commanded the place, aggressively intimidating animals and people. When they meandered into the parking lot, the ad team avoided the intruders as if they were rabid dogs. The team even named them after their least favorite clients.

He thought about the challenge of managing two offices. Such a drain. He was finally used to the long drive twice a week. The radio, bouncing between classic rock and the morning news made the drive bearable. The worst part of his commute was seeing an increasing number of drivers on cell phones drifting over the lines on the highway. It infuriated him terribly, especially in the construction zones.

The swans had waddled to the pond. Lucas checked himself in the rearview mirror to straighten his tie. The small wrinkles around his eyes always seemed bigger in the morning and the patch of gray hair above the ears was more pronounced. He grabbed his laptop and a sack of granola bars for the week, unlocked the office back door, and turned off the security alarm.

He scanned the messy break room and put his hand on the Keurig machine.

"I bet... one thousand dollars there's a K-cup in here."

He opened the lid. Sure enough, a used, Almond Roast K-Cup greeted him and he threw it in the garbage. His messy team members here were apparently raised by monkeys. He wished the company would pay for a cleaning crew to come more than once a week. He filled his thermos with fresh filtered water and went to his first-floor corner office.

As his laptop fired up, he glared at the ugly, flowery wallpaper that some dentist put up over twenty years ago before MediaCast leased the space. There were rumors circulating that his office would *finally* get upgraded. Things were good. No... they were *really* good.

He'd never felt overwhelmed by *goodness* before, but it made him pause. His oldest daughter Riley, a structural engineer, thrived in her job. Her outdoor wedding in Michigan had been spectacular and enormously festive – a perfect 72 degrees in July, how lucky. Aspen, his youngest, who had graduated from Wisconsin in only three years, was passing those tough actuarial exams fast and furiously. Her wedding date would be announced soon. His wife Kim's career in corporate finance, his own career in sales management, all good. His charity work for the St. Jude golf outing raised more money than in any prior year. His marriage was *exceptionally* good.

Like speed bumps, a sudden realization made him jolt to attention. *Surely, this can't last. All good things come to an end. The other shoe is about to drop. The law of averages will swing the other way. Right?*

His "crisis rule," a concept he reasoned out years ago to help explain why some people feel there is too much tragedy in their lives, came to mind. He calculated that each person has a tragedy every five years – car accident, laid off, major surgery, etc. That's one every sixty months. So, if one has sixty close friends, relatives, churchgoers, neighbors, etc. there *should* be a crisis, on average, every month. It made mathematical sense to most people, but it was worrying him at this very moment. Was he *due* for a tragedy? *I can't think like that.* He shoved this feeling aside and went to work.

He deleted forty-five emails after giving each maybe three seconds of his attention. One that included an agenda for a sports programming training got a full ten seconds before he dragged it to the "to-do'" folder. He replied to eight emails and saved a handful of attachments that he might possibly need for future reference.

He glanced at a yellow Post-It note he had stuck on the bottom of his monitor dated over two years ago: "228." That was his personal one-day record for most emails received and it had happened on a Monday. Sure felt like he was on pace to break the record today.

Around 8am, he heard his team arrive one by one, said a few quick "good mornings" and pressed onward. He was fully absorbed in typing a narrative for his monthly sales report when Molly appeared at the door.

"You ready?"

Lucas glanced at the clock. *How could it be 9am already?*

"I'm sorry, Molly, could you give me five more minutes?"

Every few weeks, despite coming in early, her boss was so slammed on Monday mornings he'd forget to stop and prep for their one-on-one meeting. She nodded nonchalantly and went back to her desk. Lucas pulled two reports on Molly's sales activity, cursing the slow, in-house software, and sent them to the printer. He eyeballed her annual and quarterly performance numbers as two I.M.s popped up and the phone rang. Three more emails arrived. He turned off his monitor and ignored the call but as he glanced at the phone, he saw there were four messages from the weekend he hadn't listened to yet.

He closed his eyes and took a deep breath. As hectic as the pace of this job was, Lucas had come to embrace it, reveling in the challenge and the hopelessness of keeping up. In a way, it was a sickness. He came to work needing to get a hundred things done. He would complete eighty of them throughout the day, hoping the twenty he missed weren't urgent enough to cause harm. Prioritizing had become the *real* skill of his role as Sales Manager. Some days he failed miserably.

Lucas glanced out the massive window, deeply appreciating the animal wild kingdom just a few yards from his desk. It proved to be quite the mesmerizing distraction. He often wondered if his team's sales performance would jump five points if their view was a simple, bland parking lot.

He walked to the printer in the bull pen area, passing six sales executives hard at work in their outdated cubicles. He nodded to Molly on his way back. She followed him into his office, shut the door, and settled in for a half-hour of sales coaching and discussions on her accounts.

Lucas noticed that Molly's blouse was wrinkled and a size too small, and her blondish hair was curled but still messy. He could smell she was smoking again, which upset him a bit because she was an ovarian cancer survivor. She had no verbal filter and loved her independence. Not surprisingly, she was single. If some people's lives were an open book, Molly's pages were spread out on the city square for everyone to view 24/7. And to Lucas's surprise, under all that "I'm right" attitude and "My life is a mess, so what?" mantra, Molly had the biggest heart of any of Lucas's co-workers – ever.

"Did you see there's only eight left?" Molly pointed out the window at the greenish-yellow goslings. "There were twelve last week. Something got four of them."

Molly was obviously upset by this, but Lucas tried to stay on track.

"No, I hadn't noticed. I'd like to get to a few of my agenda items first today because we've got *a lot* to cover. Let's start with planning. I see only six appointments last week. We need to talk about your appointment strategy."

"No, we don't. I had three cancellations and remember, I went to Jerry's funeral, which ate up my entire Wednesday afternoon. The training in Champaign took up most of Friday. I'll get my ten this week. Don't worry about it."

Lucas relished that she always had her activity covered. There was no laziness here, but there was always some sass coming. Other managers would argue she wasn't suited for a corporate environment, but Lucas saw an arrogant "sales confidence" in her during her interview, and he took a chance. She proved to be solid. She just needed a manager who would stay out of her way.

"What we really need to talk about is this stupid software we're supposed to use to build client schedules. Look at the reach and frequency that RETRN built for Dixon's Appliances. It placed only three commercials a week on eighteen networks. My reach is only 23% and the frequency is 1.2."

Lucas scanned her software printout. The company was always looking for ways to make the complicated process of TV ad schedule-building faster, but the good reps still spent hours trying to find the bargains and handcraft the most effective schedule they could for their clients.

"So, I built *this* from scratch. Same price."

She put her work in front of him proudly. Lucas saw that the new schedule placed at least eight commercials per week on more of the popular cable networks for women – HGTV, Lifetime, E!, Food Network, Hallmark, TLC, and of course, Fox News – always a big number in Central Illinois. The reach was 54% and the frequency was

2.9. With a smug look, she dared him to say anything positive about the RETRN software.

Lucas reminded her, "Well, what do I always say we'll do in this office?"

She smiled. "What's best for the client and what makes sense."

She took the papers back and glanced out the window. One of the goslings was struggling, fighting to stay above water. Molly jumped to her feet, watching like a hawk. Lucas knew he had lost her focus and peeked out the window. At first, it appeared normal, just a gosling bobbing for food, but Lucas quickly realized the young bird was being pulled under. He had seen this once before.

Lucas said, "I think a snapping turtle's got him."

With no regard for where she was professionally, Molly sprinted out of his office, through the break room and out the door. From the window, Lucas watched in astonishment as she flew around the corner, picked up a fallen branch from the silver maple, kicked off her heels and ran several steps into the pond. She used one hand to hoist up her skirt to keep it dry, the other to hammer the stick at the turtle repeatedly, knocking him around to disorient him.

Five other sales reps watched her through their own windows, screaming encouragement, high-fiving, and howling with laughter and applause, even though the double-paned windows kept Molly from hearing any of it. The turtle finally let go of the gosling and Molly scooped it up.

Lucas watched as she cradled the injured bird as if it were her long-lost puppy. She left her shoes in the grass and walked the bird back to the building. Certain she would bring the wet bird to his desk, Lucas raced to the break room door to intercept her. He opened the door right as she was about to come inside.

"Whoa. What's the plan here, Molly?"

"He's hurt. His mama won't care for him now. There's an animal sanctuary on Clear Lake. Can I run him over there?"

Lucas noticed streaks of mud and algae on her legs and the front of her blouse was wet. She gently set the bird down on the concrete to see if it could walk. It collapsed to one side and chirped in pain. It reminded Lucas of his older brother Reggie. How many times he had watched him tilt to one side as he walked, sometimes in pain, sometimes not, but never complaining or making any noise about it. He had never had to rush to Reggie's aide. Nor his nephew Lincoln's, either.

The bird's leg was obviously broken. Molly picked it back up.

"OK, go get your shoes."

She took a step to enter the building. Lucas blocked her from stepping inside.

"I need my keys."

"You're not bringing a wet, injured goose into the office. I'll get your keys."

She nodded, as if they were both following some imaginary standard protocol in the company handbook.

Lucas thought about what would have happened had he worked in Bloomington today or had he been at a client meeting. Molly would have dragged that soaked bird through the office and disrupted the staff for twenty minutes while she explained the evils of the vicious animal world.

Lucas had been trained to be accountable. The last thing he needed was the story getting out that an injured, wet goose invaded his office. He would be teased to no end by his boss, Toby, for his inability to control his staff.

Lucas hustled to Molly's cubicle, found her purse, grabbed an ESPN towel earmarked as a gift for a client and hurried back to the door. He shook his head – this whole ordeal was *so* like Molly. Utterly amazing she could hit her budget every year when she was so easily distracted by... life.

Molly appeared back at the door wearing her shoes. Lucas gave her the towel expecting her to wipe down her legs, or at least dry her clothes, but she cradled the scared bird with it for comfort instead.

"Molly, you have a big heart. But there's so much I needed to go over with you today."

She stared at him as if he had just sprouted fangs and a horn. "He was in trouble, Lucas. You don't hesitate. You just... help!"

CHAPTER 6

Stage Four

Reggie smiled in wild amazement at how easy it had been. *Does it get any better than this?*

He had spent the last hour sending messages to former classmates in Mr. Carvell's homeroom and was currently messaging three of them simultaneously. Of the twenty-six classmates, he had found all but two of them on Facebook or LinkedIn. Fourteen still lived somewhere in Illinois, the furthest being a two-and-a-half-hour drive. The idea of a Mr. Carvell lunch gathering over the Thanksgiving holiday, a full six months from now, was met with joy, anecdotes, and excitement.

These friend reconnections comforted Reggie. His old classmates seemed almost desperate to catch-up, the conversations so easy it felt like they had picked up their 8th-grade diplomas last week. Stories flooded back about Mr. Lacey's strict rules, Mrs. Greendale's lavender smell, the Silver Tea annual concert, terrible school plays, the shenanigans in P.E. class, and the art teacher who got fired due to a "scandal," even though no students really knew why. Tom Dulge became famous the day he tried to erase the Wonder Woman costume off of Lynda Carter in a magazine photo, Bernie puked during the spelling bee, Anson had a lice scare, and the Huffman twins set off a smoke bomb in the lunch room right before Christmas so no one had to take the math final.

But amidst the mounting stories, Reggie was alarmed at how interested his classmates were in how *he* was doing, and how much they remembered about *him*. He had always felt invisible, just a kid who sat in the corner and watched. He never excelled in school, didn't play an instrument, and was certainly not gifted at sports. His family couldn't afford Boy Scouts or any clubs for that matter. And church? Not a big deal for his family. There was no youth group where kids might meet and hang out with friends. It was more of a "write a check, endure an hour on Sunday, and go home" type of spiritual arrangement.

And yet, Reggie's efforts so far led to full participation. Everyone hoped they could make the meeting. They all wanted to connect with him on social media and get his phone number so they could text. Surprising.

Anne walked in and set a brown paper sack in front of him apologetically. He knew the fun had to end for now.

"Mix it with Crystal Lite. Green Gatorade will work too, so I bought both. I don't want any part of this. I'm going to visit Mom."

Anne grabbed her copy of *Learning to Speak Alzheimer's* and left for Evenglow, where her mother Alice had lived for three years. Reggie could sense Alice's memory was getting worse by the day. Each time she couldn't recognize Anne, it tugged at Anne's heart a little harder. Lincoln was hanging out with Zoey tonight and wouldn't be home until 11pm, so Reggie was now alone and happy about it.

He opened the sack and found a bottle with a label featuring unnecessarily large letters: "Movi Prep." He chuckled – sounds like he's putting on make-up to shoot a Hollywood film. He read the instructions, which for some reason felt like he was digging his own grave. *Suck it up, everyone must do it.* He mixed the bottle contents with Gatorade and over the next 30 minutes he drank the entire liter of the overly sweet, chemical-tasting mix.

Ten minutes later, his colon was empty, and he plodded out of the bathroom. The experience wasn't as miserable as he expected, but tomorrow morning he would have to do this again as the last step before his colonoscopy.

He started digging through a tall stack of plastic bins in the living room. He hated the lack of storage in the house, though his brother

Lucas reminded him constantly what was really missing wasn't space, but the ability to throw things away. Reggie, a garage sale fanatic, couldn't resist buying up merchandise for practically nothing. Reggie once showed Lucas a three-tiered ashtray and bragged that he only paid a dime for it. Lucas took one look at it, knowing Reggie didn't even smoke, and proclaimed, "You got ripped off." They had a good laugh about it, but later Reggie threw the ashtray away, thankful for the lesson that even dirt-cheap merchandise can still be a rip-off.

In the bottom bin, he found the *Centralio*, his grade school yearbook. His parents couldn't afford to buy every year's offering, but they promised all five of their kids to buy eighth grade and high school senior yearbooks. He remembered being upset and feeling left out that he didn't get one annually like most of his classmates, but thinking about it now, he had only looked at these books maybe three times in forty years. Perhaps Mom and Dad were onto something.

He flipped through the pages, remembering all too clearly that there were only two pictures of him in the entire book. Mr. Carvell's class was split evenly – thirteen boys, thirteen girls. Short hair seemed mandatory for all the gals, reminding Reggie that Dorothy Hamill's cute hairdo started the craze when she won the gold medal in figure skating. He admired the girls' photos, every one of them pretty as a hibiscus bloom. Reggie counted the girls who wore sweaters, realizing he had crushes on over half of them at one time or another.

He flipped pages. The theme of the year was video games. He enjoyed the trip down memory lane, reading colorful references to Pong, Tank, Death Race, Heavyweight Champ, Shark Jaws and Breakout. Even now he rated them forgettable, crappy games compared to Pac Man, Asteroids, Space Invaders and Galaxion – games he spent way too much time playing in high school.

Finally, he found the photo of the basketball team. Reggie found it interesting how almost all sports team photos featured one of two looks: tough guys with intense snarls trying to look intimidating, or "all smiles" like they really enjoy the sport. This team had chosen the tough guy look, and Reggie laughed aloud. None of them, as thirteen and fourteen-year-olds, could pull it off, even with the dark navy-blue uniforms that looked menacingly black in the photo.

And there was Reggie. Front left of the photo, the typical spot for team manager. He was on one knee, wearing jeans and a collared shirt and holding a Spaulding basketball. He sported a huge grin, looking as happy as one of the Bad News Bears after beating the Yankees to win the championship. Reggie stared at it for a long time. Exactly *opposite* of how he remembered it. The basketball team had always seemed on top of the world, laughing, joking, bonding, and getting flirted with by the cheerleaders. They achieved a 17-3 record that year. All Reggie could do was hand them cups of water, towels, and occasionally record stats for the coach. He stared at each face and started wondering what kind of home life each of them had, what fears they held inside, if they had secrets they needed to keep buried. *How is it that he looked genuinely happy in this photo and they looked abysmally sad?*

Reggie hid the yearbook in the piano bench for easy access later and re-stacked the bins against the wall. He wondered if he had news articles or pictures of his classmates, but figured even if he did, he wouldn't be able to find them. The yearbook would have to be enough to jog memories at the Carvell gathering.

His stomach gurgled loudly. The sound of the back door suddenly opening and slamming shut took his mind off a possible return trip to the bathroom. Reggie saw Lincoln climbing up the four steps inside the back door. The boy used furniture as support to shuffle into the living room. Watching his son struggle with mobility, Reggie cringed like he always did. To Reggie, it felt like a family curse. They had never once talked about their disability; they just silently shared it. Reggie wished he had talked to Lincoln his whole life about it, but at this point, it just seemed too late.

Reggie checked the clock -- only 8:15pm.

"Hey, you're home early. Everything alright?"

Lincoln looked up. He had been crying but was trying to hide it.

"Yeah. Zoey was tired. I think I'll just hang out and play *Call of Duty.*"

He moved into the game room. Years ago, this room had been packed almost to the ceiling with children's toys for the daycare. Reggie had to squeeze through little paths to get around. When Anne closed down the daycare, a natural transition was to make it a hang-out room for Lincoln and his friends. Although Lincoln never asked for much, the latest gaming system was always hot on his list and it served his friends well.

Reggie hated to see Lincoln, who was obviously upset, walk into the game room alone.

"Do you mind if I watch? You guys love this game – I'd like to see if it's as cool as you say."

"Really? OK, I guess." Lincoln thought this was odd. His Dad had never shown the slightest interest in modern video games.

Reggie grabbed a bag of potato chips and a Coke for Lincoln and a glass of water for himself, the only allowable pre-colonoscopy beverage. For ten minutes, Lincoln played and neither said a word. Strategically, Reggie started saying, "Nice shot!" and "Watch out!" here and there. Reggie felt Lincoln and the game were such unlikely partners. Here was the nicest 18-year-old anywhere. So gentle that Reggie had watched butterflies actually land on his shoulder and squirrels run up to him in the backyard as if he were Cinderella. At this moment, he controlled a militant shooter killing everything in sight!

In another ten minutes, Lincoln started explaining the game.

"They took away double jumping and wall-running, such an improvement."

"The shooter is so much more realistic again. I hated the futuristic shooters!"

"Now you can burst through a door or open it slowly. Strategy is super cool here."

Reggie listened to every word, more interested in learning why Lincoln loved to play the game than in the game itself. Could it be Lincoln secretly wished to be that avatar? That he could wield power over the universe in a strong and stable body?

In the middle of a massive war battle in which Lincoln appeared to be winning, he suddenly set the controller down.

"Zoey and I had a big fight. She says I act like I own her and I'm too controlling... Really?! Me?!"

Reggie let it sink in so they could both process this.

"Well... is she right?"

"How can you take her side?"

Reggie was used to a thoughtful, lovable son. Passions were definitely running amok here.

"Hm, maybe we could analyze why she would say that. Or think that. Is there something specific she was upset about, or was this thrown out as an overall general thing?"

Lincoln hated talking about this stuff with his Dad. He was eighteen already and felt he knew enough about girls – probably more than his Dad. He picked up the controller to start playing again. He knew, however, that he needed help. He set it back down.

"I don't know. We've been talking about going to Bloomington and ride the paddleboats at Miller Park for months, so I said we should go Saturday and then she went all psycho on me."

"I see... But that doesn't really follow though, does it? It's not really a logical reaction. Are you sure you didn't leave something out?"

Lincoln snorted, but it came out more like a spit, and Reggie saw a bit of spray hit the TV screen.

"Are you sure?" Reggie added.

Lincoln sighed deeply.

"Well, she's supposed to work on Saturday. I might have suggested she change her hours."

Reggie had a thousand things he could have said or asked, but each one would have sounded like, "Wise up you stupid kid." He stayed silent while his stomach made another terrible growl. He sipped his water slowly, hoping Lincoln would come to his own conclusion.

"I suppose I should call her... and apologize."

Lincoln sulked for another minute, then picked up his Coke and cell phone and walked to the front porch for privacy. Reggie watched him, wondering if his tactics were helping or hurting. At times, they loved the idea that Lincoln found a gal willing to accept him as her boyfriend. But he was still so young – maybe they shouldn't encourage any of it. Reggie wondered how his own history would have been different if his parents had given him life advice. Herb and Ruth Nichols, his parents, offered no such wisdom or ever talked about relationships with *their* five children. It was knowledge you had to learn on your own, wherever you could find it. Reggie was tired of hunting for it. When he dished it out, he usually felt like he had no idea what he was doing.

*   *   *

Reggie and Anne woke the next morning both feeling especially well-rested and ready for the day. Reggie repeated the Movi Prep colon blast without incident, and they soon found themselves in the hospital prep area. Reggie changed into the hospital gown, answered a dozen questions, and finished the routine pre-op poking and prodding.

A veteran nurse and a peppy anesthesiologist walked them through the steps of the upcoming procedure and told them another nurse would be back for one last check. Anne was extremely calm for a "medical" day. Reggie noticed it, grateful to see her relaxed inside hospital walls.

But then it happened.

The new nurse appeared with a clipboard. She read Reggie's chart, and as casual as she might have commented on whether it was a sunny or rainy day outside, she said:

"So, Mr. Nichols... you're taking Zestril for stage two hypertension and you are in stage four kidney disease."

That hit Reggie in the face like a wicked upper cut. He was stunned. He knew he was itchy, had too much protein in his urine, couldn't give blood and the doctor asked him to see a specialist, but no one had put it to him like – *that!*

This family knew kidneys – Anne already had one of hers removed due to a severe infection eight years ago. She struggled with a tough recovery but thank God her experience as a nurse helped with tips to

40

get through the suffering better than most. She was exceptionally knowledgeable on the topic, which Reggie feared mightily at the moment. She would know this didn't happen overnight. She would know there were only five stages, and that Reggie had trudged through stages two and three silently. She now knew Reggie had been hiding a lot from her, starting with a prescription for Zestril.

Anne slowly stood and stepped in front of the nurse, blocking her from the conversation and forcing Reggie to look solely into her bedeviled eyes. He felt helpless lying on the gurney. She glared at him, and with more anger, frustration, love, and incredulity than she had ever crammed into the space of just one word, she exploded with:

"WHAT?!!"

CHAPTER 7

18% Capacity

Anne was silent the entire drive home. Reggie sat in the passenger seat trying to figure out damage control. *How would he explain this? Could it be explained? Is an apology anywhere close to enough in this case?* He thought he must be the first person in history to be driven home from a colonoscopy with absolutely no questions thrown his way by the driver. How ya feeling? Can I get you anything? Are you hungry? Nope – nothing from his wife of twenty-two years whom he loved dearly. He had royally pissed her off by being... silent. He realized the radio was on, but the Chugga Chant drowned out whichever artist dared to entertain them.

Anne pulled the SUV into the driveway and walked quickly into the house without looking back. At least the colonoscopy results were good, Reggie thought. The gastroenterologist found only three polyps. The doctor appeared unconcerned they might be cancerous but needed to send them off for biopsy – standard procedure. Reggie couldn't help but think *that's how they get ya... send 'em to a lab, send the patient another bill.* He shook his head – angry with himself because this was the type of thinking that got him into trouble in the first place.

He opened the lift gate and grabbed his walker. As he wheeled to the back door, his back hurt and he stopped to stretch it out. He always thought the pain was related to his legs or hips but now he reasoned that much of the pain had been from his failing kidneys. He remembered the TV commercials he'd seen over the years for OSF Medical Center in Peoria. Cardiac Care classes. Birthing Unit classes. Classes on the disease of the day. Surely, they held a class for people like him with failing kidneys. If he was going to get his wife to speak to him again, he'd better take responsibility and figure out a plan for his own health. Fast.

He climbed the four steps and into the kitchen where Anne was sitting with her head in her hands, looking down at the table. He couldn't tell if she was crying, had a headache, or needed to sleep.

"OSF has a class I can go to... it will cover all the options on dialysis, medicine, costs -- all that stuff. I'll find a time I can drive over. Do you want to go with me?"

She looked up with disbelief. He could see the angry demon of death leave her body, her entire demeanor changing. Before she spoke, he knew he had chosen his words perfectly to diffuse this tension and create a new, positive direction for them.

"I don't care if the class is at two in the morning. We're going to the next available class!"

She stood and marched out of the kitchen. OK, she was still a bit angry, he thought, but at least we are out of the doghouse for now. He had better search for these phantom classes. He would be in a real pinch if they didn't actually offer them.

He moved into the dining room where his computer sat. Anne walked back in, threw her arms around him and held him. Silently. For at least ten seconds, they hugged without a word. She walked away. Reggie treasured this moment, but it left him with a rise of self-anger. *Why did he put her through so much? Wouldn't she better off without him?*

In twenty seconds, he found the OSF schedule. The "Kidney Disease and Dialysis" class was held Tuesdays and Fridays at 11am. Easy. Anne would be happy even though it meant Reggie would have to take a day off work. Maybe he could pick up a Saturday shift to make up for it.

Then he spent a full hour mesmerized by the intense world of dialysis terms, statistics, and general information: "GFR and how it's calculated." "Hemodialysis. Fistula. Grafts." "Peritoneal Dialysis." "Dialyzer. Hemolyzer. Nephrolyzer." There were pages and pages of "Getting Enough Dialysis," "Caring for Your Access," "Self-Management," "Managing Other Health Problems," and much more. It was overwhelming, scary, and so complicated he turned off the computer as if stopping the onslaught of unknown terms would help him decide what to do. The class should certainly help him make more sense of it, but... if a half million people in the U.S. could handle dialysis, why not him? He breathed easier knowing a solution was out there.

He heard a loud knock and saw Grace and Gavin walk in the front door. They were the only relatives who would let themselves in, which used to irritate Reggie. He soon learned it kept him from having to move to the door so he had a change of heart. It also trained him to yell, "Come in" when he heard a knock... sometimes gambling he was welcoming in a salesman.

Grace looked just like her mother, shoulder-length hair with the same beautiful swirl to it. She carried maybe fifteen extra pounds – Anne's great cooking came at a price. Gavin, six feet tall, towered over Reggie and most of his relatives. He hadn't shaved. Reggie noticed the beard was rather patchy, but the mustache looked good. Reggie considered himself an expert because he sported a Burt Reynolds mustache for many years in his twenties.

Anne rushed in to hug her children.

"Hi guys! What are you doing here?" Anne asked. "I thought you were moving Gavin today?"

Reggie felt bad. He had totally forgotten it was a big day for Gavin. Grace spoke with joy and enthusiasm.

"We had to bring Dad something to commemorate this historic occasion!"

She handed Reggie a coffee mug that read: "Your colonoscopy results are in. They found your head." Reggie belly laughed, enjoying the ribbing but more so that his stepchildren felt comfortable enough to join like this. Gavin and Grace laughed with him before giving him a quick hug. Anne inspected the mug and gave Reggie an "inside-joke" look. Reggie understood... *yes, I've sort of had my head up my ass lately.*

"Can you stay for lunch? I can whip something up?"

There was no such thing and they knew it. If Anne offered food, a 20-minute minimum commitment followed while she made it simply perfect.

"We can't," Gavin explained. "The first truck is already packed and we're unloading in ten minutes. We just wanted to give Dad a hard time."

Reggie offered, "Can I help transfer the cable, phone, or electric bill? I could call the city for you." He felt helpless at times like this. He couldn't move boxes, landscape, hang curtains, or any of those needed tasks at the time of a move.

"All taken care of. Anyway, you need to rest, colon boy," Grace added.

"I'm so glad you got to see me," Reggie quipped. "I'm a lot less full of shit today than normal."

They laughed, waved, and rushed out. Reggie watched them hustle to Gavin's pick-up truck. Despite a sketchy diet and never really exercising, Gavin somehow looked strong and fit. How sweet was it that Grace agreed to help her brother move?

As they drove off, they turned and waved at Reggie's front window, even though a reflection of the trees and sky was all they could see. They knew Reggie was behind that window, waving like he always did until his loved ones were out of sight. They were right – Reggie waved until he watched the truck disappear around the corner, wishing again that he could be more helpful. *Shame on me for forgetting that was today.* He made a mental note to find them the perfect house-warming gift.

Anne sat down on the couch. Reggie noticed her defensive posture and braced himself. He hoped it would be a clearing of the air. She was calm, but intense.

"I am so sick of this. Why would you keep it a secret?"

"We both know you have a lot of worries. I just didn't want to add to them."

Anne's face grew a deeper shade of red.

"And what do you think the SHOCK of all this is doing to me? You have two kidneys, and together they're functioning at eighteen percent. This is a *turn-your-life-upside-down* medical nightmare! Do you have ANY idea how serious stage four kidney disease is?"

Reggie didn't know. He had no argument. No excuse. All he truly knew was that Anne had an infection years ago, they took out a kidney and she was doing fine living with just one. He kept thinking that maybe they'd remove one of his and he'd be fine. It would somehow work out. He hadn't yet faced up to the fact that his kidneys were *both* failing.

"Anne, we are signed up for the Tuesday class. Do you need me to do something more?"

"I want you to promise me the silence stops now! You need to tell me what's going on with you medically no matter how much you think I'll freak out about it. I was a nurse. I can deal with it."

"But you quit..." Reggie stopped himself, realizing his word choice was a colossal mistake. He needed to recover but luckily, she hadn't even heard him and she pressed on.

"Dialysis is no picnic! It's a rough road here. We need to work together – better. Start communicating with me like an adult or... or I'm going to lose it and you will probably die!"

That was as blunt as she had ever spoken, but he knew she had every right. She stood in a huff.

"Yes. I promise."

She walked away. He moved right back to the computer determined to learn what he could about dialysis in all its different forms. For three hours, he researched. Testimonials. Trends. Doctor insights.

Recommendations. Companies involved. YouTube videos of dialysis in action. Improvements made over the years.

But he kept returning to and re-reading one article that got under his skin. It kept his mind from truly processing the other articles:

"Six Reasons Why You Should Never Go on Dialysis."

CHAPTER 8

Scrubs

Anne sat in the passenger seat hopeful the class on dialysis would showcase incredible improvements since she worked in the medical field. She had witnessed massive strides from the sidelines since she left medicine: the growth of the role of the nurse practitioner, more men becoming nurses, increased specialization, the new ethical code launched in 2015, and even nurses pushing to get on the boards at some hospitals. Nurses were no longer housekeepers; they were collaborative healthcare providers and commanded much more respect and responsibility than in generations past. And the medicines – so many new discoveries. Surely, the dialysis field had advanced and her husband was in for a pleasant surprise in terms of the patient experience.

Reggie steered the SUV onto Highway 116 feeling as if he was totally wasting his time. Though the article he read warning patients against dialysis was aimed mainly for those over 75-years-old, Reggie's mobility issues, small, cramped house, fatigue level, and living an hour away from the hospital put him smack-dab in the same boat as their intended readers. Reggie was exerting a lot of energy trying to convince himself to keep an open mind about dialysis, but deep down he was 90 percent sure it was going to be a terrible option. Hopefully, the class would surprise him.

Anne reached over and held his hand, an automatic response these last several years when they were driving together. Both had tension running through their veins. Reggie pulled his hand away just long enough to hunt through three AM radio stations and settle on the best topic he could find – the history of cereal in the U.S. He cranked it up so it could be heard over the Chugga Chugga Chant. That helped the drive go by faster.

They pulled into the OSF parking garage which was packed on all six levels. It felt like its own bustling city on a Saturday night instead of a parking deck, late-morning on a Tuesday. Reggie cherished his handicap parking placard and quickly found a spot by the elevator door. They had to wait for a dozen cars making the trek to the upper levels to drive by before it felt safe to get his walker out of the back.

"Where are we, downtown New York?" Reggie laughed as they entered the elevator.

"We sure got a lot of *sick* people in Illinois," Anne joked.

They made it into the plush classroom with only a minute to spare. Sunflowers and daffodils rested in sleek glass vases, beautiful landscape wall-hangings featured the four distinct seasons in Illinois, and a wide assortment of fruit, salt-free snacks, and water bottles filled a countertop.

Five other couples were already gearing up for the class. One of the ladies sat in a wheelchair. Reggie relaxed in one of the oversized, comfortable chairs, noticing that he felt more at ease here than he did in his own cluttered living room. He sat back hoping to be dazzled. Anne grabbed two water bottles and sat next to him just as three medical professionals walked through the door.

All three were women. One wore a casual skirt and blouse, one wore nurse's scrubs and the third, who Reggie thought looked like a bank president in her business suit, began the class.

"Hello and welcome everyone. I'm Doctor Kiper, Director of the Dialysis Center. We are happy you've joined us today to learn the real facts about dialysis, when it is and is not the right decision for you, and how it could impact your lives. If you are in stage four or five kidney failure, you need to make some decisions very soon. I'm going to get us started, but Jenni, our Nephrology Administrator and Sahana, our Renal Dietitian will be teaching the class today."

Each lady waved as she heard her name, and the class looked left to identify them. Reggie stared at Sahana in her scrubs. Though Indian, she looked so much like Anne did when she used to wear scrubs. It reminded him how lucky he was to have a wife who knew the world of medicine. He fell in love with her while she wore scrubs. He often wondered if his fascination with the medical attire was caused by constant doctor visits growing up, or the dozens of photos of WW2 nurses with their cute white hats that he saw in magazines in grade school. Sahana scanned the group catching Reggie's eye, so he quickly looked away, realizing he was missing Dr. Kiper's speech.

"...our patients are often their own worst enemies. You do research, but unfortunately the tool you use is the internet and there is just as much misinformation in that space as there are accurate facts. So please, try to forget any preconceptions you have. Whatever you've read, whatever you believe in your heart at this moment about dialysis, we're here to make sure it's correct."

Reggie and Anne exchanged looks. Reggie felt foolish – was his three hours in front of the computer a complete waste of time?

"Just last week we had a patient who read an article on the many disadvantages of doing dialysis at home. It was written in England five years ago. Every fact he brought to the table was outdated. Keep in mind, we are not here to talk you into anything today. We are not selling anything. We are here to share information on your options and how our program works, insurance and expectations. As the Director, I feel personally responsible for every patient, whether you end up using our services or not. There are pads of paper on the tables... please write down your questions as they come up, any questions at all, and we'll do our best to make sure you leave here completely informed."

Reggie opened a water bottle and relaxed further. This was much more pleasant than he expected and the professionalism was through the roof. Anne grabbed two pads of paper and pencils and smiled at Reggie. She obviously liked what she was hearing.

"We're going to start off with a twelve-minute video and we'll go from there. I hope you enjoy your time with us today."

Having completed her mission, she left. Jenni worked the video projection and Sahana turned out the lights.

And that's when Reggie and Anne felt the punishment began. For them, the remaining time in the class was like getting slapped on the hand and punched in the gut again and again. The video started with the details of trying dialysis *at home*, but Reggie and Anne instantly hated it. Their house didn't have a room they could dedicate to it, especially where a water source and a drain for the equipment was accessible. They also didn't feel they could deal with retrieving and managing the products and equipment. Any expected improvement for Reggie's health from home dialysis felt minimal at best and was not "guaranteed." The time commitment alone felt outrageous -- four times per week for three hours. The expected return didn't match the effort. In fact, everything about this option stunk. They both rolled their eyes and waited for the "on-site dialysis" segment.

That was only a hint better. Reggie would be required to drive to a dialysis center three times a week and spend four hours there each time. That's a minimum twelve-hour weekly commitment. He could never work full-time and pull this off without feeling as if he didn't have a life of his own. In Reggie's research, one consistent note was that people on dialysis would often feel great for just a day, but then start to feel progressively worse until their next treatment. Many complained they were often drained by the experience, wanting to sleep after going through it each time. *Would he be even more tired? What kind of a life would that be?* Both he and Anne shut down the option because, well... it would be fantastically unpleasant.

And then the information got *personal*. The beautiful Sahana started a Power Point for her portion of the presentation on diet and nutrition. At first she talked about diabetes, which didn't interest or affect them, so Reggie just concentrated on how pretty Sahana's ebony hair looked against the bright blue scrubs. Then she started talking about sodium, a big nemesis for the kidney.

51

"The recommended daily sodium intake for any person over fifty, or with hypertension or kidney disease, is 1500 mg. Now let's look at how much sodium is contained in some of the common foods we eat."

Reggie and Anne had rarely ever looked at food labels. Before Lincoln was born, Anne and Reggie went through a swimming phase and she started looking at calories, but that got old fast. And in 2013, new guidelines from the American Heart Association were announced causing a lot of national news and conversations about cholesterol, so for a couple of months they looked at those numbers. Neither Reggie nor Anne even knew sodium was a mandatory measurement on today's food labels.

Sahana listed dozens of common brands and foods which are harmful to the kidneys. She started with dark colas. Makes sense, Reggie thought. I can start avoiding those. But it started to get so confusing. White bread is better that whole wheat bread? White rice better than brown rice? Bananas and avocados have a lot of potassium, so they are... "bad?" Then she moved to processed foods.

One can of Campbells Cream of Mushroom soup – 870mg of sodium. Anne sulked. She used four cans of it in her famed Tuna Casserole. Reggie could gobble a third of the dish in one sitting. Anne did the math... when you add the tuna, he was surpassing his total sodium intake for the day in just one meal.

Heinz Ketchup – 190 mg in just one *teaspoon.* Reggie would sometimes squeeze what seemed like four tablespoons of it onto his plate when they had French fries. That's almost 2,300 mg *before* we add the deep-fried, salty fries or the salted burger.

One of the classmates joked, "Hell no! I ain't givin' up MY ketchup!" Everyone in the class except Reggie and Anne laughed.

Kellogg's Raisin Bran – 350 mg per cup. Reggie probably went through two cups for breakfast using half his allotment for the day.

Lender's Whole Grain bagels – 490 mg per bagel. Reggie often ate two for breakfast or lunch with cream cheese. The lady in the wheelchair scoffed, holding firm to her love of bagels.

Italian dressing – Anne often used it because she thought it was the "healthy" dressing. 440 mg per tablespoon. She probably dumped four tablespoons on Reggie's big salads. Anne was feeling overwhelmed, ignorant, and ashamed.

Sahana changed the topic to restaurants. The news went from terrible to catastrophic. The dining out choices they loved were wildly destructive for Reggie's kidneys. Every sodium number from every restaurant that Sahana displayed on the screen smacked Anne further and further into her seat. Arby's. Chick-Fil-A. Olive Garden. Chile's. It was making Anne sick. And the final blow... Sahana's last restaurant slide showed Logan's Roadhouse, their favorite of favorites. Anne had *forced* Reggie to eat there about once a month for years to enjoy a healthy salad. They over-indulged on the unlimited rolls, but that was OK – they were eating *healthy*. It was her way of saying "we need to pay some attention to our health." And every time they went, they both ordered the shrimp salad. *Because it was healthy.*

Sahana flipped to the data screen, which showed sodium content for the Logan's shrimp salad with dressing: 3,000 mg.

Anne trembled. She had been celebrated for her cooking and love of food her entire life. She was revered for it. But she suddenly realized that maybe, just maybe she might be responsible for Reggie's predicament. She had never considered the health consequences of her cooking and now it rocked her to her core. She could not look her husband in the eye.

Anne stood and raced out of the room, frantic, upset, holding back self-loathing tears. She searched for a bathroom to hide in as she stormed down the busy hallway but couldn't find one. She followed an exit sign and pushed her way outside into a small courtyard, probably used for employee smoking, but at least it was empty. She sat on the ground, her back against the hot brick.

She sobbed, feeling she was a pathetic excuse for a wife and caregiver. She wiped her eyes, wondering how she could ever face Reggie again. She finally looked up and noticed a gazebo surrounding a bird fountain with two white, cement angels guarding it. She spoke to them, confessing her revelation through her tears.

"I've been slowly... killing... the love of my life."

CHAPTER 9

Puffs of Orange Dust

Lucas felt amazing as he sped around the two-lane track at the health club. His knees and ankles were strong today and the gym's stereo system played a great mix of classics like REO, the Stones, and Huey Lewis. During the week, the alarm blared at 4:30am. It got noticeably harder to wake up as the week went on, but on weekends, they got to sleep in until 6am. Years ago, they would sleep till 7am, even 8am. But a good friend convinced them the weekend was "their" time. *Why would you sleep it away?*

Kim rarely missed her all-women's POWER class at the gym on Saturdays, which let Lucas choose anything – weights, circuit training, running, resistance machines, whatever felt right for the day. Today he had chosen circuit training: he would run four laps, then two minutes of sit-ups. Run four laps, then two minutes of push-ups. Run four laps, squats. Ten different exercises in all ending with twenty dreaded burpees. The endorphins were flying so high after sixty solid minutes of a high-impact, elevated heart rate that he contemplated signing up to run his third marathon.

Right on time, Kim paraded out of the fitness room with the other ladies sporting athletic wear. Lucas playfully pinched her side and tugged on her ponytail as he ran up behind her. They walked briskly to the car together. It was time to get the day started.

"I was just running through my list today. I got a lot going on, what's your day lookin' like?"

Kim rolled her eyes. Lucas overpacked *all* his weekends. It amazed her that even on Saturdays when they had "made no plans," they would still be crazy busy. He was that guy that liked to get stuff done but she had to admit she wasn't far behind.

"Shopping at Sam's. I want to sneak by Meijer and get some fresh veggies." She spoke quietly on this next part, "Maybe a little *rendezvous time* this afternoon?"

Lucas smiled. There was always room for "rendezvous time," especially since they had become empty nesters. Lucas and Kim often chatted about the unexpected reaction they got from dozens of other couples after learning that Riley and Aspen were both grown and had moved out of the house. *How are you handling it? How are you filling your time, now? Are you OK?* – as if they'd had a death in the family.

"Oh, I also have a lot of Wishbone paperwork to get caught up on. Can you pick up some dog food today?" Lucas admired her for volunteering at the non-profit dog rescue. After Aspen left for college, Kim took on the task of reconciling all the checking and PayPal accounts and managing the backend accounting. Some days, she'd spend up to four hours working on it while Bali and Fiji snuggled at her feet.

Lucas grinned, reflecting on pricey dog food and the journey they took bringing Bali and Fiji into their lives. One of their neighbors had walked three Shih Tzus by their front porch almost nightly for five years and Riley and Aspen begged their Dad for one. Lucas, who resisted getting dogs for years due to their already crammed lifestyle, had a moment of weakness and asked Kim, "Can you imagine the look on Aspen's face if we brought home a dog?"

That was enough of a "toe in the door" for Kim to research the shelters, create a cost analysis, and convince Lucas in a matter of 24 hours to just go look at one. And Lucas's heart melted so fast just watching his wife fawn over the cute pup that he agreed to a second dog to make sure it had a companion. Aspen cried massive tears of joy when they brought Bali and Fiji home, cuddly Shih Tzus now living quite the pampered life.

Kim could sense her husband's mind was working on several things at once, so she asked, "What's on your plate?"

"Bob's lawn is overgrown. I saw on Facebook he's in Germany and gets home tomorrow. I hate to see a neighbor have to cut his lawn after that long trip, so I think I'll knock that out for him. I should bring the toolbox up to Mom's to fix a few things. I should probably check on her finances, too."

This was typical. An entire day of activity planned and most of it was for a neighbor, his Mom, and who knows what will come up later. At least she had some *afternoon time* on the schedule for when he got back.

The drive home took only five minutes. Lucas whipped up two quick peanut butter and chocolate protein shakes for their breakfast and he finished Bob's lawn in forty minutes. He showered, dressed quickly, and zipped up to Pontiac – a quick thirty-minute drive.

Ruth Nichols, his Mom, had four fixer-upper problems written in her notepad. As Lucas read them, he felt they were rather tame: tighten a kitchen cabinet door, replace some light bulbs, look at a tape recorder from 1977 and see if it could be fixed, and as always, look at her printer. "It's not working right." None of these were urgent but having a constant list of needed repairs was her one excuse to keep him coming up regularly so she could spend time with him. Lucas saw through the charade but didn't mind -- getting quality one-on-one time with his 88-year-old mother was precious.

After completing the list, he spent an hour chatting with her about her Writer's Club and Rosary Project. He gave her an update on his two girls, hugged her, and made a comment about how great her silver-white hair looked. On his way out the door, her last comment was "I love you. We'll see you next time." Lucas adored this about her. It was never "Call me when you get home." She somehow put all her worries about the safety of her five children in God's hands and believed life for them was wonderful until she heard otherwise.

Lucas still had plenty of time to get home, so he stopped by County Market to buy dog food and added a big bag of Chee Zees to his cart.

He penned a note, "Try the little ones – they're the <u>BEST</u>!" and stuck it on the bag. As a third grader, his brother Reggie had insisted that small, broken bits of Chee Zees tasted "the <u>best</u> – far better than the full-sized ones." He had been lightly teased about the assessment for almost five decades now, and it wouldn't stop today. Lucas's plan was to drop the bag inside Reggie's back door and hit I-55 back to Bloomington.

He parked in Reggie's driveway and took one step inside the gate, pausing to admire the amazing hibiscus plant bursting with nine glorious tropical blooms. Lucas had thought of planting a hibiscus in his own yard, but there was something magical about how this plant looked at Reggie's place – he felt he'd never be able to duplicate it. He shook it off and walked towards the door.

"What are you doing?" The voice came from his left.

Lucas had been so distracted by the magnificent plant that he hadn't noticed Anne sitting at the picnic table reading a book on Alzheimer's. Her question was said with accusation – far from her normal friendly greeting.

"Oh - Hi Anne. Didn't see you there. Thought I'd remind Reggie of his stellar contribution to the world of party snack reviews," he said with a big grin. He handed her the bag so she could read the note. She knew the story well and had taken in dozens of Chee Zee bags and jokes over the years – all in good fun from the Nichols family. But Lucas intuitively knew from her stoic body language that something was seriously wrong.

She took the bag and read the note. She stared at it for several seconds, then turned the bag over and read the food label. She glanced at Lucas as if he had brought her husband rat poison.

"This contains 290 milligrams of sodium... per serving!"

She opened the bag and put a handful of the orange snacks on the table, counting out a pile of exactly twenty-two Chee Zees. Lucas thought the pile looked small.

"That's one serving. You realize Reggie will eat three, maybe four times that watching a Bears game?"

She glared at Lucas who felt as if he had entered the twilight zone. Nothing like this had ever happened with his gentle, loving sister-in-law, and he'd never once known her to care what food *contained.* Taste and emotional attachments were the only benchmarks that mattered.

He watched her put the twenty-two Chee Zees back in the bag, neatly center the bag perfectly on the picnic table and pull on the corners, trying to erase all the wrinkles. She held the top shut where she had opened it.

And without warning, she made a fist and slammed it down on the bag. Again and again. Violently – for a full minute. The bag finally burst on the bottom, but only a few puffs of orange dust flew out. Convinced she had completely pulverized the contents into powder, she handed it back to Lucas.

"There. No little pieces left. Don't ever bring salty food to your brother again." She grabbed her book and walked to the back door.

Lucas finally came out of his shock. "Anne! What the hell!?"

"I found out Reggie hasn't given blood in three years. His blood pressure is too high. It's not my place to say anything more. Ask your brother. He picked up a shift today – he's not home."

She walked inside, leaving him shell-shocked. Reggie had *always* felt a strong duty to give blood but thinking about it now, Lucas realized it had been a few years since he and Reggie had discussed blood donation. He pulled out his wallet and hunted through it to find his Red Cross donor card. He and Reggie had proudly carried their original donor cards for decades. It was "their thing." They even had a race between them long ago to see who could first donate twenty units. Each time they had donated, Lucas and Reggie hand-wrote the date. Lucas read his twenty dates: May 1982 to October 1988.

He turned the card over. It showed his blood type: O negative. His brother was O positive. Their blood was always in high demand – the Red Cross often hounded them to schedule their next appointment. It felt severe that Reggie couldn't donate. And Anne led him to believe there was a more serious medical issue to be revealed. What events had unfolded to turn Anne into a demonic destroyer of innocent Chee Zee bags?

Once home, he sat at his computer to figure out the mystery. Lucas recalled that his own blood pressure was borderline high, but his doctors never expressed concern about it. He didn't even know what medical issues high blood pressure might cause.

He typed "high blood pressure health problems" into Google.

"746,000,000 results." *Really?* He used Google daily, but these numbers were ridiculous. He thought about Reggie's overall health. He had dealt with so many medical issues. Now there was more? It was so - *unfair!*

He clicked on the first link. An article appeared listing six serious health issues prominently displayed in bright red circles. Because Reggie had picked up a shift today, Lucas could immediately rule out Stroke, Heart Failure, Heart Attack, and probably Vision Loss. That left only two. Lucas read them closely, wondering, wondering, reliving Anne's meltdown. She was angry. Unwilling to discuss it with him. Anne said, "ask your brother." What issue caused by high blood pressure could logically be the answer?

Kidney Disease?

Or Sexual Dysfunction?

CHAPTER 10

Only 7,000

A massive semi-truck barreled up I-55 behind Reggie. He watched it nervously in the rear-view mirror heading directly toward his back bumper as he merged onto the interstate. Reggie was up to 60 mph coming off the ramp and tried to speed up but the Enclave only had so much giddy-up in her. Would it bash his Enclave and toss his family into the ditch? His heart skipped a beat as the semi showed no sign of switching lanes.

"Get over. Get over!" Reggie yelled.

Just as Reggie was about to crank the wheel to veer to the shoulder, the semi ducked into the left lane at the last possible moment, screaming past the Enclave like she was standing still. The Enclave shook as if a 747 had flown directly overhead. Anne covered her eyes, clutching the passenger door tightly, trying not to make matters worse by screaming. It was obvious to Reggie that as Anne was aging, traffic made her increasingly nervous. In this case, that semi had plenty of room to get over. At least she wouldn't blame him for the near miss.

"Why do they have to go so fast!" Anne said through gritted teeth.

Reggie glanced to the back seat to check on Lincoln. Ear buds and a cell phone dominated his entire being. He had no clue a semi came a stone's throw from smashing into them, and Reggie was relieved his son was oblivious to the danger. At least today's trip was only seventy miles to a small office in Orland Park with easy parking. For Lincoln's more serious operations and doctor evaluations, Reggie had to drag his family thirty more miles to the University of Illinois-Chicago and deal with I-94 maniacal drivers, hectic city streets, skybridges and crowded parking decks. The doctors and staff there were brilliant, but the family was always exhausted from the long trip.

Despite the semi, today would be nicer. The highway was clear for now. Reggie figured Anne could relax a bit – a great time for a chat before they hit the heavy traffic in Joliet.

"Can we talk about what happened after you left the class in Peoria?"

Now it was Anne's turn to check the back seat. Lincoln was still buried in his phone so she felt OK talking about another one of her meltdowns. Lincoln was still mad at her because she used the recent health news as an excuse to say "no" to bringing Zoey. She felt super about that decision now. Had Zoey been in the back seat, she would probably have seen that semi, screamed bloody murder and freaked out everyone in the SUV.

"Sure... I guess."

"I was able to meet a few people after the class. The guy who sat right behind us? He's at 15% kidney function, but he has been that way for almost eight years. Maybe we won't have to do anything for a long time."

"Well, that's comforting, but we both know every person is different. No one *really* knows how much time your kidneys have left. It's a lot more about how your body *feels*."

"But what about our diet. Maybe it won't get worse if we eat less sodium, drink a lot more water, no sodas, no chips, stuff like that."

This stung a little but Anne knew he wasn't trying to blame anyone, just state facts.

"Did you save all the information?"

"Of course. I've never dieted in my life. I never felt I had to. I'm sure I can do this, but I'm gonna need your help."

She felt proud of him for taking control of his health. It was still daunting though – what in the world would they eat every day? Shopping was going to be a nightmare, she thought, as she mentally rejected all their typical, favorite foods due to the saturated sodium content.

"OK, but that list of bad foods is huge. We're going to have to find a list of things you *can* eat, which I'm guessing is a small list and includes a lot of stuff you won't like."

Reggie smiled, happy to be on the same page with his wife and working well with her.

"The last five minutes of the class were actually the most helpful. It appears we're doing it backwards. We should have gone to a class on kidney transplants as our first option. Dialysis is really the *last* choice if you can't get a transplant. What do you know about them?"

"I never worked for a transplant team, but... let's see... what do I remember from the other nurses? First, the numbers were always stacked against anyone who needed a kidney. You had to get on the transplant list and basically wait for someone to die from a stroke or heart attack while in the hospital. Or get in a bad car accident. But... what you *really* needed was for the car accident victim to be brain dead but not have ruined their internal organs. It's heartbreaking. Recipients have to sit around for years waiting for someone.... to *die*."

"Years? Really?"

"Yes. And it's not like, *Hey, you're the next contestant on The Price is Right.* They don't go in order. They go by all kinds of things: geography, age, how good of a genetic match you are, all kinds of data points trying to find the best match. The goal is to make sure the kidney isn't rejected. So, one guy might wait only two years, leapfrogging up the list over people who have waited for three or four."

"I bet the rich and famous make out nicely here."

"Actually, that's not supposed to happen. They're pretty serious about keeping the list according to medical data only. It's protected with a vengeance from what I hear. Of course, you have to live your life like you're on call. Once a matching kidney is found, you just have to hope the phones are working and you're not on vacation."

"That's a lot to take in. You remember anything else?"

"I'm sure a lot has changed. We should try to get you on the list right away."

Reggie wasn't encouraged by any of her answers.

"Well," he said, "I signed us up for a class next week on kidney transplant and I have an appointment with a nephrologist. He's on the transplant team at OSF. I'm told if the nephrologist feels I qualify, his office will get me on the transplant list."

Anne suddenly felt cold, a new fear grasping at her throat. She peeked into the back seat and watched her son, totally pacified by one of his many phone games. Lincoln had inherited vertical talus. What are the odds he will also have kidney failure? His eating habits were exactly like Reggie's and she didn't see him welcoming health into his diet. He shared so many physical traits as his Dad. *Is this nightmare going to be repeated later?*

They drove for a long time in silence listening to WLS debate whether downstate Illinois would be better off if they separated from Chicago and formed their own state. Reggie had thought for years it was a crime that the Illinois border states – Iowa, Indiana, and Wisconsin – were three of the top-thriving states in the union, while Illinois had credit just above junk-bonds and charged him crazy-high property taxes. Illinois was always listed as the worst state in which to open a new business. And so much corruption -- it held the record for sending Governors to jail. The hotly debated topic took Reggie and Anne's mind off all things medical for the remaining hour-long drive.

They arrived in Orland Park, pulled into the handicap spot only ten steps from the door, checked in, and the nurses quickly got Lincoln prepped for his surgery. For most people this would be outpatient, but they wanted Lincoln overnight given his long history of infections and sometimes violent reaction to anesthesia.

Reggie and Anne watched their son expertly instruct the nurses about everything from the gown, to the gurney, to how to re-set the alarm on the heart rate monitor. There was a funny sadness in the fact that he knew their job better than they did. He proved year after year he had the good heart to want to help. The nurses adored him.

The medical team finally wheeled him back to the surgical room and Reggie and Anne found themselves in the familiar waiting area. They made friendly small talk with many of the staff, all of whom they knew on a first-name basis. Bartholama, the receptionist with the funny name, kept them updated. When the room quieted down and there was just one other couple waiting, Reggie had a new thought they hadn't discussed yet.

"Hey, I forgot to ask about *living* donors. What do you know about that?"

Anne knew plenty, but she was cautious. "Living donors are rare – a special class. Let me look it up."

She pulled up her phone and did a quick search.

"Let's see. Over one-hundred-thousand people are on the transplant list, but only seven thousand are expected to step forward this year to donate a kidney."

She thought about Reggie's options. She was already down to one kidney so she couldn't be a donor. None of her children were matching blood types, but what if they were? How could she possibly live through a day where one of her own children or family members might try to step forward? She'd have to live through a day where two of her dearest loved ones were in surgery together. Unthinkable!

She closed her eyes and reached into her memory bank: she was wearing full nurse's attire – the scrubs were light purple back then. She stood in the hospital hallway with dozens of other nurses, doctors, janitors, office employees and patients. All clapped sincerely, demonstrating the utmost honor and respect as they wheeled a kidney donor through the halls and out of the hospital – a *living donor* who volunteered for surgery but had died on the operating table. This was her most devastating memory from her career in nursing – she wished with all her heart she could forget it.

Although that happened years ago and she knew living donor deaths were rare these days, she didn't dare reveal this sad memory. In the end a *living donor*, a term that scared her to no end, may be his only hope for a healthy, quality life.

"You have to have a matching blood type," she said. "We'll learn more in the class. I don't know anything else."

CHAPTER 11

O Positive

Scott and Emma Nichols played an epic point of badminton in their backyard, laughing as they volleyed the birdie back and forth for two solid minutes. They sent each other left, right, to the net and stumbling backwards. Scott held a Miller Lite in one hand making mobility harder, but it didn't stifle his competitive spirit. Finally, Emma smashed the birdie in a clean, vicious line drive at Scott's nose. He moved just in time, but the birdie landed a half inch inside the line. The point, which they played every year at this exact moment, was their kick-off to celebrate that the backyard was finally party-ready.

It promised to be another spectacular Fourth of July bash. Badminton and volleyball nets were ready, corn toss games, frisbees, footballs, and soccer balls were spread out, and four massive coolers held beverages on ice. A crate of small American flags, hats and noisemakers sat next to four tables covered in chips, fruit, and assorted candies, and soon to be filled with over fifty side dishes. The fire pit was stacked with logs for late-night chit-chat, singing and s'mores. An extensive fireworks display waited patiently in the garage. The shiny chrome grill reflected a perfect sun, ready for the dozens of steaks, brats, and chicken that Emma would cook up in a couple hours. Their cat, Billie, sensed the imminent invasion and was already curled up in a ball in the master bedroom.

Scott swooped under the net, picked up his wife up and kissed her. He resisted the urge to pull her to the ground for a more romantic smooch -- Emma might get grass stains on her new shorts. They wore twin red, white, and blue tank tops and were perfectly matched. Though thin and fit, they lived large lives - Scott was a partner in a Chicago law firm and Emma ran three organic foods stores. Today, they felt at the top of their entertainment game.

The work was done, the yard perfect, and they were ready to let loose for their annual gala. This party was their chance to invite neighbors, friends, and the entire Nichols family for a day of fun for all ages. They cherished this moment of pure anticipation.

Even though it was ten minutes before the *official* 1pm start time, Reggie, Lincoln, and Ruth Nichols appeared around the side of the house, early as usual. Reggie and Lincoln pushed their walkers, each carrying a bowl of Anne's renowned potato salad. Like many 88-year-olds, Ruth shuffled along but was steady and moved under her own power, carrying a plate of homemade vanilla cupcakes.

Scott hugged Reggie, "Hey big brother!" Then his Mom, "Hi Mom. Happy Fourth!" He hugged Lincoln, "And there's my superstar!" Emma, right behind him, gave hugs and greetings, collected the food and took it into the house. Anne had stopped coming to the party several years ago, something about anxiety around the Chicago expressway traffic, so they didn't even ask where she was.

Ruth exclaimed, "Oh, my! Scott, the hedges look amazing." A new growth of perfect hedges lined Scott's south fence. Ruth adored gardens and genuinely appreciated the backyard features. Emma's father had managed a landscape business for decades. Nothing irked Emma's family more than a home with shoddy exterior design and her yard proved it.

"Thanks. Our new neighbor, he's Russian, has two Rottweilers. They try to dig under the fence every time they see our Billie so we blocked their view." Reggie couldn't remember what Billie looked like. All of Emma's cats had been named after Jazz greats. Billie was her most skittish ever -- sightings were rare, especially at packed parties.

Reggie sat down at the patio table under a massive orange umbrella to escape the sun. He scanned the glorious backyard - perfectly landscaped with hedges on his left, a gorgeous rainbow of colorful flowers in the back, and a garden with tomatoes, oregano, basil, thyme, and cilantro in the corner. A lilac bush graced the entrance to the sunroom giving guests going into the house a whiff of floral elegance. Reggie wished he might someday have a chance to own something so inviting. He guessed there would be at least fifty people here today, a number he couldn't even fathom visiting his home at one time. *But... why would they want to come there anyway?*

"Uncle Scott, can I check out the sunroom?" Lincoln pushed hard to get here early every year to get first shot at the 70-inch TV and the Xbox or PS4 console -- Uncle Scott owned both. Last year was the first time Lincoln had ever stepped further *away* from a screen to play a game. He was tickled by the rad experience of playing with his entire peripheral vision engaged.

"Of course. Let's check the batteries first."

Scott walked Lincoln into the house and Ruth followed to use the bathroom. Reggie stepped over to the dark wood fence and opened a cooler. All beer and wine. The next, Sprite, Coke, Pepsi, and their diet counterparts. Normally, he'd choose a Coke. The next - a variety of sodas and energy drinks. He opened the last one. For the first time ever at this annual party, he thought of his health and grabbed a water bottle. *What did that say about his choices over the years?*

He scanned the yard again, noticing two massive green bins -- one for garbage, one for recycling. Both would be full by the end of the party. He thought more about recycling and how donating a kidney is *kind of like recycling. Is it possible someone here today would "recycle" a kidney for him?*

Reggie sat back in the same shaded spot that he did every year. As people rotated around, the party would come to him, but it felt different this year. For two wonderful hours, he watched guests arrive, doled out hugs and greetings, and shared updates. His younger sister Ava, usually the bitter pill at family events, had flown in from Seattle with her quiet, genius husband Levi and their two sons. She shocked

Reggie by actually thanking him for his advice on raising a teenage boy. It helped her and Levi transition their son into high school.

Reggie's older sister, Harper, an engineer about to retire from the city of Charlotte arrived. A small crowd laughed as Harper shared the story of Reggie growing up – terrified to sleep in his room alone after *Close Encounters of the Third Kind* freaked him out. She had developed a stronger hint of a southern drawl, which Reggie found delightful.

The stories mounted. Gavin showed off pictures of his new house and thanked Reggie publicly for the awesome housewarming gift, a shiny new grill set they desperately wanted. Reggie felt smart – a $90 value that he found on clearance for $28.

Dozens of neighbors and their kids arrived, filling the entire backyard with games and chatter. Reggie tried to put his medical predicament out of his mind. It was difficult to observe the tremendous love, bonding, and joy being displayed and to have to fake it. His mind was elsewhere.

Grace introduced Anthony, her new boyfriend-of-the-day. Reggie disliked him instantly because his tattoos were so poorly done. Ben came late, and though technically he wasn't related to anyone, they welcomed him like family. Even Scott's neighbors knew that Reggie had raised Ben as his own son for eight years before the truth of his paternity came out. When asked, Reggie would tell you Ben and his stepsister Skylar were two of his five children. He insisted the rest of the family treat them that way.

Reggie saw Lucas and Kim arrive, both carrying extra beer to ensure the supply wouldn't run low. They were "floaters" at this party, preferring to separate to give them more stories to share on their drive back to Bloomington. Lucas's daughters, Riley and Aspen arrived separately. There was much reminiscing of Riley and Mason's wedding in Michigan and speculation on Aspen's possible wedding date with her boyfriend, Carter. Reggie wondered if he'd still be alive by the time the wedding took place.

At 3pm, Emma served up the first round of brats and the line for food circled the yard. Every chair, step, the front porch, and even the coolers became seats for guests to sit on and indulge in a variety of picnic foods. Most went back for seconds and thirds, but not Reggie. He analyzed each dish, trying to estimate how much sodium it contained. He filled his plate with fresh fruit and salad, using only a teaspoon of ranch dressing. He dared to add one small slice of a burger and continued to drink water as the day pressed on.

At 4pm, Scott sang an amazing version of *Red Solo Cup* while Emma accompanied him on guitar. The crowd boisterously joined in, laughing and clapping. The junior-high kids instantly turned into Country music lovers, singing the song for hours. Reggie kept hearing the word "solo" repeatedly. He felt solo. Alone. Though four of his five kids were here, he missed Anne. He had never missed her at this jam-packed party as much as he did today.

Reggie found himself paying extra close attention to his siblings. What were they eating? Were they drinking beer? *Would that be bad for a kidney?*

A neighbor's two-year-old wandered too close to the volleyball action. Reggie watched his sister Harper let herself fall hard against the net pole to avoid crushing the kid. When Reggie saw Harper's back slam into the metal, he thought, "don't hurt your kidney!" *How could he think so selfishly?*

Around 5pm, Ben walked up with a beer and sat next to Reggie. The others at the patio table were in a deep discussion about how to best kill Illinois mosquitos so the floor was open for a private chat.

"Hey, Dad. Can you weigh in on something?"

"Sure."

"Samantha's been a greedy little shit lately. It's like she has to get her way *every... single... time.* I'm really sick of it. I'm done. She's fucking impossible!"

Reggie didn't know Samantha well, but he liked her. Very spirited. She had some great street smarts and he thought she was a great complement for Ben.

"Hm... have you talked about it? Like, have you told her how you feel?"

Ben felt stupid and took a swig of beer. He obviously hadn't.

Reggie thought about Samantha. She was a common-sense type of person, just a bit obstinate. She had this insatiable need to be *right*.

"I have an idea. What if you asked her, when everyone's calm and no one's blood is boiling, what percent of the time she expects to be right. And also, what percent of the time she expects to let you have your way. Write it down – heck, you should both sign it. Then when these things come up, show her the percentages. Hopefully, she'll see that she's trying to get her way every time."

Ben thought it through, nodding. "That's a bitchin' idea. And I can track that shit on my phone. Fuck, if I get my way twenty percent of the time I'll feel like a boss. Hey... gratitude."

He fist-bumped Reggie and walked off. Reggie wondered if his advice was helpful, if his kids even followed up with it or if they asked for his thoughts just to make him feel useful. He found himself alone at the table. To his delight, Lucas walked over – they hadn't connected yet.

"Reggie! Happy Fourth of July! How's it hanging?"

"A little to the right. Call your wife over, we'll have her adjust it for me!"

They both laughed. Reggie could get away with innuendo with his brothers, but only with his brothers. It was never tested outside the family. Reggie felt instantly comforted yukking it up with his Lucas though he was still hungry after his plant-based meal.

Lucas started, "Hey, you know what I've noticed walking around here all day? The Nichols all come to this party, eat too much, watch fireworks, and destroy Scott's house, but we rarely have any *real* conversations. You ever notice that?"

Lucas waited intently for his reply and Reggie noticed how closely his younger brother was tuned in to his response. Reggie laughed inside. He *just had* a real conversation – or at least he thought he did.

Reggie replied, "Real conversations? Sounds like a movie of the week on Lifetime."

Reggie appreciated Lucas's gift of gab, storytelling, and sense of humor and thought he was well suited for a career in sales. But this felt a bit off – like he was directing the conversation. Lucas was obviously digging for something. It wasn't like Lucas to be evasive. His gift was getting to the point -- being direct without coming off as pushy.

Lucas waited. The biggest lesson in sales is learning when to shut up.

"Hey, here's a real conversation for ya," Reggie said. He reached into his wallet and pulled out his Red Cross donor card, "I never truly verified the dates on your card."

Lucas pulled out his wallet, suspicious of Reggie's true intent. They prided themselves on still carrying their cards, but Anne had said he hadn't given blood in a few years. *Why would he bring this up now?*

They exchanged cards. Reggie pretended to read the back of Lucas's card, but quickly turned it over to see the front. "Blood type: O Neg."

Reggie sulked. His own blood type was O Positive. Not a match. And at that moment, he felt slimy. Disgusting. *Did he just trick his brother into giving him his blood type?*

"Interesting that you're O negative," Reggie said. "Do any of us have the same blood type?"

"Harper and Ava. They're both A positive. You and I, of course, have blood that is in much higher demand. We are so much more *valuable.*"

Lucas looked around the yard for Scott who was clearing dirty dishes off the tables.

"Scott! What's your blood type?!"

"B Positive. As in, Will *any* lawyer ever get into heaven...? Be positive!"

Lucas smiled but noticed Reggie's reaction had a hint of disappointment in it. *What was Reggie thinking?* At that moment, Lucas was ready to ask him flat out about blood pressure, his kidneys, even his sex life – though that question would probably come out as a joke of some kind. But his Mom sat down next to Reggie, and the strategy suddenly needed delicate work.

"So, what's going on, Reggie? How've you been feeling lately?"

"Not great. To be honest, I'm tiring out easily. Work is getting harder on me and all I seem to want to do most days is take a nap."

His Mom winced, concerned. Lucas could see she muttered a silent prayer for him.

"I hear ya. This over-fifty club sure has a lot of hidden fees, right? And you and Anne? Still crazy lovebirds after all these years?"

"Well, you know. We're doing fine."

Lucas assessed his comments. There was nothing super serious here. His brother was simply getting older. Lucas's beer was empty so he walked to the coolers to grab a new one. On his way, he felt relieved. He agreed smugly with his own diagnosis.

Oh yeah. It's gotta be sexual dysfunction.

CHAPTER 12

One Year at Most

Reggie poured milk onto his second bowl of frosted mini wheats, his favorite, and took in a big whiff of the aroma of sugar and wheat. It was a shocking surprise that *this* cereal turned out to be the one breakfast option with no sodium. He felt smug as he gobbled up the bites ravenously as if he were getting away with something sinful. Recently terrified of food and what it might do to his kidneys, Reggie had lost three pounds in one week.

Anne ate next to him, relieved. They had just researched Wheat Chex, which she assumed might be at the top of the healthy list. She never cared for how the cereal seemed to turn to mush halfway into a bowl of it, but knew Reggie had an emotional attachment to it – a big staple in his house growing up. It was terribly sodium-heavy: 357 mg per one-cup serving. She wouldn't be purchasing any more of it, probably for the rest of her life.

Lincoln joined them and scanned the kitchen table. Blueberries, fresh cut apples, and cereal. No amazing bacon. No fluffy banana pancakes drenched in butter with Anne's blend of syrups. No decadent cinnamon rolls, star-shaped cream cheese coffee cakes or Mom's famous homemade breakfast sausage. Usually Lincoln would be pampered with Anne's ultimate cuisine for two full weeks after a medical procedure, getting steel or titanium hardware removed included. Not this time. He could tell his mother was daring him to even ask for anything special, so he decided to eat whatever his Dad was having and be quiet about it.

Lincoln sat and poured himself a bowl. The table was eerily quiet. He could tell his Mom and Dad were panicky, trying to figure out a new diet that could work for the whole family.

"So, I heard you guys talking last night about dialysis."

Reggie and Anne exchanged looks. There was no "talking" last night. It was a heated argument but they thought Lincoln's headphones would have prevented him from hearing any of it. They must have been louder than they thought.

Anne had tried to convince Reggie that if he retired they could make dialysis work. That infuriated Reggie – he was a provider. He was willing to work even through the pain. He would not consider living on disability. For decades now the topic came up here and there, and it did appear the disability laws and insurance rules were written specifically for people like Reggie, but he dismissed the conversations. His worth was tied to being a provider. If he could work, he would. If he didn't have that... well... *what was he?*

Reggie was apologetic. "Sorry if we upset you, Lincoln. We're just a bit on edge right now."

Anne added, "This is a new health problem for the family. We're trying to figure it out and we won't necessarily agree on the best way to do that. We see a nephrologist later today." She felt silly, figuring Lincoln had probably never heard the term before.

Lincoln ate a handful of blueberries. Bland. Flavorless. He closed his eyes and imagined they were chocolate chips. He weighed his next words carefully. He wasn't leaving the table without saying them so he might as well blurt 'em out.

"So, after you guys went to bed, I did some research. Dad, if you don't do dialysis, won't you... die?"

His voice cracked saying it, trying to sound pragmatic but revealing a deep fear of the future. Hearing the words, Anne gulped. She had been so preoccupied with stage four kidney disease, sodium content, Reggie's options, and Lincoln's titanium that she had ignored Lincoln's mindset through all of this. In fact, Gavin, Grace, Skylar, and Ben should all get updates with a chance to discuss how they feel about it – soon.

"No, Lincoln. Don't think that way. We'll do whatever necessary to keep this family together. Right, Reggie?"

Reggie felt an unexpected rage watching his son work through the concept of his father's death. Theirs was a way of life they had no choice but to accept. It was a shitty deck of cards they were both dealt but they kept their chins up and learned to make the most of their struggles with legs, feet, hips and mobility. They still had a life, a family, a home, and many of the things a *normal* family enjoys. But this was the first *internal* medical problem. *Was this the future? Suddenly, we add kidney, liver, heart, pancreas, and lung issues?* His son should not have to resolve a whole new world of medical worries.

Reggie spoke with assurance, "That's right. Look, we don't have to make any decisions today. We might be able to go several years without making any decisions. It'll all be fine. Business as usual for now."

Lincoln wanted to believe that there was nothing pressing, that options were numerous, that everything would work out. He couldn't shake this strong uncertainty about his Dad's health, a vulnerability that scared him. He made a decision – he would search for a more stable job that afternoon.

Two hours later, Reggie and Anne parked in a lot they never knew existed. It was on the far east side of the OSF Medical campus in front of a special wing they had never heard of before.

They met with Dr. Sahill, a nephrologist who was everything you wanted in a surgeon. Meticulous. Experienced. Well-respected. He was calculated with his speech. He had a six-foot frame, deep brown eyes and a full swoop in his hair that made him look like a muscular Ritchie Valens. Anne thought she could listen to his mellow Punjabi cadence all day.

"I see nothing in your file that indicates any... psychiatric issues?"

He waited for a reply. Reggie had a dozen jokes he could have spewed forth but resisted the urge. This felt similar to saying "bomb" in an airport. Reggie and Anne both shook their heads.

"Reggie, do you drink alcohol?"

"Almost never. A glass of wine or maybe a beer once in a while. I don't like the taste."

Anne thought she could see Dr. Sahill smile – he *really* liked that answer. He cycled through several pages of Reggie's medical history, X-rays, and notes.

"And no evidence of any heart issues, correct?"

"That's right," Reggie said, feeling more and more nervous, each answer building on the last.

"If you were to receive a kidney transplant, who would take care of you in the recovery?"

"I would," Anne chimed in. "I'm a former nurse and I'm at home full time. Our son will definitely help out, too."

Anne thought he liked that answer even better. Let this be over, she thought.

"Reggie, you have chronic, irreversible kidney disease. You have responded well to Zestril which has helped you manage hypertension. I'm going to schedule a series of exams and for you to meet with our transplant team. It appears at this time you could be a candidate for a kidney transplant, but to be sure, there is more work to be done. If everything goes well, we will get you on the transplant list."

It was such a small step but for some reason it meant the world and Anne held back tears. Reggie had a different reaction. He suddenly felt like he was hogging someone's spot, even though he wasn't even guaranteed to get on the list yet. *Certainly, someone more important, someone with more to offer, or someone younger was worth saving before him?* Should he even bother to complete the "work to be done?"

"Here's what's going to happen next. I'm going to put in an order for labs and we'll have you come in every six weeks after that so we can keep an eye on your numbers. I also want you to schedule a full day with our kidney transplant team."

"I'm sorry... schedule a whole *day?*" Anne asked.

"It is a six-hour appointment. You will watch an educational video, tour our facility, meet our transplant coordinators, nurses, our dietician, social worker, and financial advisor. You will want to get to know everyone, trust me. You don't want to sit around and just... wait, do you? If we approve you as a transplant candidate we need to seriously consider finding a *living* donor. Reggie, is there someone in your life who might possibly give you a kidney?"

This sounded incredibly silly to Reggie, like asking who would take a bullet for him.

"I would think so," he answered. "Most of them have already given me the finger."

Dr. Sahill belted out a huge laugh. In his twenty years in nephrology, no one had responded humorously to this all-important question. The joke told him Reggie would have a good attitude about the inevitable roller coaster ride in the months ahead. Anne simply smiled to cover up a mountain of anxiety building within her.

"Be thinking about a donor. A kidney from a living donor can last fifteen to twenty years, sometimes longer. A kidney from a deceased donor will give you much less. If all goes well and we can approve you as a candidate for transplant, your first move will be to go public and ask family and friends, friends of friends, and even enemies if they would be your donor."

Reggie thought of the group photo taken at Scott's Fourth of July party. He counted fifty-six people in the picture. Reggie had already come up with a reason why each one of them could not or should not be his donor – too young, too old, sickly, psycho, not a match, and so on. His brothers and sisters were not a match. His friends were all mid-50s and older – would they even qualify? And what did it matter? Reggie had a hard time returning merchandise to the store that was defective or that wasn't exactly what he needed. How could he possibly ask someone *to give him a kidney?*

"But Doctor, wait a minute. Is this really *necessary?* Couldn't I go for years living at 18% kidney function?"

Dr. Sahill saw hesitation in Reggie for the first time. But this was common. Anne looked at the floor, slightly perturbed with Reggie for trying to delay dealing with his circumstances.

"Reggie, my gut tells me you have one year at most before your kidneys shut down and you will find yourself on dialysis. That's just my opinion but I'm fairly confident given your fatigue, your history and your numbers. If I'm wrong, at least you will be prepared and you'll know what options you have. If you find blood in your urine or if it ever appears foamy, you'll need to call us right away."

Dr. Sahill handed Reggie a packet of information and invited them to exit the long way through the transplant center. They slowly inched past a dozen private consult rooms, peeking in as they passed. There were four doctor offices, a large conference room and a massive waiting area. It felt surreal to Reggie.

"I feel like we're in some magical, medical kingdom all its own," Reggie admitted.

Anne felt the opposite, knowing that some big city hospitals performed hundreds of kidney transplants per year. If she remembered right, OSF completed under forty. Back when she was a nurse, the stigma of small-market hospitals being inferior to their counterparts in major cities initially bothered her. She soon learned it all boiled down to how dedicated and skilled the surgeons and staffs were – the size of the hospital just allowed for more errors. She had met dozens of highly skilled surgeons who chose to live outside crowded urban centers despite the expected lower salary. She had a good feeling about Dr. Sahill and was looking forward to coming back for their full-day appointment.

Worn out from the long hallways of the hospital, Reggie asked Anne to drive home. This allowed him to rest and admire the historic farmhouses and small towns on Route 116. He was feeling *especially* good now. He watched his wife drive, amazed at her strength and how much she could make up for his deficiencies. He thought about her standing by his side as they get help from an army of people: surgeons, nurses, administrators, dieticians, X-ray machine techs – there must be at least twenty professionals doing their special part to help him get his health back.

Then he thought of the cost. *Must be crazy expensive.* He would have a chance to talk to the finance advisor next week to discuss what his health insurance might cover. Right now he was overjoyed that he was lucky enough to have health coverage through work, even if it was crappy. He told himself to remember to send his medical insurance information to the transplant center before the big day of meetings.

A nasty aroma shook him from his thoughts. He glanced right and saw they were driving past the massive white picket fences of the Porter Hog Farm. Anne made a foul face as if trying to plug her nose without taking her hands off the wheel. Reggie thought it was funny and lifted his phone to capture her twisted face with a photo. It was turned off, so he powered it up and noticed he had one voicemail.

"Reggie, this is Jelly Man. Um... hey, I'm sick to my stomach over this and I might get in big trouble for saying anything, but... they're going to fire you."

CHAPTER 13

Notice of Right to Sue

Nervous. Scared. He was getting fired tomorrow. Reggie sat at the piano and glanced at his cell phone wishing his brother Scott would return his call and dispense some free legal advice.

He began to move his fingers methodically over the old piano keys, playing chords a bit slower than the sheet music demanded. He had been teaching himself to play over the last two years and could fumble through about a dozen songs by heart. A huge life-long Elton John fan, the most soothing by far on his playlist was *Rocket Man*. It was easier for him to perform than *Für Elise, The Entertainer*, or the other beginner favorites. Even though the piano begged to be tuned, he thought it sounded pretty good. It also gave him a good excuse not to talk to his wife yet.

Anne understood her husband often played piano when stressed and she probably attributed this session to his kidney issues. She rested on the couch scrolling through Facebook on her phone, nibbling on grapes instead of the usual pretzels or potato chips. She softly sang, "Rocket Maaaaaan...burning out his fuse up here aloooone..." which delighted Reggie. She was relaxed.

Reggie expected to struggle with his fingering but somehow the music flowed through him smoothly and he nailed the entire song with no flubs. He had decided to tell Anne the news about Drucker's later, but he needed a game plan first. He didn't consider his employment to be "health news" so it didn't fall under the promise he made to be more open with her. She had too much to worry about already.

Earlier, when they arrived home from the hospital, Reggie called the transplant center to book the entire day of appointments for next week. Once Anne confirmed that the necessary X-rays, tests, and appointments were set, she felt comfortable heading to Wal Mart to pick up fruit and any other low-sodium items she could find. That's when Reggie called Jelly Man to get the full story.

Three Drucker's bigwigs from corporate met with local managers early this morning. Two of their niche magazine clients were abandoning print and switching to an on-line-only format, which was a growing trend. This sparked corporate to reduce staff in order to be better suited for their future workload. In the past, Reggie knew it was almost always the least experienced, the last ones hired who would be let go first. Six employees were considered expendable – five fairly-recent hires who were let go today and Reggie with his twenty-six years of service. It didn't make sense.

Jelly Man speculated that maybe some of the new top brass didn't like having an employee using a walker in the plant. Or perhaps it was his age. Or that Reggie was paid a higher wage than most of the front line workers. All could be possible, they thought.

But Reggie had a deeper concern. It was true he made more money per hour than every other floor worker due to his years of service but it wasn't by much. His expertise, ability to train, and just the fact that he showed up on time and sober every day was certainly worth a couple extra grand a year. Reggie convinced himself his slightly higher earnings didn't matter.

However, when submitting his request for this last day off, he had been honest, perhaps stupid, and wrote, "Nephrologist appointment" as his reason. Why didn't he just type "Medical" or "Dentist appointment?" Did they suspect Reggie had serious health issues? Is it possible Drucker's wanted to prevent a potential insurance premium hike from something like an expensive transplant? Reggie didn't know for sure how corporate medical insurance *really* worked, but the timing here made this suspicious. Either way, his firing felt illegal for a hard worker who had paid premiums for twenty-six years and whose life literally depended on having health insurance.

Reggie heard a raucous roar of laughter spill out from the game room down the hall. Lincoln had invited Zoey and another couple their age to play *Cards Against Humanity* and the game was in full swing. Reggie and Anne had played with their friends, laughing uproariously at the naughty innuendo, political humor, and overall "that's just wrong" feeling they got from the cards. They were both happy that Lincoln needed nothing from them at the moment.

An hour later, 9:30pm, his phone finally rang. Luckily, Anne had gone upstairs and was in bed reading. To be safe, Reggie took his phone to the front porch.

"Hey Reggie. It's Scott. Your message floored me. How are you doing?"

"Terrible. Nervous. It feels unfair."

Though Scott was a product liability attorney, his firm covered wrongful termination cases. He knew Illinois was not worker friendly. Scott leveled with him.

"Reggie, here's the scoop. You don't have an employment contract so we can only defer to state law. Illinois is an "at-will" employment state. This means an employer can fire you for any reason. In fact, for no reason at all if they choose as long as it's not illegal. Now, I take it you are not being let go due to any of the following: national origin, ancestry, order of protection status, military status, sexual orientation, marital status, race, religion or gender?"

Reggie was impressed Scott could just list this off the top of his head. This wasn't even Scott's specialty. He wished he had the smarts or skills to be able to provide services like this, or of any kind, to his siblings.

"Correct."

"And you're not... pregnant... right?"

They both laughed. Scott was happy to have lowered Reggie's tension a notch. It was Reggie who usually got the room laughing.

"OK, that leaves us with two angles. Age and disability. Do you feel you are being fired because of your age?"

Reggie thought about it. There were a handful of workers older than he was in the trenches at the plant. One co-worker was already sixty-four, even though she looked much younger than Reggie.

"Probably not. There are several people older than me. It would be hard to prove that."

"I agree. We'd almost have to prove a trend, anyway. What about disability? Do you feel there's any chance you're being fired for having to use a walker?"

Reggie thought about how he listed "nephrologist appointment" as the reason for taking a day off. He wanted to share this with Scott but couldn't. Or maybe, he didn't want to share it.

"That's got to be it," Reggie replied, happy that his brother had another viable reason to explore.

"Then why now? You've worked there for twenty-six years and have used the walker for, what, seven or eight years now? Help me understand what has changed where it would suddenly be important to your employer. Are you slower than the other workers? Less productive?"

Reggie was quiet. He wasn't ready for these questions. He had hoped his brother would somehow have a magic answer to save his job and he could go back to just worrying about his health.

"Reggie, let's switch gears. If you noticed, I haven't asked you the big questions yet. Why do you *think* they want to fire you? And the next question is: What will they *say* is the reason they're firing you?"

"I think they need to reduce costs so they're firing six people. But in the past, the ones fired were the last ones hired. I'm worried they're going to say I'm less productive than my co-workers."

Scott's reply would sound just like their Dad talking. Their father had used this strategy countless times in conversations where his kids didn't want to accept blame or sometimes the truth. Reggie used it often with his children. It was effective, but he hated that it was thrown in his face at this moment.

Scott said, "Well... are they right?"

Reggie tried to be open with himself to what the real answer could be. Yes, he was slower moving around the equipment, acquiring tools to fix machinery, getting to and from the hoists, but overall his job requisitions were completed faster than most the other employees.

"I am slower, that's obvious, but my productivity isn't slower. My jobs finish on average faster than most the other guys. They gave me good reviews. I won't know until tomorrow what their excuse is, but you're saying they don't even have to have a reason?"

"That's the law. You have a couple options if they terminate you. You could tell them that your brother is an attorney and that my firm is going to represent you as you file for wrongful termination. Sometimes that will scare a company into changing their mind, especially if you are close to retirement."

Reggie didn't care for this. He wasn't the go-to-war type and threatening his employer didn't feel right. *How could he work for them after that?*

"The other option is to *actually* sue them. I could offer my services to be your attorney, pro bono, but there's no guarantee anything will come of it. And it would take a while. The first step is to file a claim under the Americans with Disabilities Act. To do that, we need a Notice of Right to Sue from the EEOC. That alone can take up to one-hundred-eighty days."

Six months? Reggie suddenly felt desperate. He thought about his kidney function and where it might be in six months. What if it dropped to 15% by then? Or 5%?

"But I wouldn't have any health insurance for all that time, right?"

"Only if you win and they work backwards to cover any payments. You'd qualify for COBRA, but that can be very pricey."

Reggie felt sick to his stomach. He heard another burst of laughter from the game room. He wondered if he'd ever laugh with such carefree gusto again. *Was his usefulness on this planet shriveling up? Was the universe just pushing him out?*

"Reggie, there's really nothing we can do until we know for sure how Drucker's is going to play this. Can you call me tomorrow night and we'll go over your options again?"

"OK. Thanks so much, Scott. You're a great brother. Love ya, bro."

"I wish there was more I could do. Good luck. Love you too."

Reggie moved across the living room and looked up the stairs. He dreaded it, but it was time to tell Anne. She wouldn't be able to sleep after this and he knew they'd be up for hours speculating blindly over their options. He walked past the game room entrance. When he peeked in the kids didn't even notice him, but it comforted him that they ate snacks and drank sodas instead of beer or drugs like a lot of kids their age. He made it up the stairs and to his relief, Anne had fallen asleep with a romance novel still in her hand. He set her book on the nightstand, turned off the lights and snuggled up to her, completely terrified of what tomorrow would bring. Ninety minutes later, he fell asleep.

*   *   *

Looking stylish and smart in her oval, maroon glasses, all eyes were on Vanessa as she walked through the Drucker's plant to the main entrance. She always wore a dress or a skirt to work. Today's choice was a bright banana, empire waist dress. She moved with a slow, methodical purpose as if to make sure her long, jet-black hair would stay in place. Her shoulders were always square. She wasn't overly thin, attractive, or flirty but men couldn't help but watch when she moved. As Reggie walked into the plant, Vanessa was waiting and walked right up to him like she had done to five other employees the day before. Dozens of eyes were suddenly on him, not her.

"Mr. Nichols, can you come with me please? Mrs. Eyre needs to see you in her office."

This was it. All eyes followed him as he pushed his walker a third the way through the plant to the hallway leading to the administrative offices. Jelly Man watched closely, pretending he hadn't warned Reggie what was going to happen. Reggie saw him shake his head in protest, probably upset he'd be losing a solid worker with a positive attitude.

Reggie lightly slapped his right ear to make sure it was working. The usual buzz and chatter in the plant was missing – all he could hear was the hum of the machines. It was an eerily quiet, somber day for the workers in the trenches, each of them fully aware that one of their veteran employees was about to get sacked – walking out the door behind the five who were sent packing yesterday. Reggie felt like an injured football player being removed from the field as the crowd waited in silence.

Vanessa held the door for Reggie as he entered the HR office, then disappeared. Mrs. Eyre sat at her desk, her dirty blond hair raised into a big bun that, combined with her "smoker's wrinkles" made her the butt of a lot of company jokes. In a lounge chair in the corner sat an attorney from corporate with white hair who looked like a smug George Washington in a modern suit. He wouldn't say a word through this whole ordeal but somehow controlled the entire exchange. Reggie figured he was already pissed – Reggie's absence yesterday for a doctor visit probably meant he had to stay in Pontiac an extra day.

Mrs. Eyre started: "Reggie, thank you for coming. Please have a seat."

There were two chairs in front of her desk but the thick rug, placement of small tables, floor sculptures, and two big planters made it impossible for him to get to the chair with his walker. The attorney finally moved two plants so Reggie could get to his seat.

Mrs. Eyre began her speech... something about the future of the company, on-going trends in the industry and the need to adapt or go out of business. Reggie registered none of it. He'd never been fired before and he was in a fog. What about Anne? His kidneys? How he would pay the credit card bill this month. His mind went straight to his life insurance policy with COUNTRY Financial – he didn't even know the value of it.

He looked down and noticed a folder in front of him with his name on it. He opened it and saw a one-page termination agreement, his name and date already filled in with a line for his signature. He looked up and started to feel deep anger as Mrs. Eyre droned on.

He didn't know where she stood in her speech but he blurted out, "Why am I being fired?"

"Again, you're not being fired. We are under strict rules from corporate to eliminate six positions."

"Then why me? Tell me why I was selected. I train people. I'm considered an expert on the floor. Is it because I use a walker?"

She exchanged a long look with the attorney. It appeared he gave her the answer telepathically.

"Reggie, your physical condition has nothing to do with this decision. We based it on metrics. We reviewed the poly bag project efficiencies over the past month for the 8am until noon time frame, and those employees with the lowest scores are subject to termination. You were sixth from the bottom, and as I said, we have to remove six employees."

This was total bullshit. Reggie was an expert on that machine – he was on it nearly every day. He struggled three times in the past month, twice when it broke down more than usual and once while training a new employee. Though he had fallen behind early in the day, he finished all the jobs ahead of the scheduled time in the afternoon.

He had a fleeting thought – perhaps he could just re-apply for a position when the next one opened up. But... if he got re-hired, he would have to start all over. His insurance wouldn't start for six months and his benefits would be reduced big time. He felt railroaded.

"So, you're saying, I was the last to be let go. If we had one open slot, I'd still be safe?"

She nodded. "We're not lost on the fact that you've worked here for two and a half decades. Even though we've only owned the company for three years, we are offering a generous eight-week severance package. You will have insurance and receive paychecks for two more months."

That was unexpected, unprecedented for Drucker's, but eight weeks was not helpful. He stared at the paper. *Who's going to hire a 56-year-old man who needs a walker?* There were no other commercial printers in Pontiac. He thought about tearing up the paper and storming out. But if he didn't sign, he might forfeit the eight weeks of pay and insurance.

They had said all the right things. It wasn't about age. Or his limitations. They seemed to have all the bases covered even though Reggie knew he was a strong performer on the job. He wished Scott were here, if for nothing else, to wipe the subtle little smiles off the faces of Mrs. Eyre and the lawyer.

He was whipped. He picked up the pen and read the paper. He glanced at the clock: 8:04am. He felt numb as twenty-six years of history in this building was about to come to an end and it only took them four minutes to push him out.

He hated to do it but he played his only card left. "My brother is an attorney and his firm is going to represent me in a wrongful termination suit."

The attorney shifted, crossed his arms and looked pissed. He shared another long look with Mrs. Eyre. She matched his anger but kept her voice calm.

"I'm sorry you feel that way. If you don't sign the agreement, you will forfeit the eight-week severance package."

His threat did nothing. He had no cards left. He could kiss a kidney surgery goodbye. *Would he even be able to afford dialysis?* He stared at the signature line and felt as if he were about to sign his own death certificate.

The door suddenly burst open, startling everyone. Harry Schott paraded in.

"Harry – we're in the middle of a meeting!" Mrs. Eyre yelled.

Harry ignored her and sat in the chair next to Reggie, who suddenly realized he didn't know which five employees were released yesterday. Was Harry, a recent hire, one of them? Had he been fired yesterday and was now about to go "postal"?

Harry gave Reggie a calm look as if he were smiling without really smiling. Reggie could see the rabbit face again but he looked more like an arrogant Bugs Bunny this time, and his expression said to Reggie, "I'm going to wipe those shitty grins right off their faces."

He looked at the attorney, then at Mrs. Eyre, and with full confidence announced:

"I quit. I want Reggie to have my job."

CHAPTER 14

Drucker's Jacket

Filled with angst, Skylar hopped into her aging Honda Civic. She clicked her seat belt and sped out of St. Mark's where she taught a summer program for a dozen Catholic children. She had asked permission to leave immediately after she learned the shocking news. Her "stepfather" was fired today from his job of twenty-six years.

One of Skylar's students was Candi Wesson, the only troublemaker she ever taught who she openly called a horrible little snot. All Candi blabbed on about today was that her Dad was fired yesterday morning from Drucker's. During today's late snack time, Skylar ducked out and made several phone calls to hunt down the full story of the cutbacks, a feat one might be able to accomplish in a small town if you have taught children of key people.

It was extra easy for someone as pretty and pleasant as Skylar. She never asked for the attention, but her huge brown eyes, milky-white skin and soothing voice made it easy to get answers when she wanted them. She hated *these* answers. Six employees in all, and Reggie was on the cutback list. She needed to be there for him. He had done so much for her over the years. Though he technically wasn't family, he *was* family.

She told her car phone system to call Reggie – no answer. Then Anne and Lincoln – no answer. Terrible visuals of the family suffering ran through her mind: fret, betrayal, freaking out financially, worried about insurance, wondering where the next meal might come from. She called one last number, and her stepbrother Ben answered.

"Hey girl. What's up?"

"Hey Ben. Have you heard from Reggie or Anne today?" She hated that she sounded upset. Her goal was not to reveal anything if Ben hadn't heard yet.

"I have not. But if you see him, tell him he's a genius. Samantha and I are mint. She even let me pick the restaurant tonight. Arby's Roast Turkey Ranch and Bacon! I am *the boss,* baby!"

"Sounds great. Thanks Ben." She hung up, wishing more peace for Ben. He often sounded angry, even when he was talking about things going well for him.

She remembered how Reggie and Anne had consoled her eight years ago when she hit rock bottom. Anne helped tremendously with the medical side of it, but Reggie gave her courage. Inspiration. When Skylar unfairly threw too much blame at her husband Jack, Reggie got her to believe in hope again, which she thought impossible for anyone after a devastating miscarriage. Three years later, she gave birth to a healthy girl. Thanks to Reggie's efforts to help her believe in it again, she named her Hope.

She noticed the sign for County Market and decided she shouldn't show up empty handed. Though her summer earnings were laughable, she was feeling generous. She was certainly better off than someone who just lost his job. She would bring food. She parked, admired the perfect mid 70's weather – unusual for July, and walked inside. Then she found herself at a loss. *What groceries do you buy for a guy who was just fired?*

She settled on a variety of brats, burgers, and chicken breasts, then some Chex Mix, bananas, and a box of fresh cookies from the bakery. On her way to the checkout she passed some plump, juicy peaches. She couldn't resist and bought two bags, planning to keep one for herself.

Stocked and ready, she drove to Reggie's house, practicing a speech that would convince him he could find a new job... a better job. That he was a conscientious, fun employee. That any company would be lucky to have him. And like he had taught her -- to have hope.

As she pulled up to the house she saw about twenty people packed in his backyard, which she had never seen before. Obviously, she wasn't the only one wanting to console the family today. She had to park way down the block and braced herself for a sad afternoon. She stepped out of her Civic and heard a song blaring: *Take This Job and Shove It.*

The chatter was boisterous. Laughter echoed off the walnut and oak trees. Reggie was actually... *grilling?* This was not a sad occasion. As she strolled up to the gate, she realized Lincoln and Anne were the only family members in the yard. The rest must be co-workers who were... *having a party?*

She strolled through the gate. Two of the younger Drucker's employees stared her up and down – she was used to it and had mastered the art of looking like she didn't see oglers. Confused, she walked up to Reggie with her bag of groceries.

"Hey Reggie. How's everything?"

"Skylar! What a surprise. What are you doing here?"

"Well, I came here in a panic 'cause I heard you were fired today. What's up?"

Anne broke from a big group and ran up to Skylar for a hug, then checked the bag of groceries.

"Skylar – this is perfect! How'd you know? I'll get this ready. Reggie, no brats for you." Anne set out the Chex Mix and cookies on the picnic table and took the rest in the house.

Skylar looked at Reggie, even more confused. Anne had never *limited* food.

"We're cutting back on salt. Hey – thanks so much for adding to the party. You should hear the whole story."

He introduced her to Harry Schott. Skylar couldn't help but think he kind of looked like a rabbit but he sure told a story with vibrant enthusiasm. The others gathered around as he told the saga which turned out to be their collective triumph.

"About fifteen of us, I guess, met before work to talk about Reggie losing his job. We were all torn up about it. The least we could do was take up a collection. We raised fourteen hundred throughout the plant."

Skylar choked. She managed fundraisers during the schoolyear for her second-grader class at Central. They were hard. Once it took them four months to raise fourteen hundred dollars.

Some guy in the back yelled, "I threw in all my weed money, man!" Big laughs followed.

Harry continued. "But then we started wondering if there might be a way we could *save* his job." A few of the guys started pumping their fists, yelling, "Reggie! Reggie! Reggie!"

"Jelly Man wanted to use the old, *if he goes, then we all go* ploy but none of us thought management would bite. We were dead in the water until Vanessa came to bitch at us to get back to work. *She* spilled the beans. She told us exactly six people had to be cut – didn't really matter which ones. With five already gone, Willow had the idea that as an incentive, if anyone quit and saved Reggie's job, he or she would get the fourteen hundred. Well, I just started a month ago. Wouldn't be that hard for me to find another job. My wife has great health insurance. I was the logical choice."

He put his hand on Reggie's shoulder, towering over him with his six-foot three-inch frame. He shot him a pure genuine look and Reggie nodded his thanks. Harry raised his glass.

"To Reggie Nichols! May the bastards never drag you down!"

Everyone raised their drinks, including Reggie with his water bottle. High fives all around. The comradery was bursting as if the team had just won a major championship. Skylar shook her head, impressed but not surprised Reggie incited such support. She hugged him, then wandered over to chat with Lincoln.

Reggie turned to his grill and stared at the hot dogs and burgers. They became blurry as he turned them aimlessly over and over again, reflecting on Harry's story. For his entire life, Reggie had refused special treatment. He wanted no favors. Yet, here was a man who gave up *his job* for him, and there was absolutely no way Reggie could refuse it. Reggie had been faking joy ever since management agreed to keep him on board around noon today, almost four hours after Harry announced that he quit. Though his family and co-workers were ecstatic with the ending of the story, Reggie felt more unworthy than ever. *Why is it that others always have to step up to take care of him?*

He noticed Lincoln sitting at the picnic table, engaging Skylar and other adults in pleasant conversation. *"Hospital time" sure ages you and makes you mature in a hurry.* Four of Reggie's co-workers would tell him by the end of the party what a polite, fine young man Lincoln had become. Relieved his son didn't have to hear that his father had been fired, Reggie agreed wholeheartedly.

Reggie moved the hot dogs and burgers onto plates right as Anne returned with Skylar's brats, burgers and chicken prepped for grilling. She soon followed that with three pitchers of delicious peach margaritas. Over the next three hours, the booze and food disappeared, and the guests started to leave with joy in their hearts.

Reggie and Anne rested at the picnic table as the party wound down and said a few last goodbyes. Anne turned to Reggie and in a huge effort not to ruin this amazing high from the party, she forced a smile and said quietly, "It finally happened. The honeymoon fridge died."

He grimaced. A new one would cost a grand, at least. They had caught a huge break. He would have been fired yesterday morning had he gone to work instead of the hospital appointment. But he instantly got pulled back under the muck by the fridge. This just seemed the way of the world. Life happens.

She continued, "At least it was mostly empty – our guests pretty much cleaned us out."

He admired her effort to be positive. "I guess the honeymoon is over."

They both half-smiled knowing their honeymoon fridge had a good run. Anne picked up the last of the dishes and took them inside. Reggie noticed only one guest remained, Harry, who was cleaning the grill. Reggie yelled to him, chuckling:

"Haven't you done enough for me today!? Get away from there!"

Harry continued until he had scraped the entire surface, then looked to make sure no one else was around. He untied his jacket from his waste and walked over to Reggie. The jacket boasted the familiar blue plaid with the yellow Drucker's logo, but was obviously too small for Harry.

"If that's *your* jacket, you must look great in a bikini."

Harry laughed, "Never tried one on! No... when I was hired, I got the traditional free jacket but all they had left were smalls and mediums. I can't wear it. I want you to have it, but you have to promise to wear it at least three times before you give it away or throw it away. Deal?"

Reggie nodded, thinking that was an odd request. He wished that Harry lived in town so he might see him around more but he lived in Flanagan, an even smaller town a dozen miles away. Reggie drove through it on the way to Peoria – maybe he could set up a visit.

"Amazing things are going to happen for you Reggie Nichols, I can feel it. Fun party – thanks for the invite."

He shook Reggie's hand, gave him the jacket and left. As he walked off, Reggie searched his brain for a funny quip but a joke didn't feel right. He felt nothing but respect as he watched his rescuer walk to his car. Reggie could feel in his bones that Harry was going to land on his feet quickly and that their paths would cross again.

The sun was setting. Reggie noticed a breezy chill for the first time. Good timing, he thought, and he put on the Drucker's jacket – a perfect fit. He observed an amazing sunset filled with purples and reds. The hibiscus, which received many compliments today, took on a new glow under the colored light.

Reggie knew he had dodged a *big* bullet today. His company never felt so unimportant to him, but the insurance had become everything. He still didn't believe the poly bagger bullshit. He wondered what had *really* happened in the decision rooms at Drucker's. Had he been a target? Was it just pure coincidence they selected him for firing when dialysis or a transplant stared him in the face? Mrs. Eyre and the attorney had said if there was one slot open, Reggie would have been safe, so is that why they *had* to keep him when the slot opened? Why did it take four hours for them to tell Reggie he still had his job? Did his threat to sue actually help? He would never know.

He looked at the gorgeous, darkening heavens. He wished for a sign that things were going to be fine going forward. One shooting star. A flickering star. Something celestial to give him comfort that his life and his health would get back on track. He waited for a full minute but nothing came. He thought about the unexpected expense of a new refrigerator and shoved his hands into his jacket pockets in despair.

He felt an envelope in the jacket pocket. He pulled it out. Enclosed was a note signed by Harry: "I never agreed to take funds that were collected for you. Do what you want with it. Maybe fix your muffler."

And behind it was fourteen hundred dollars in cash.

CHAPTER 15

Appointment Day

Reggie pulled a sealed bowl of green grapes out of the new appliance and grinned like a trouble-making schoolboy. The refrigerator was a beautiful, chrome beacon of delight - side by side doors, door-in-door storage, slide out, easy to clean shelving, tilting, adjustable bins, multiple crisper drawers for the fruits and vegetables that had become so important to him, and an automatic ice and water dispenser. It smelled like a new car. They could have bought a simpler model for a grand, but when the guys at work refused to take any of their money back, Reggie and Anne decided for the first time in years to pamper themselves. This was a $1900 fridge but on sale with tax and installation -- just $1401.

The final total prompted Anne to jokingly give Reggie a hard time for "going over budget." They playfully renewed their vows after the install and nicknamed it "the Wedding Vow" fridge. It beautified the kitchen, reflected the shine and strength of their marriage, and with their pride and spirits lifted for a few days, it even improved their sex life.

Reggie refilled a water bottle just for fun to watch his new toy at work. The sensors automatically knew when the bottle was full and stopped dispensing. Reggie laughed, impressed with the technology and giddy that he and his wife owned it outright. He brought the grapes to the garage where Anne was waiting in the passenger seat for the drive to Peoria and a full day of appointments with the transplant team.

As he climbed into the driver's seat, Reggie thought about the request he submitted to Drucker's for this day off work. He had written "vacation" as his reason for absence just to be safe. Reggie and his loving wife both cycled through a labyrinth of emotions before they finally reached the parking lot in Peoria.

They started the day with the Transplant Coordinator, Rah, shortened from "Deborah." A tiny spitfire wearing shiny wire-rimmed glasses with thirty years nursing experience on her resume, she was the go-to girl 24/7 and could get stuff done. Reggie thought of her as the Radar O'Reilly of the whole operation. She made sure meetings got scheduled. She managed post-care labs, meds, and follow-ups. She seemed an expert on the anti-rejection medications taken post-surgery and explained the process of experimenting to get them exactly right. She couldn't stress enough, "The better the genetic match, the less medication needed so we want to find a donor who's the best genetic fit."

She got them started on a 45-minute video – an overview of the history of transplants, the doctors, staff, and the reputation of OSF St. Francis Medical Center. The current performance numbers at OSF appeared stellar. They were up to almost 50 transplants per year and their surgeons were skilled veterans who had a lot to brag about.

The video also explained the most exciting development since Anne's tenure as a nurse – the growing popularity of "donor chains." A potential donor and his recipient who weren't a match were thrown into a pool to find other pairs that didn't match. And donor chains could involve a lot more than two pairs if necessary – the record was a whopping 34 donors and 34 recipients. The possibilities seemed promising.

The next agenda item was a cancer screening. Because his father had died of lung cancer, he had to answer dozens of questions. Reggie also admitted he had smoked in the past. He thought it complimented his Burt Reynolds mustache back in the day, but he had been smart enough to quit after just one year. Because he had a colonoscopy recently, they let him skip that section of the medical survey and went straight to a thorough physical. It was just like the one Dr. Basson performed recently. So far, so good.

Feeling tired already, Reggie was relieved to be sent to Radiology. He thought it would be easy and quick but there were several X-rays taken, even a chest X-ray to look for infections or abnormalities. The office also had to verify that Reggie had dental X-rays taken in the past six months. After a full hour, he got to return to the consult rooms.

The stress test was next to ensure his heart would be strong enough for surgery. Because Reggie couldn't run on a treadmill like many patients, they injected Lexiscan into his vein to simulate the response to exercise. Reggie felt some dizziness and tingling throughout but the technician showed no concerns. Reggie figured he must have passed.

Next, Dr. Singh, a nephrologist and transplant surgeon, stopped in to chat with Reggie and Anne. He had star power. He was personable. He told a few jokes, chatted about life and health in general, his fascination with smaller markets like Peoria and his love of the Pittsburgh Pirates. He explained that Reggie would keep his two existing kidneys and they would just "plug in" the donated kidney in front. That is just one of the reasons why his recovery would be easier than the donor's. Dr. Singh was busy, though, and politely moved on.

Reggie joked with Anne, "I'm gonna have three kidneys and you have only one? You're such an underachiever!"

Next, they met Lori, the Dietician. She talked about food she loved – a *lot*. She handed them several brochures and discussed sodium at length, which they politely sat through even though they had already painfully self-educated. Lori picked up on their sodium fear and the extremism with their recent diet.

"It's not *life or death* to eat a banana or avocado once in a while – just try to *limit* high potassium and high-sodium foods." Going stir-crazy from their own militant dietary rules, this was a huge relief.

Finally – a break for lunch. Two dozen fast food places rested within a mile of the hospital, but Anne walked to the car and brought a cooler to the lounge filled with grapes, chicken sandwiches, sliced cucumbers and red peppers, salt-free potato wedges and Kit Kat fudge. Reggie savored every bite and when he raved about it, Anne beamed sheepishly. She missed the adulation terribly as she re-learned how to cook in a low-salt world.

After lunch, they were nervous walking into their most dreaded meeting - how to pay for all this. They met Donita, the Financial Advisor. A dedicated professional who fought for every penny for her patients, she had thoroughly reviewed Reggie's insurance plan before the meeting. They were surprised to learn it was standard for the recipient's insurance to pay for both the donor's and recipient's surgeries. The donor only paid for travel to and from the hospital. Reggie sighed heavily when hearing this - that should *really* help when seeking a donor. Reggie would be responsible for his usual deductible, but everything else was covered. No extra costs. Reggie and Anne eased back into their chairs and relaxed slightly. It would still be a significant hit -- a large deductible, lost wages, travel, and there would be a lifetime of anti-rejection medications to think about, but it wouldn't wipe them out.

Donita also shared that transplants were performed on Mondays. If all went well, the donors usually went home on Wednesdays and recipients on Thursdays. Anne gasped. You donate a kidney and two days later you're on your way home? Modern medicine was miraculous. Reggie's mind was elsewhere. He added it up. Two major surgeries, five nights minimum in the hospital, the surgeon's fees, you add in the salaries for everyone they had met today - how expensive *was* this? He suddenly needed to know the overall cost to society for him to get a new kidney.

"We don't give out that number," Donita said. "It varies so widely with each case."

A standard answer. Reggie felt "managed." It must be a hundred grand, he thought. And mentally, he plunged into the chasm of his own negative thinking, *I'm not worth that.*

Reggie and Anne were then sent to a waiting room where they checked their phones for a while before an aide came and asked Reggie to follow her. Just Reggie. She took him to one of the consult offices. A lady in a stylish orange suit with gorgeous ebony skin greeted him. She was tall, fit, and her office was dominated by golden retriever photos. She seemed a bit surprised to see a kidney transplant candidate pushing a walker but was patient while he got settled.

"Hi, Reggie. I'm Melissa. Nice to meet you. I'll be your last meeting today. My job is to help you understand some of the common reactions we see with kidney transplant patients. We want to make sure you are emotionally prepared for a surgery of this magnitude and are suited for a life with a new kidney."

Reggie tried not to look insulted. This was the psychosocial exam. Despite dragging a walker wherever he went, Reggie would describe himself as normal, well-adjusted, and currently wasting his time talking about whether he was mentally fit to receive a kidney.

"OK. I'm ready. I don't know what to tell you except that I would be thrilled to have a transplant and not have to go on dialysis. It will definitely save my life. I know I will live longer. I have my wife and son to help me with the recovery."

"Excellent," she replied, and looked at her notes. Reggie felt like she was just humoring him.

"Let's try a little exercise. Please close your eyes."

Reggie figured he might as well play along – this had been a long day. Maybe he could rest with his eyes closed.

"OK, now, I want you to picture a person you admire very much. Not a celebrity, but someone you know personally who is over eighteen. Tell me if it's a man or a woman."

Reggie had several to choose from in his life, but Harry came to mind as he was the most recent hero to come to his aid.

"OK. He's a man."

"Wonderful. Now, I want you to visualize that this person donated a kidney to you one year ago. His journey was a long one. He had to explain to his family and friends that he was *volunteering* for a major surgery, which was a risk to his health -- possible blood clots, infections, or heaven forbid, even his death. His loved ones were scared for him. Some of his friends tried to talk him out of it. Some asked if you would do the same for him. He had to undergo a myriad of tests to be sure he was healthy enough for surgery and was a good genetic match. He missed several days of work to do this, probably using his own vacation time. He then endured a scary, traumatic operation, leaving his loved ones to care for him and bring him back to health. The first week of recovery was especially painful. He had to use short term disability and missed at least three weeks of work, maybe more. After all that, he's now committed to living a life with only one kidney. Controlling blood pressure and sodium, and staying hydrated suddenly take on a vital importance. He probably had to change his diet and if he drinks, he cut back on alcohol. Now... take your time with this... really think about it. Can you tell me what you want to say to this person?"

Reggie didn't dare open his eyes because they were starting to well up. Everything she had mentioned had passed through Reggie's mind in pieces but listing it all together made the sacrifice seem colossal. Epic. Fucking gargantuan! Who would possibly do this for *him*? How the hell would he even ask? And what in God's name would you say to this person? He berated himself for dismissing this session earlier because he was obviously NOT mentally prepared. He knew deep down he didn't feel he was worth it, but suddenly it felt crucial he didn't dare let her, or anyone else, know this. It was illegal to pay donors or give them valuable gifts for a human organ – that had been stressed repeatedly – but how would he thank the donor? The donor's family?

After what felt like five minutes, he finally spoke.

"I guess the only thing I could say is... thank you. Like, a million times."

He opened his eyes. She was smiling.

"That is an excellent answer, Reggie. Probably the best there is. It's so important for your own health that you explore all the possible emotions that could come of this, and even more important to feel and express gratitude. So, let's talk about one year later. Two years later.

You could be living a life made possible by another person's sacrifice. How will that make you feel?"

"Like every day is a gift."

She smiled again as if she had a star pupil in the room.

She added, "And just my two cents – maybe every day should feel like that anyway, right?"

Reggie sat up straighter, excited to work with her further. The rest of the hour was just as informative and insightful. Together, they considered the possible outcomes if he were to find a donor. What if the donor chickened out? What if the donor had complications? What if the donor got sick a year later? What if Reggie's body rejected the kidney? He figured she was "assessing" him through all this but felt confident she'd sign off on him as a transplant candidate.

And then Melissa asked a final question that jolted him. It would nag at him on several levels for months. He couldn't answer it – heck, no one could. He would have to reconcile this question, maybe put it in a corner of his brain and revisit it over and over until an answer presented itself.

She asked, "Though the odds are very slim, how do think your donor would feel if you don't make it home from the hospital?"

CHAPTER 16

Dilly Bar

The slice of banana had the perfect amount of tangy sweetness and radiated a powerful, delectable fruit flavor. Reggie munched with his eyes closed to savor the fresh aroma. The texture was wonderfully soft – not mushy or too firm. No hint of that chalky, leafy smell you get when underripe or the mustiness when overripe. He had been afraid to eat bananas for weeks but now that he had "permission" to eat one, he realized what a gift they were to the food world. Still careful about potassium intake, he gave the remaining half of the plate of sliced bananas to Lincoln, who sat with him at the kitchen table preparing for an interview.

"So, what do I say if they ask me what my weaknesses are?" Lincoln asked.

Reggie tried his best to coach him. "Well... what are they?"

"I don't know. I got C's in math."

Reggie wished Lincoln was a little further along with self-awareness and confidence. He could pass for age forty with his mature personality but his ability to brag about, or even talk about himself was lacking – as if he were barely a teenager.

"I'm not going to feed you the answers, but you'll be asked to do math if you get the job. Please don't say math. Whatever you say, follow it up with how you're working on it so it will no longer be a weakness."

"Driving?" Lincoln said, but it was more of a guess.

"No – that's not what they're looking for. Focus on things like patience, how you learn, computer skills, that kind of thing. Speaking of driving, you should drive to the interview. How is it going to look if you're the only job candidate whose parents drop you off? I'll talk to your Mom about letting you have a set of keys again."

Lincoln tried to hide his excitement. He slinked into the game room to practice his responses with a printout Reggie gave him: "The 30 Most-Asked Interview Questions." Reggie wished his own father would have shared this simple tactic with him – to practice. He had struggled mightily to land a job in his twenties and knew he interviewed poorly. It was one of the biggest reasons he stayed with Drucker's all these years. He scratched his legs, feeling especially itchy today.

His cell phone rang – it was the OSF Transplant Center. It had been a full week since their exhausting trip to Peoria. He took a deep breath. Then another. There were 500,000 people on dialysis in the U.S., but only 100,000 or so on the transplant waiting list. So many people don't qualify for the list for a host of reasons. Would he be one of them? Would his leg and hip issues force him into a draining life on dialysis. Would he be forced against his will to retire? To go on disability? He answered on the sixth ring.

"Hello, this is Reggie."

"Hello Reggie. This is Rah at the Transplant Center. I have great news. You are officially on the national transplant list."

Reggie gulped. Hurdle one, cleared.

"That is excellent news. I was so worried but I guess I didn't need to be."

"Not only did you qualify medically, but you made quite an impression on the team, Reggie. The staff is excited to help you on what will be an epic journey."

Reggie tried to internalize her comments, but felt she probably said that to everyone.

"Rah, can you... can you tell me... what does this really *mean*? Like, if you were in my shoes, knowing what you know, how excited should I be?"

"Hmm... that's an insightful question. I guess – it means that all sides of the medical community agree that a kidney transplant could dramatically improve and extend the life of Reggie Nichols. With a transplant you should live longer and have a higher quality life. It's hope for a less medically invasive future. I will stress that the waiting list is extensive – it'll most likely be a couple years, maybe more before you are called. And you are O positive, a wait list that tends to be even longer. But – you are on the list and we should celebrate that. The best move you can make is to tell the world you need a kidney. We call it *the golden ticket* – when you have a *living* donor lined up before you need dialysis."

"I see. Well, this is great day. Maybe you and I should go dancing."

She laughed – never expecting the man with a walker to suggest such a thing.

"You need to let us know if anything with your health or your health insurance changes. We'll review your lab results every six weeks to stay on top of how those kidneys are doing for you."

He hung up and suddenly felt invincible. He was officially on the list. He had made an impression on the transplant team. Drucker's tried to fire him, but he *still* had his job and health insurance. He glanced up and was reminded that he owned the Cadillac of refrigerators. Dr. Sahill had predicted one year, but with his focus on eating right, he could probably go several years. He was at 18% kidney function and felt he could make that work – maybe for the rest of his life. The long waiting list? *No problem!*

Reggie agreed with Rah – he should celebrate. He walked to the game room to ask his son if he'd like to take a drive and get a treat. Lincoln had taped a picture of Ben Franklin on the computer monitor and was talking to it.

"That's a very good question," Lincoln rehearsed. "I feel my biggest weakness is being assertive when it matters. A lot of people will say I'm a nice person, but sometimes at work that might not be best for the company."

Reggie was impressed. Lincoln sounded so much smoother than *he* ever had in an interview. Practice was paying off and he felt it best to let Lincoln continue. He walked out quietly and used his walker to get to the garage, feeling less pain than normal.

The Enclave was missing. Anne must have taken it to visit her mother at the nursing home, leaving him with their Ford Ranger pick-up. Reggie liked how easy it was to hoist the walker into the back and to climb into the small truck, but that's where the love ended. Heating and AC were weak, there was a hole in the floorboard and it took forever to get up to 30 mph. At least she had been remarkably reliable through most of her 144,000 miles.

Reggie drove to Dairy Queen and joined the line at the drive-through. One of the first food items he researched when this health nonsense started were Dilly Bars, a family favorite. Only 220 calories and 80mg of sodium, just five percent of his recommended daily intake. He would buy a dozen and surprise the family with a treat. The line was short and he looked forward to the look on Lincoln's face when he returned with a celebratory treat.

As he slowly moved up in line, he thought about the reunion planned for David Carvell over Thanksgiving break. His classmates had been so eager to talk to Reggie. Perhaps there would be a real angel in *that* group who might step up and be his kidney donor. Or perhaps he'd magically fit inside one of those long donor chains. Maybe one of his non-matched siblings would step forward and be part of a small donor chain. Maybe he'd be a match for one of those "altruistic donors" – people who walk in off the street to volunteer to donate a kidney to a stranger to save a random life. There were so many possibilities and at this moment, Reggie was confident everything was going to work out. He felt like Charlie in *Willy Wonka and the Chocolate Factory*. He was about to buy chocolate and he would find that *golden ticket.*

He ordered a dozen Dilly Bars, impressed at how clear the drive-through speakers were these days compared to the muffled, garbled noise that used to confirm his drive-through orders. He drove forward to the second window and paid, but his Ford Ranger suddenly stalled. Reggie took the bag from the DQ employee, a high-school girl with short, spiky hair that reminded him of his wayward, rebellious sister Ava. He tried to start the truck but all he heard was the familiar "click click" that indicated the starter had gone bad. His first thought was how angry the customers behind him would get and he checked the rearview mirror. He counted five cars – all customers he would be pissing off. He turned to tell the DQ employee his truck wouldn't start but she had left the window.

How could this happen? *Really? It had to stall right here in the DQ drive-through?* Again, he had been on top of the world dreaming of possibilities but got sucked under the surface. Is it *him?* Is it his *luck?* Is there *any way in the world* he is worth a new kidney and an entire team of people coming to his rescue?

He looked in his rearview mirror again and saw five people running out of the restaurant side door, all wearing the same bright red DQ collared shirts. The oldest, most likely the manager, approached Reggie and said, "Put her in neutral, Bud." They positioned themselves in the back and sides of the truck and quickly pushed him out of the drive-through to the back of the parking lot. It was such a light-weight vehicle, Reggie thought they probably could have easily moved it with two people. They left him under the shade of a gorgeous oak tree, parked at an angle so a tow truck could easily access the hood if he needed to jump the battery.

"Can we call a tow truck for ya?" the manager asked.

Reggie shook his head, showing the man his cell phone.

"No – but now I know how cool it would be to drive into a pit stop at the Indy 500! Thank you!"

The employees laughed, high fived and skipped back into the building – like moving the truck had been a short, fun recess for them. It was as if Reggie helped them by needing their help.

It was a hot August day, but cool in the shade. He noticed a steady breeze coming through his window. Parked at this odd angle, he had a perfect view through the backyard gate of the neighboring house, where a healthy hibiscus plant waved in the breeze at him. He stared at it, feeling trust, poise, and good karma. With his good luck today, maybe a tow truck would just happen to drive by. Or maybe he'd call one after having a Dilly Bar. He opened the bag and grabbed one, not caring if the others melted. He unwrapped it, leaned the seat back, and admired the cool steam rising off the glistening chocolate. He placed it near his lips and absorbed the chill emanating off this perfect treat.

He thought about Harry Schott's parting words, *Amazing things are going to happen for you Reggie Nichols, I can feel it.* He winked at the waving hibiscus and took in the peaceful scene as he filled up on fresh ice cream, decadent dark chocolate, 80mg of sodium, and a ton of faith in his future.

CHAPTER 17

The Berly Factor

Kim zipped up her sleek, light green party dress in the front leaving the slightest hint of cleavage visible. Half of the dress's back was cut out, showing off just enough skin to be acceptable at a corporate function. The dress hugged her form perfectly and complemented her chestnut hair with auburn highlights, expertly curled as if she had just come from the salon. Her heels were strappy and reeked of elegance. She slid on a lace jacket to cover her bare shoulders and applied a layer of pink lip gloss in front of the mirror.

Lucas wondered how she continued to find these flawless outfits that balanced professionalism with just the right amount night-life style. He glumly checked the weather app on his phone for the umpteenth time, wishing they could just stay in the hotel room all night.

"Now it says the rain is supposed to last twelve more hours. We're gonna be stuck inside the boat the whole time."

She kissed him and whispered smugly, "Berly Factor."

Ah yes... the "Berly Factor" – his wife's superpower. Shortened from "Kim-berly." For three decades, Kim had gone to a multitude of outdoor events where the forecasts called for rain, snow, howling winds, even tornadoes. But if Kim attended a Cubs, Sox, Bears, or college football game, a music concert, graduation, a festival, or a parade, even her daughter Riley's wedding, the storm systems magically cleared and the sun appeared in its full glory. Often at the last possible moment. Every... single... time. Fans would get full value for their money and maximize their experience simply because Kim showed up. And the weather often returned to its ugly forecast the minute Kim sat back in the car for the trip home. The Berly Factor was legendary, envied by family, co-workers, and her wide circle of friends. She received free tickets to events in hopes she would attend and deliver a good-weather guarantee. Some of her co-workers would ask to touch her arm or shake her hand before leaving for the weekend, hoping to take some of her good-weather luck with them.

Lucas was positive the streak was over. He had driven through wicked rains earlier today on their trip upstate to Chicago, and the forecast gave no hope that this slow-moving pressure system would let up until 9am tomorrow. This would severely hamper the Lake Michigan dinner cruise for the two hundred guests invited by MediaCast.

Lucas noticed that Kim didn't bother to check her weather app all day and never once considered wearing something rain appropriate. By the time they stepped out of the hotel, it had stopped raining. As they walked the three city blocks to Navy Pier, they watched the clouds blow out to Lake Michigan. When they stepped in line to board the gorgeous Odyssey yacht with clients and Lucas's fellow managers, the sun shone brightly and a massive rainbow appeared as a gateway for the ship's journey. The Berly Factor streak was alive, taking care of her husband and his clients.

The pre-dinner cocktail hour was festive. Lucas shook hands with his clients and their spouses from Bloomington and Springfield, and two ad agency contacts from St. Louis and Kankakee that he'd never met in person. He thanked them for their business with his smart, corporate-analyst wife by his side – completing step one from Lucas's "client-entertainment handbook." Now, for step two.

Kim watched the master at work, admiring Lucas's ability to move each conversation along at a fluid pace. His clients were oblivious to the fact that Lucas never talked about himself for more than a sentence. He'd react. He'd make them laugh. Then he'd ask more questions about them. Which led to deeper questions. The focus always remained on the client, their spouse, their business, families, and their hopes and dreams. She could tell they sensed his sincerity. It confirmed for her once again his real secret to success: he genuinely cared for his clients and could always identify something about their lives that he found interesting. None of them would realize until they woke up the next day that they learned little about Lucas Nichols, but for some reason, they *really trusted him.* This skilled craft went on for almost an hour before the Captain announced dinner was served.

The Odyssey staff had perfected dinner logistics and the banquet kept the guests busy gushing about the cuisine and quick access to their favorite booze. The salads, all four choices, were amazingly fresh. Each individual steak was prepared to the clients' preference and spiced with their choice of Fajita, Balsamic & Herb, or Korean – all tender. The buttery lobster tasted as if it were caught off the coast of Maine that morning, and the potatoes somehow remained hot on their plate for the entire meal. It was difficult for the clients not to rave constantly about the exquisite meal. The waiters hustled to refill wine, beer, specialty drinks, and even suggested concoctions called *MediaCast Cranberry* and *TV Tequila* to promote their client.

Lucas kept a close eye on how hard the staff was working. He greatly appreciated stellar customer service because it was his job to demand it from his team. Dessert would be next and then the boat would disembark, sending almost everyone to the upper deck to take in breathtaking views of the famous Ferris Wheel, Willis Tower, AON Center, the red CNA building and more.

This was the perfect "go time" for Lucas. Being a manager downstate didn't give him much visibility, so he had to maximize his chances. The clients were not yet drunk, his bosses were trapped at their tables, and the timing was ideal to shake hands with upper managers, meet a few clients from other markets, and open doors for his career down the road, if he ever needed them. He shared a knowing look with Kim, who acknowledged his need to work the room. He excused himself and stood up to leave but noticed one client who must have already finished eating. She sat outside on the middle deck alone in a wheelchair, admiring the city skyline.

Kim knew her husband well. Lucas was *that* guy – the guy who would find the one person in the room not participating or seemingly unhappy. He would storm a path directly to that person to draw them into the fun. Sure enough, Lucas left the table and negotiated the tricky path out the cabin, around the tight walkway to the middle deck.

Lucas was instantly impressed by her wheelchair. A stunning bright yellow, very modern, it looked lightweight – made of some aluminum alloy he thought he probably couldn't pronounce. He watched the client gazing at the beauty of the Windy City. The cool front had pushed the storm eastward and washed away any evidence of pollution or humidity. The colors had never been sharper.

"Hi there. I'm Lucas, MediaCast, downstate offices. You know, we paid extra to have that storm removed."

She turned, smiled, and gave him a long, serene look.

"You doing OK? I wanted to make sure you didn't need anything. I can leave if you prefer."

She was probably mid-30s, he thought. Her hair was black and extremely short with a choppy cut as if she had trimmed it herself. She wore a plain, olive t-shirt, a casual floral skirt and tennis shoes, all out of place for this party. Yet she held a Mamiya Leaf camera. The producer in Lucas's Bloomington office kept pictures of this brand on his cubicle. He called it his dream camera. Lucas remembered only one fact about the device – it cost over thirty-grand.

"No. You can stay, but can we just watch for a few minutes?"

She pointed at the city. Lucas nodded and sat on a cushioned bench, still a bit damp from the earlier rain. Though he was missing some prime career-building opportunities inside, he told himself to live in this moment. They watched the skyline for several minutes, the lights of the city slowly emerging as the sun set behind the massive skyscrapers. Every thirty seconds or so, she would snap a photo or take video – he couldn't tell. Lucas could only see about forty buildings from this close vantage point, though he knew there were over a thousand more out there and that Chicago was the home of the original skyscraper sometime in the 1800's. The light grew brighter near the land, most likely due to the streetlights. He had seen these powerful miracles of glass and steel dozens of times but realized this was the first time he had *really* noticed how the light affected the sheer architectural beauty. Even the laughter and chatter from inside the dining area faded away. Surely, dessert had been served by now.

He was almost disappointed when she spoke. "Thank you for sharing that with me. My name is Bexley."

She had a touch of an accent – possibly German. He found himself highly interested in her story. He shook her hand.

"Nice to meet you, Bexley. Are you one of our Chicago clients?"

"My father. He owns eleven jewelry stores."

"I don't see any jewelry. You rebelling against the family business or is your father just really... stingy?"

She laughed. "I used to wear it. Now it just seems silly. What's the point?"

Lucas found that a bit passive-aggressive. She was fishing for him to dig. He thought of a few comments but maybe it would be best to remain quiet. A full minute went by before she spoke again.

"I'm not supposed to be here."

"Oh, of course. You're an illegal alien! Alien here! Illegal alien here!!"

She laughed again. She hadn't expected to have any fun tonight.

"I wish. That would be exciting, no?"

She studied him, as if trying to give herself permission to say her next line. "I was supposed to die over the winter but my cousin gave me part of her liver. I was ready to go but her gift saved me. I'm still working out how to live again."

Lucas was stunned at the severity of her words compared to the nonchalance of how she said them. He knew it wasn't his job, or even his business, but he felt compelled to make a positive impression. To help her take one step toward "working out how to live again." He chose his words carefully, knowing this statement might change his entire plan for the evening.

"Bexley, my wife is eating dessert, probably desperate to get away from my clients. What do you say I go get her and we all watch the spectacular views together as the boat tours the shoreline? We'll enjoy the fireworks and then we'll all dance the night away. Hope you like classic rock – it's all the DJ plays."

She didn't object at first so he started to walk back toward the cabin entrance.

"Lucas! Stop! Dancing?! Can't you see this wheelchair?!"

Lucas turned and walked up to her slowly. He didn't want to piss off the daughter of a major client so he was cautious, but there was an innocence in her eyes. He could sense her anger, but he felt it really wasn't directed at him. He was confident she didn't want to be confrontational.

He spoke slowly. "Do you – *want me* to see the wheelchair?"

He waited for a response, but she was nowhere near prepared to give one. He continued.

"My brother and my nephew have used walkers for... wow, it seems forever. For the first couple years, it's all I saw. But now, I don't see the walkers anymore. You know what I see? Their mood. Feelings. Attitude. How healthy or sick they look. Their souls hiding behind their warped humor. You can dance, I guarantee it. Anyone can dance. But... I'll ask again. Do you want me to see the wheelchair?"

It felt like a trick question. She was angry that a total stranger had rocked her entire belief system in a matter of minutes. People usually felt sorry for her. She was used to getting her way. She wanted to be treated special when it suited her, yet, thinking about it now, she often told the world to ignore the wheelchair and *not* treat her differently. Here was some random guy who asked her to dance – ignoring it completely. Treating her like a regular person. She was energized, even empowered by it. She shook her head.

"OK, be right back," Lucas said, and walked toward the cabin.

He entered the dining area to rescue his wife and found a full dish of delectable tiramisu waiting for him. He guessed right. Kim was quite anxious for a break from his clients so he took one delicious bite and they exited.

He introduced her to Bexley. Together, the three relished a remarkable night of stellar skyline views and dazzling fireworks. As the DJ rocked the late-night bash on the upper deck, Lucas coaxed over twenty people to share a dance with Bexley. She bee-bopped with her arms and twirled her wheelchair to the music. When the final song blasted, Bexley pumped her fists high in the air and jerked and twirled with pizzazz in the center of the floor. She was the star of the show surrounded by over sixty revelers of varying degrees of drunkenness. She even led the crowd as they belted out...

"Whoa – we're halfway there!
Whoa, livin' on a prayer,
Take my hand and we'll make it. I swear!
Whoa, livin' on a prayer!
Livin'... on... a prayer!"

Kim watched the boisterous crowd from the corner of the boat's deck with her arm around her husband and the stars twinkling above them, courtesy of the Berly Factor. Their feet too tired to dance even one more song, they both sipped water, calming down after some tasty Flor de Caña Rum and Cokes. She adored Lucas at the moment, remembering past family weddings where he ensured Lincoln got to be part of the fun by lifting him up in the air and dancing with him. She could still see the joy on Lincoln's face. And here Lucas was, at it again, fully responsible for elevating Bexley's evening – maybe even her life. He didn't even seem to care that had confused his bosses, who wondered why he was hanging out with the wheelchair lady all night – she wasn't even his client. He had sacrificed a chance to get ahead.

Kim stood up and faced him, then slid her dress zipper down another inch. She kissed him deeply, and in her head planned for some significant rendezvous time in the morning.

CHAPTER 18

Not Supposed to Happen

Reggie shuffled to his SUV after a blissful day at work. He had anticipated a few problems early with the poly bagger and fixed them before they happened. The business magazines were printed, sealed and in the mail two full days ahead of deadline.

And they wanted to fire my ass.

Reggie's invincibility was undeniable. Ever since the impromptu get-together in his backyard, the first actual party held at his house in over a decade, the guys at work treated him differently. Having outsmarted management, the crew felt a collective feeling of power. Reggie still had a job because they had *protected* him, and now it was only logical to continue. The guys strolled over more often than before to chat and ask how he was doing. They asked about Lincoln. They even offered to help on some of his more difficult job loads when they had a spare minute. News of Harry Schott getting hired by another company the week after he sacrificed himself spread faster than hay fever in the spring. Seven different employees ran to Reggie when they first heard the news to share it with him. The team had bonded and Reggie was the glue.

It didn't stop there. Mrs. Eyre called him into her office again to inform him that Drucker's marked off two additional handicap parking spaces and she insisted Reggie start using one. Years ago when Reggie worked second shift, all four spaces were often taken when he arrived so he got used to parking a few rows back in the corner. He didn't mind parking further out back then, but today it would be helpful to have a closer, secure spot. Done. Front row all the way, every day. He also noticed new handicap grab bars had been installed in the hallway to the break room and in the men's bathroom.

Reggie stepped into the Enclave and took a deep breath. Today the results were due from his first blood panel since he changed his diet. As he sat alone in the SUV, he pictured all the guys he'd seen over the years checking their phones for sports scores, stock prices, the weather, election news, etc. But this glance at his phone meant *his life*. This email meant everything. Would he hover at 18% or were his kidneys losing ground? He was eating right. He was trying supplements which were believed to be natural ways to lower blood pressure. He checked his phone – no email from the doctor's office yet.

He turned on the radio and *Beautiful Day* by U2 filled the air – one of his few favorites *not* sung by Elton John. His itchiness had gone down and this past week when he walked, his pain seemed more tolerable. He headed home to pick up Anne, then they would head to Gavin's new house for a game night. Life was frickin' good!

He pulled into his driveway. Anne walked up with a large cooler, opened the lift gate and set it in the back. She lifted three large sacks into the backseat, went back in the house for a massive casserole dish wrapped in a towel. She kept it in her lap as she strapped on her seatbelt and glanced at her husband. He had that look. He couldn't resist giving her sass.

"The invite said bring a dish to pass. Who are you, Tom Brady? How many passes do you plan to make?"

She laughed. "Stop it. Everything I made is low sodium. What if the kids don't like it? I had to bring a variety. Any news?"

He shook his head. She was just as anxious as he was to hear the medical report. He backed onto the street and headed for Gavin's – only a mile away. After a moment of quiet, Anne got curious.

"What about work? Did you put a note in *Hot Off the Press?*"

That was Drucker's company newsletter. It was popular – read cover to cover by most of the employees. It had been a great resource for them in the past. They found used furniture, computer games for Lincoln, yard tools, clothes for the kids, even great recipes. They had agreed that Reggie would announce his need for a kidney there to start getting the word out.

"I didn't place anything. It feels like we're jumping the gun."

"Reggie! You're impossible! This isn't like going to the phone book to find someone to paint the garage. Any little angle could be the one that leads to finding a donor."

"Right," Reggie agreed. "*A* donor! We need just one person to step up."

"They explained the numbers; weren't you listening?! There are only about seven thousand living donors a year in the entire country. That's like, one donor for every forty thousand people. Pontiac has ten thousand residents, so I could argue there's only a twenty five percent chance that any person in town would step up to donate a kidney for anyone."

Reggie found it hard keeping up with her math, but he believed her. She didn't make mistakes when she was angry like most people – she actually got *more* accurate. He breathed deep as he pulled the SUV up to Gavin's new house. It was a cute starter home with a nice bay window in front, just like Reggie and Anne's house. Reggie felt that was a compliment – as if Gavin had chosen this house to have a memory of Reggie and Anne in his new home. Skylar and her husband Jack, Ben and Samantha, and Lincoln and Zoey should all be in there waiting.

"Look," Reggie retorted. "I just have this feeling that everything's gonna be fine and we don't have to worry so much right now." He turned the car off and looked at her. She was disappointed. She wanted him to be right but she'd lived a life overwrought with medical challenges. Every fiber of her being told her to move on it. *Fast!*

Reggie's cell phone rang. It was Dr. Sahill's office. They both saw the caller ID.

Anne asked, "Why are they calling? They said it would just be an email?"

Reggie could hear the panic in her voice and quickly answered.

"Hello, this is Reggie."

"Good evening, Reggie. Dr. Sahill here. We just got your lab results back. I know I told you this isn't supposed to happen, but we want to know what you've been up to."

Reggie and Anne stared at each other. This didn't make any sense.

"Your numbers went... *up*. You're at 21% kidney function."

CHAPTER 19

Doors You've Opened

Reggie parked the Enclave directly in front of The Cup and Scone, the best coffee shop in the county and smack dab in the middle of historic downtown Pontiac. The city had been chosen for several movie and TV shows in the past decade due to its old-time downtown charm and the famous courthouse built in 1842. Reggie admired the coffee shop's vintage entrance and the 150-year-old brick. He had waited a long time for this day – eager to visit with grade-school classmates and visit with Mr. Carvell, who insisted via text that Reggie call him "David." *Like that's gonna happen.* Reggie knew his childhood instincts. Respect for the man would never allow for such casualness.

Fourteen former classmates would be meeting today. Three of them Reggie saw occasionally because they lived in town, but he had not seen the others since high school. Reggie would serve as the local expert. He suggested this coffee shop for the venue. He could personally vouch for every scone, muffin, and deluxe sandwich choice, though he no longer ate pickles or ham due to their sodium levels.

Reggie glanced to the back at his walker. It was such a part of his life that depending on it rarely bothered him but this was one of those times when it did. His former classmates would remember him with a limp, some may have seen photos of him with a cane on social media. They might be disturbed by the walker, possibly pitying Reggie for being *worse off* than he used to be. He hated that.

Reggie had analyzed every aspect of this reunion and how to handle it because today took on much more meaning than it had the day Mr. Carvell first called. Every few days for the past three months, Anne had nudged Reggie to start telling the world he needed a kidney. He had committed to inform people on a few occasions already, but the moment never felt right. It was unexplainably difficult, as if needing a kidney meant he wasn't *whole*. It made him feel inadequate and needy. Or maybe he wimped out because his subsequent lab report dropped to only 19% kidney function, and six weeks later, it was still at 19%. He held onto the hope that he would never need a kidney.

Two days ago, Anne expected Reggie to inform the children at Thanksgiving dinner. He chickened out. Sick of his delay tactics, she made him *promise* he would inform the group today that he had stage four kidney disease and would need a transplant. She certainly didn't expect a former classmate to volunteer to be his donor, but Reggie needed to practice saying it out loud. Then she made him promise it *again*.

He grabbed his walker from the back. With the *Centralio* tucked in the pouch, he walked to the classic distressed-wood door that featured a coffee mug for a handle. The rich aroma hit him before he pushed the door open and he strolled in with a satisfied grin as if he'd already tasted his favorite java. He came early so he could choose his chair at the far end and tuck his walker out of the way.

"Look who it is. You a gonna make a big trouble in my store?" The voice belonged to Chen, who had arrived in America a few years ago from Taiwan. Reggie admired how hard she hustled. She covered the counter and all the tables herself and had served Reggie countless times, even slipping him a few free scones now and then for the helpful advice he doled out about living in America.

"I don't *make* trouble. It just sort of follows me," Reggie said smiling. He turned to look at the door to see what might be following him. On cue, a man sporting a full gray beard entered and Chen and Reggie laughed together. It was Mr. Carvell. Reggie hadn't seen that beard in any of the Facebook photos and he was barely recognizable.

Chen had already moved the tables so their large group could sit together, and she served up two cups of delicious cold brew.

Reggie was ecstatic to get a full fifteen minutes with his former teacher before the room filled up. Natalie Murray and Zane Schmidt were the first two arrivals. They had dated in high school and the world thought they made the perfect couple based on their hotness, but they had nothing else in common so it ended quickly. Natalie, still beautiful, was married with four children and six grandkids, and bragged a little too much about her successful yoga center in Naperville. Zane had raised two boys and was Fire Chief in Carbondale, a logical move given that, on Christmas Day when he was nine, his home burned to the ground.

They were followed by Christian Quintana and Blake Dakan, both of whom, like Reggie, had thought to bring the yearbook. Christian still lived in town and managed the Pontiac Library and Blake became a lawyer like his Dad and was now managing partner for a big firm in Rockford. The coffee was flowing as fast as the hugs, stories, and laughs. Reggie was in a deep conversation with Mr. Carvell about some photos and captions in the *Centralio,* causing him to miss Mary Herges and two more people that he didn't recognize as they joined the group.

As the rest of the roster arrived and filled out their cluster of tables, Reggie feared he wouldn't get to connect with those at the other end. Because he had spoken briefly to each of them as he set up the event, was his attention not needed? He hoped people would shift seats to have personal one-on-ones with everybody. After Mary Herges finished her Triple Berry Paleo scone, she walked over and stood behind Reggie so she could catch up with him. Then Cole Staab did the same. One by one, the party came to him whether there were open chairs or not.

After a full hour and much shifting of seats, every classmate had come to Reggie to reminisce and share laughs. Reggie relished the upbeat conversation. The only sour notes of the day so far were the reminder that a few of the classmates had lived through bitter divorces and that Minnie Carvell had died of a widowmaker heart attack. Reggie shuddered – that word "widow" got to him.

Reggie gave his phone to Chen to take a few group photos and promised to email them to everyone. With the attention on him, he thought this might be the right time to announce his need for a kidney but it didn't feel right. Mr. Carvell stood up, stealing the moment from him, to move the meeting into a new light.

"I'd like your attention for a moment. First off, a big thanks to Reggie. I asked the famous *Yankee Doodle Dandy* soloist if he would help me organize this gathering and before I knew it, he had contacted every one of you and booked this nice venue. Nicely done, Reggie." The group applauded robustly.

"I need to express how rewarding it was to teach this group. I was afraid of going into teaching because I wasn't sure it was the right choice for me. One year with you junior high yahoos and I knew I was in the right place."

Laughs and smiles followed. Melinda Ray, a kindergarten teacher herself, wiped away a tear.

"And I hope none of you are offended by this, but I also need to know if each of you would give me permission to use... this."

He showed a digital recording device he had hidden under his napkin.

"One of the reasons we're all here is that I am writing a book. I don't intend to use any of your names, but if you listened carefully today, you heard some powerful dialogue. Zane has warned several of you of the dangers of kitchen fires and storing flammables in your home. Christian has forwarded four links already of books that can help some of you with issues you're having. Blake has given out legal advice to many of you."

Blake interrupted, "What kind of book is it?"

"It's a self-help book and I think you'd all be proud to be associated with it. The current title is *Remembering the Doors You've Opened.* Perhaps I can best describe it this way – would anyone volunteer to let me show the pictures on your phone to the group?"

Reggie thought of offering his but there was one picture of Anne in her underwear on it, so he stayed quiet. Melinda offered hers freely. Mr. Carvell scrolled through and quickly found what he was looking for.

"Thank you, Melinda. I'm writing about a theory I have. It's about the way we record our lives today, how that changes how we feel about ourselves and our overall self-identity. Let me explain."

He showed a dozen pictures of Melinda and her family – a beach, a concert, her daughter's barbecue, a bed and breakfast in Oregon, an aquarium, a parade, and several restaurants. The group scooched closer together to view them on the small screen. He showed several more photos of her running a 10k race, taking a tour of Mackinac Island, and a glamour shot with her husband at a charity event.

"Now, based on these beautiful photos, would you all agree that our dear friend, Melinda, is living an amazing life?"

The group responded with strong affirmation, confirming that her life did indeed look amazing.

"But now let's look deeper. What we've mostly seen is the record of Melinda's travel and entertainment, which I maintain is what most of us capture in our photos. Is this really her *life*? Is it who she is? Is this what makes her truly *happy*? I could argue these photos simply show rewards for her success. What about the million little things she's done for people that didn't get recorded. The advice she gave. The cookies she made for her neighbors. The hugs she gave to cheer people up. Her *goodness*. And to the title of the book, how many times she opened the door for someone just to be helpful or friendly?"

Reggie immediately looked down. He grew flush. He never held the door for others, he couldn't. Others always held the door for him. Being handicapped reared its ugly head in dozens of ways and now he felt singled out of this discussion. The timing of this sucked and was draining the joy of the day away from him.

Mr. Carvell continued. "Reggie will forward the group photos we took today. But what will that help you remember? That we got together, had great conversation, some laughs, some amazing scones and lattes? That's what the photos will show, right? But what it won't show is all the help you gave each other today. My book will hopefully teach ways we can capture and record just how much good each of us is doing so we can remember it, honor it, and let it be a bigger part of who we are. And that will further justify the rewards that we already record. Imagine how much better some lives would be if only they focused on the little things they do like opening doors for people."

The group agreed with this concept and their collective goodness continued. Everyone gave permission to use the recording. Mary offered to introduce Mr. Carvell to a publisher she knew. Cole had been an editor for Men's Health magazine years ago and offered to review the rough draft. Blake's office worked with a PR firm and he offered to set up a meeting. Reggie watched from the end of the table, wishing there was something he could do to help. He thought about his promise to Anne – he still hadn't announced his news.

Then Mr. Carvell switched gears.

"I've really kept you here longer than you expected. Thank you so much for coming, for your help and for spending your valuable time with me today. I enjoyed reconnecting. Before we go our separate ways, could we each give a quick update to the entire group on what's happening in our lives?"

He looked to his left. Reggie was right next to him.

"Reggie, you want to go first?"

This was his chance. All eyes were on him. He had promised Anne. Twice. Chen cleared plates and silverware, distracting him, indicating it had been a long meeting already and it should be winding down. Her cleanup told Reggie to "keep it short."

"I'm so happy to have seen everyone today," he started. "What an amazing group of successful, wonderful people. I have a good job at Drucker's. I tell people I have five wonderful kids and I'm so blessed they all live close by."

He looked at the group. They were genuinely interested in his words. It had been a wonderfully positive day. He couldn't bring this group down. *Why was this so hard?*

"And I consider myself one of the most happily-married men on the planet. That's about it for me."

He tried to listen to the others speak but he was too disappointed in himself. The updates went by quickly and the group said their goodbyes. Mr. Carvell paid the bill and there were hugs and much talk of meeting again next year. Just like being the first to arrive, Reggie wanted the be the last to leave so his walker wouldn't get in anyone's way. Mr. Carvell walked him to the door.

"Thanks again, Reggie. Hey, was there something else you wanted to share with the group? You looked like you had something on your mind."

How does he do that? Reggie thought it must come from decades of being a teacher. Reggie gritted his teeth as if the following statement needed help coming out.

"Mr. Carvell... actually... I have stage four kidney disease. I need to find a kidney donor." Reggie exhaled as if he had been drowning underwater for a full minute. His body tingled with relief.

Mr. Carvell scratched his beard as he contemplated the enormity of the statement, fully realizing how hard it must have been for Reggie to say it aloud. *Why didn't he mention it to the group?*

He led Reggie back to the table, ordered more scones, and listened to Reggie pour out his soul until the restaurant closed.

CHAPTER 20

Teardrop in the Harbor

Reggie arrived home late feeling energized and buzzed from too much caffeine. Lincoln was having a game night at a friend's house and Anne was in bed. He figured she was probably awake, anticipating news from the grade-school gathering but he needed to fulfill his promise before he saw her. He immediately drafted an email to the Cup and Scone group. He thought it would be easy with a group list already established, but he fumbled over the wording for a full half hour. He finally settled on the right phrasing to explain his need for a kidney. Hoping someone might step up to donate, he mentioned that any potential donor could be part of a donor chain, but a direct fit would have O Positive blood.

He felt proud, but also foolish. This wasn't really *that* hard once you got started. He attached the group photos and hit *Send.* There. He had fulfilled his promise. The news was finally out. He figured it would spread faster than Anne's famous apple butter.

He immediately received two emails. One from Melinda Ray thanking him for organizing the reunion and wishing him luck with the kidney issues. The shortness of the message depressed him, as if he were in sales and this was the first customer to say "no." The second was from his mother. Her phone had stopped working. She wanted him to come right away if he could – she would wait up.

Reggie had been her emergency phone repairman for a couple decades now. He was rather proud of her for how she tried to keep up with technology, even if new software and devices frustrated her. He felt jittery anyway and wouldn't be able to sleep, so he walked back to the garage and drove a few miles to his mother's house.

As he climbed up the slanted wooden stairs on the back porch, he looked in the window. Ruth worked on a puzzle in the dining room with her back to him, her usual spot when waiting for a loved one to visit. Her white hair glistened under new, bright LED lights. He thought Lucas must have installed those. She was surrounded by boxes, clutter, and twice the furniture that she needed. Greatly influenced by the Great Depression, she found value in every object and didn't dare throw belongings away. The library is giving away free books? Someone put a perfectly good coffee table by the curb? Ruth would be first in line, stockpiling merchandise in the hopes someone somewhere could use it. And with the mere mention that you wanted something in her house, no matter what it was, it was yours.

Reggie walked in the back door. Her children were not expected to knock when coming home.

"Mom! I'm here!"

She greeted him with an angelic smile. He liked that there were boxes and furniture everywhere – they became his cane, his support as he moved through the house.

"I'm so grateful you came. The phone has stopped working and I have so many calls to make."

She wasn't exaggerating. Reggie knew that between her writer's group, her rosary project, and her family, combined with the fact that she didn't text, his mother spent more time on the phone than any other 88-year-old on the planet. On Mother's Day, it was routine to get several busy signals when reaching out to her.

"Let me have a look."

Reggie weaved through the small path between the furniture and boxes to the phone stand. He picked up the receiver – no dial tone. He called his Mom's number on his cell and he heard an incredibly quiet ring. He turned the phone on its side looking for a volume setting. He raised the volume. Phone fixed.

"Mom, this dial is for volume. You must have somehow turned it way down."

"Oh... I'm so... I took a nap yesterday and the phone kept ringing. I forgot I turned that down so I could sleep. Thank you so much. I get nervous. What if I had an emergency?"

"It's OK. I'm glad it was an easy fix."

She wanted to ask him to stay but felt guilty. It was late and he probably wanted to get back to his family. Reggie, however, thought a chat with his mother could prove helpful.

"Do you mind if we visit a little?" Reggie asked.

They sat together at the table and worked on the puzzle. There were maybe a hundred pieces left to complete a picture of Sydney Harbor with the iconic Opera House basking below an orange and red sunset. Reggie stopped to gaze at the five high school senior pictures lined up neatly on the walnut built-in sideboard. He thought of the roles his siblings played. Harper, the engineer, helped everyone in the family with mechanical and house issues. Lucas, the party planner, tried to keep everyone involved and having a good time. Scott took care of legal issues. Ava bitterly fought with family members regularly and considered herself the black sheep of the Nichols clan, but she knew computers. Though she avoided her siblings as much as possible, she would still remote into their computers to fix problems. And there he was, Reggie, right in the middle. *I guess fixing Mom's phone was... something.*

His Mom put in five pieces in a row – she was on a roll.

"Mom, I need to tell you something. I'm having some medical issues that are pretty serious."

She gasped and gave him her full attention. She suddenly looked very tired. The look in her eyes wasn't a mother's fear that one might expect, but rather anger and fatigue. Resentment that Reggie, her son who had already dealt with the lion's share of the family's medical issues, was about to reveal yet another health nightmare. And fatigue – she was just weary, worrying about him. If only she could take this on in his place.

"What is it?" she asked.

"I need a new kidney. The doctor said in a year I'd need dialysis, and that was a few months ago. I am on the waiting list for a transplant. I know I shouldn't feel this way but the road ahead looks so rough. And expensive. I don't know if I can take it. A transplant feels like such a huge fuss for someone like me."

She stared at him as if he just announced he wanted to commit suicide. A large tear formed, rolled down her cheek, and fell on the puzzle. Reggie didn't mean to upset her and tried to replay his words in his head to figure it out. All he could focus on was that her wet teardrop missed the Opera House and landed in the harbor. His mother walked to the hearth and grabbed a tissue to dab her eyes and wipe the puzzle dry. She stared at the puzzle and spoke quietly.

"As you grew up, we didn't have the grit to be hard on you, to challenge you. Your father knew how important keyboarding would be, but when you didn't like typing, we let you quit. We were harsh with the others if they came home with a bad grade, but we simply asked you to try harder. We should have been twice as demanding of you. We should have found *something* you could have worked for – to be proud of what you could accomplish."

She put in a puzzle piece, trying to find the right words. More tears were forming.

"Reggie, I wish I knew how to fix it, but I don't. I have one hope for you. My hope is that you could somehow learn your genuine value, so that no one, especially your mother, would ever again hear you say the words, *I'm not worth such a fuss.*" Another tear fell down her cheek.

Reggie tried to understand why this little comment meant so much to his mother. *Was the statement really that powerful?* He tried to picture how he would feel if his children, Lincoln, Skylar, Ben, Gavin, or Grace had said those exact words. He agreed with her. It was insensitive.

"I'll work on it, Mom. Can we finish this?"

He picked up a piece and found its home right away. His mother stopped crying and together they completed the pretty picture.

CHAPTER 21

Rh Factor

Reggie steered the Enclave through the peaceful streets of Bloomington to the annual Christmas Eve bash. One foot of pristine snow covered the front yards of the beautifully decorated homes that Zoey thought looked like mansions. Lincoln commented that the snowmen, inflatable reindeer, and wreaths all looked brand new while Anne sat awestruck at how every sidewalk was meticulously shoveled and the road perfectly clear. She held a casserole dish of a low-sodium version of her famed twice baked Mexican potatoes, hoping Lucas and Kim would have room in their oven. It required forty minutes at four hundred degrees to heat up properly. Not a minute less.

Reggie admired the idyllic Norman Rockwell winter neighborhood basking in sunshine. He was excited to see his relatives and super pleased it had stopped snowing unexpectedly a couple hours ago. But he needed a mental jolt. He had spent the last month disappointed at the speed with which his news travelled. His former classmates had replied to his email with sympathy, shared the news on social media, but the overlap was surprisingly non-existent with his family, co-workers, or his inner circle. The news trail died quickly. He kept remembering "one in forty thousand gives a kidney." His brothers and sisters were still in the dark but Reggie had a strategy. He would break the news today in person and would tell everyone right at the start. This way, he wouldn't have the excuse of not wanting to bring the party down.

The Chugga Chugga Chant weaved past fifteen cars parked in the street, into the driveway, and came to a stop right in front of Lucas's garage door, which immediately opened. Lucas dashed out, doled out hugs and helped Anne and Zoey carry presents inside. Reggie and Lincoln grabbed their walkers and moved through the garage toting homemade cookies and fudge.

Reggie asked Lucas, "Did you know it was supposed to snow all day today?"

Lucas simply shrugged. "Berly Factor."

They entered the house to the aromatic waft of baked turkey and joined almost forty other relatives in reds and greens who were already partying. Six in the piano room worked on a puzzle depicting Christmas in New York, a dozen sipped wine, chatted and nibbled on goodies in the kitchen, ten youngsters played in the basement. Another ten guests laughed and talked in the great room with upbeat holiday music behind them, guessing what the presents under the massive tree might be. Bali and Fiji were already worn out. They snored loudly in the corner by a heat vent wearing bright red Christmas bow collars.

Lincoln rushed to the basement where the younger kids traditionally gathered to snack, play video games and make a mess. Anne bee-lined to the kitchen to negotiate oven space with Kim. Reggie, determined, walked right up to Lucas and Scott who were reminiscing about the brilliance of Scott's valedictorian speech in high school. Reggie listened carefully – the first time he had heard Scott tell about the inside jokes hidden in his speech and the double meaning of half the phrases. They laughed, awed by his ability to do this publicly and not get caught. No wonder Scott had become a successful attorney.

Reggie was on a mission. He jumped right in at the end of Scott's story.

"Hey, I've got a doozy for you, but it's not funny. I've been struggling with blood pressure for a long time now. I have kidney disease and my doctor says I'll need a transplant in less than a year. I'm supposed to tell everyone I know. My blood type is O positive, so neither of you is a match, but spread the word."

His brothers stood stunned. They exchanged a surprised look, each secretly hoping Reggie would yell "April Fools!" Finally, Reggie broke the silence.

"Well, times-a-wastin'. I better tell the others."

Thinking his sisters should hear it next, Reggie walked to the kitchen to find Harper, snatching a piece of fudge on the way. He would have to text Ava – she never flew in for the Christmas party and she rarely answered his calls.

"Holy shit! What was that?" Scott asked. "Did you know anything about this?"

"No. Anne mentioned over the summer that Reggie stopped giving blood, but I thought..." He trailed off, not wanting to admit his misdiagnosis. He remembered Reggie fishing for blood types at the Fourth of July party. His kidney issues must have been driving that.

Lucas continued, "People joke about how we should be nice to our family because we might need a kidney someday, but who actually *does* that? Do you know *anyone* who donated a kidney?"

Scott replied with a shrug. "Must be a legal nightmare for the surgeons and the hospitals."

They watched Reggie float between groups. Each time, he would wait for a conversation to lull before broadcasting his newsflash. He shared it with everyone, making his way to the piano room and even downstairs to the younger set. Lucas took this opportunity to confront Anne.

"Hey, thanks for bringing the Mexican potatoes. I know they're a lot of work."

"Oh, it's nothing. We love this party. I think Lincoln looks forward to this more than Christmas at home."

"So, what's the real story on Reggie? Is this what you couldn't tell me that day in your backyard?"

"Sort of. I felt it wasn't my place. He's been such a scaredy-cat about telling people. You know how proud he is."

"Of course. Um... Anne, how are *you* doing?"

It always shocked her when people asked. Her life was one of giving and caretaking. She rarely got the luxury to analyze how her life, health, or attitude were faring.

"Not great. You know I love him dearly, but I worry. Sometimes..."

She was getting emotional, feeling as if she were failing her husband miserably.

"Sometimes, I feel there just isn't much fight left in him. Like, he wouldn't care if something bad happened to him... I don't know what to do." She struggled to hold back tears.

Lucas hugged her. "Shhhh! Hey... it's gonna work out. Hang in there."

Lincoln and Zoey walked up hoping Anne would be the deciding vote on who was the best James Bond actor of all time. Lucas stepped away into the great room and stood in front of the fireplace, his own personal tradition. From this view, he could see the entire great room, kitchen, the piano room, even up the stairs. Each year, this view reminded him how blessed he was... a moment to observe his loved ones enjoying each other's company and making memories in *his* home. The party took tremendous planning and effort and it wasn't cheap to host, but this filled him with satisfaction and the inspiration he needed to do it again next year. Today, it simply felt lost on him. His mind was on his brother.

He signaled Kim and moved to the kitchen. She forced everyone away from the island so they could have room to make gravy. They cooked it together as a tribute to Kim's grandma who had taught them her hearty recipe years ago. It was their ritual – wouldn't be Christmas without it.

Together, they prepared a roux of butter, flour, poultry seasoning, pepper, and thyme. Lucas lifted the perfectly golden-brown turkey from the oven, prompting several immediate compliments. He slowly scooped the juices one ladle at a time into the skillet as Kim whisked. She sensed Lucas was "off" and gave him a quizzical look. After decades together, communication with a glance was second nature.

"Someone in this family needs a kidney transplant."

She sighed, as if defeated.

"Not Reggie! Please say it isn't Reggie."

Lucas nodded. She put an arm around him as she stirred.

After the gravy was perfected and Lucas sliced the turkey, the relatives filled up plates and dispersed to all areas of the house to enjoy the feast. Later, his Mom had the children put on a puppet show. The wine flowed, desserts disappeared, the puzzle was completed, and songs were sung as Kim played piano. A lucky youngster in a Santa hat doled out gifts to the other children. Another successful, tradition-filled party to add to memory.

The clean-up was much easier than in years past now that their two daughters were grown. With Riley and her husband Mason, and Aspen and Carter willing to help, they divided and conquered. In less than thirty minutes, the place was spotless. They found the usual cards, gifts and gloves left behind, and baby formula and leftovers forgotten in the refrigerator.

The last step was to move all *their* wrapped presents from Lucas's home office to the Christmas tree. Each year they hid them in the office so the gifts for Christmas morning wouldn't get mixed up with the big family celebration. Kim grabbed an armful, giddy at the thought of watching her children and their significant others opening them tomorrow at 9am sharp.

She noticed Lucas's computer was on. He always shut it down for the party to keep the kids away from it. In fact, she was in the room this morning when he turned it off. She wiggled the mouse and a page appeared: The National Kidney Foundation website popped up; the title read "What Blood Types Match." Lucas obviously sneaked in here during the party and started doing research. She read the entire article.

She glanced at a note on the desk in her husband's handwriting:

Reggie = O Pos
Lucas = O Neg
Rh factor does not matter

She stared at the note. She re-read the article to make sure she fully understood it. Sure enough, positive or negative Rh factor doesn't matter in kidney donation, just the blood *type*. Her husband was a match for Reggie.

"Mom, do you still hide these from Dad?"

Aspen had spoken from the doorway holding a tray of Scotcheroos. Lucas loved the taste so much that in the past he playfully asked his daughters to hide them and only allow him one per day.

"No. We don't hide anything from each other these days."

Aspen helped her move the presents to the tree. Kim was distracted, her thoughts dominated by her own comment. *We don't hide anything from each other.* She carefully analyzed the data, a skill she had honed over the years in corporate finance. She thought about Lucas's note. She remembered the effort he made to lift Lincoln's spirits at weddings, and literally lift Lincoln to dance when he was young. How he interacted with Bexley on the Odyssey.

Kim stepped back from the glorious Christmas tree after she placed the last gifts under it. Dozens of personal ornaments depicted the family's travel, interests, and accomplishments. She admired the twinkling colored lights reflecting off the presents. Because of the streetlight, she could see the perfect Christmas snow filling out the scene through the window behind it. It was a stellar night, a cozy home, a blessed family. She had gladly put a strong effort into her career and a stronger effort into raising her children. She had hoped to ride it out just the way it was. Her life was wonderfully predictable – just the way she liked it.

But given the evidence, Kim found herself trying to answer a question she never thought she'd ever have to consider. *Was her husband going to donate a kidney?*

CHAPTER 22

Anne Had More

Ice and snow covered the Pontiac streets on a dreary, drizzly Saturday in early January but Reggie refused to be dragged down by it. With Anne's help, he hadn't consumed any soda for weeks. He had eaten delicious, low sodium foods. He had lost ten pounds, which was quite noticeable for a guy who never had much of a gut. He drank water constantly to help flush his kidneys. He had been quite disciplined over the Christmas and New Year's holidays, cheating only with three pieces of fudge and two strips of Anne's bacon. Though he knew his food intake wasn't the only element affecting his kidney function, it was all he could control. He was determined to stay at 19%.

The truth will set you free kept ringing through his mind as he shared his story on Facebook. Last week, Zoey helped him start an Instagram and Twitter account. He designed flyers and delivered them to restaurants, grocery stores and doctors' offices – every business he approached posted one. Two days ago, it struck him that maybe athletes had the strongest kidneys so as a long shot, he gave flyers to the Pontiac health clubs. After Lincoln's first day at his new job as a surgery scheduler at St. James hospital, he and Zoey made a *Kidney Donor Needed – Be a Hero* sign for the front yard. Reggie found a coupon for five hundred business cards, allowing him to leave his message everywhere he went.

The marketing side was rolling. And yet, the only response so far was a single phone call. A man from Tulsa had stopped for gas in

Pontiac as he drove Route 66 cross-country and spotted the flyer. He told Reggie about his own kidney transplant a year ago and claimed he was now living life with a renewed appreciation for each day. He encouraged Reggie to hang in there and swore that things would work out great for him, too. It was a nice, supportive conversation, but the net effect was that Reggie felt even more anxious. Only one reply after all this work? From a random person who lived almost nine hours away?

Reggie was starting to have "bad" days, and the Tulsa call, unfortunately, came on one of them. Twice in the past month, Reggie felt so tired it was hard to get out of bed. His back hurt worse and twice he couldn't stop itching for the entire day. He kept thinking about the time he ran out of gas in the Ford Ranger. The truck sputtered hard, then drove for a few more miles, and died. He compared his body to that truck and could not help but think that just like that old jalopy, his body was running out of gas. Deep down, he could sense he had a time limit.

Anne walked into the living room as Reggie was about to post yet another Facebook plea for help.

"Did you expect your brother? I think he's parked out front."

Reggie checked his phone to make sure he didn't miss a call or a text. It was unusual for his siblings to just stop by without calling first. He shrugged, then walked to the front bay window. Sure enough, Lucas sat motionless in his Nissan Altima. Its shiny metallic blue brightened up the gray, cloudy snowscape. Billowing clouds of exhaust poured from the twin tailpipes into the five-degree air.

Reggie texted: "We're a bit crazy in here and we smell funny, but we don't bite. You coming in?"

He watched Lucas through the window reading the text. It was another minute before he turned off the ignition and ambled coatless through the biting wind. Anne opened the door to let him in.

"Well you sure picked a shitty day to be out," Anne said. "Where's your coat? You want some soup?"

Lucas shook his head, appearing as if he were in a daze. "No, thanks. I was in town. Thought I'd stop in."

Reggie led Lucas to the kitchen table. Though they didn't ask, Anne put out orange and cucumber slices and made tea for them. She left them alone and went into the game room to be with Lincoln.

After a few minutes listening to Reggie complain about the heat bill and compliment him on the success of the big Christmas party, Lucas got serious.

"So, for the past two weeks, I've done research on kidney transplants. Did you know that when they say the blood type has to be a match, they don't mean it has to be exactly *the same?*"

Reggie felt stupid – how did he miss something so important? He reviewed in his head all the times he had heard the doctors and nurses say, "the blood types have to match." He assumed that meant they had to be identical. Lucas showed Reggie a complete chart of the compatible options, which showed that any Type O could donate to O positive or O negative. He knew what this meant. His own brother was a match.

"Look," Lucas continued. "I don't want to get your hopes up. There's just so much going on in my life right now. MediaCast is crazy busy with turnover, training, new software launches and a potential reorg this summer. Aspen's probably going to announce her engagement. We're booked for a week in Florida in March and our summer is packed. I want to train for another marathon. Fiji needs surgery. And Kim – she's usually supportive, but I think she's really scared I'll do this. I'm not here to tell you I've decided anything, but... I am going to study it. The research says it's not up to me anyway, a whole team of people have to approve the donor."

Reggie's feelings went in the exact opposite direction from what he expected. He thought he'd be thrilled to have a family member consider donating, but he felt uneasy. What if something happened to Lucas in the operating room? How could he face Kim, Riley or Aspen ever again? How would his Mom react to having two sons in surgery on the same day? He thought of the tough question in his psych meeting –

how would his brother feel if he donated and something terrible happened to Reggie? Suddenly, it felt like this would be so much easier if his donor were a total stranger.

Reggie replied, "I don't know what to say. I'm honored you're even thinking of donating."

Lucas nodded. He sipped his tea and grabbed an orange slice, but he couldn't eat it - too rapt in thought as to what this conversation meant to both of them. They sat quietly for a full minute. Reggie was afraid to speak for fear he might say something stupid. All Lucas could muster was, "Well - I'm gonna go."

Lucas looked for his coat, then realized he had left it in the car. Still a bit disoriented, he hugged his brother and headed to the door.

Reggie offered, "If it helps, there's a class in Peoria for potential donors. They can answer all your questions and put you in touch with others who have donated. If you want, I'll go with you."

Lucas nodded, which Reggie took to mean he liked the idea.

"Love you," Reggie said. Suddenly, he thought it sounded self-serving.

"Love you too," Lucas said.

Reggie felt numb. He watched Lucas walk toward his car and slip on the ice. Reggie jerked forward as if he could catch his brother and keep him from falling, suddenly realizing what Lucas's health might mean to him. He watched Lucas catch himself on the hood and climb carefully into his car. As he drove off, Reggie waved goodbye through the bay window even though Lucas could no longer see him.

Reggie turned to go back to the kitchen. Both Lincoln and Anne stood in his path, having listened to every word since Lucas arrived. Lincoln had two massive tears of hope streaming down his face. Anne had more.

CHAPTER 23

A Class for One

Lucas sat alone in the common waiting room at the nephrology department at OSF, filling in a quick medical survey on himself. He thought he might feel added pressure if Reggie came with him to this class so he decided to go it alone. This room accommodated at least eighty people. Three dozen patients milled about at any given time. He wondered how many of them would be in the class. *Busy place*, he thought.

It had felt relaxing on the drive over knowing he had a day off work but that feeling dissipated when he pulled out his phone. As he waited to be taken back to the class, he read emails and answered questions for his team. He checked voicemail. Three were easily answered with a text. The last was from Molly. She rambled on about a deer that slammed into her client's Mercedes, how another manager had pissed her off, then reminded him the office was almost out of coffee. Three minutes for her message – not one item urgent for a boss on his day off. Typical for Molly. And yet, the one visual stuck in his mind today was of Molly with algae and dirt on her legs, cradling a wet goose and proclaiming, "He was in trouble, Lucas. You don't hesitate. You just... help!"

He followed a nurse back to the consult offices. She handed him water and a pad of paper. She gestured to the corner. "Help yourself to snacks and coffee." Right after she left, a small woman entered, moving quickly.

"You must be Reggie's brother. It's a real honor to meet you. I'm Rah, the Transplant Coordinator."

Lucas shook her hand taking note of her old-time wire rim glasses, spunky attitude, and the perfect labels on the folders she set on the table.

"Yes, I'm Lucas Nichols. Just doing research today. There's a lot to consider. I don't really know how I feel about giving up a kidney. Um... I thought this was a *class*."

"It's a class for one. Believe me, it would be encouraging if we had a dozen potential donors every week. You are a rare breed. Very few people sit in that chair contemplating such a sacrifice. But this is the fun part of my job – to see a family member stepping up for one of their own. It shows a genuine love for your brother."

He was quick to make sure they were on the same page, "I haven't decided to donate yet."

She smiled. "Doesn't matter. You're here. That says a lot."

She took his medical survey from him that he completed in the waiting room and scanned it.

"You're fifty-three and you don't take any medications? Nothing?" she asked with surprise.

"That's right. I'm sort of anti-medicine. My Mom taught us to drink water and take a walk if we ever felt sick. Once a decade, I got an aspirin. It was usually enough."

She giggled to herself. The strategy sounded silly, but she admired it.

"OK, then you won't need to meet with our Transplant Pharmacist today."

She started him off with a video filled with the latest information and technological advances. Lucas realized how little he knew about the process despite the research he'd already put into it. He knew he had to be approved by a nephrologist but learned he would have to take a battery of tests and X-rays. He would incur no costs except for travel and would spend only two days in the hospital. Recovery was anywhere from two to four weeks, so he wouldn't miss much time at work. If he was lucky, his left kidney would be the better anatomical fit for Reggie. The left could be removed laparoscopically – meaning smaller incisions and easier recovery than if they removed his right kidney. There were no long-term medications. He could live a normal life. To stay hydrated, he needed to be careful with beer and rum and cokes. Yes, he could run another marathon, just drink more at the water stations. And if he ever needed a kidney for the rest of his life, he would go straight to the top of the transplant list.

Lucas found the information daunting. When the video ended, he started with the questions.

"Rah, how safe is this, really?"

She was quick and blunt. "This is a major surgery. From your history, you haven't gone through anything like this, and..."

He interrupted, "I had an appendectomy two years ago."

She sighed. "Don't *ever* compare your appendectomy to kidney donation. They are not in the same ballpark – a three-day recovery versus maybe a thirty-day recovery."

After a moment, she continued. "I'm proud to share with you that 99% of all our donated kidneys are still functioning a year later, most of them last a minimum fifteen years. The statistics for each transplant center are published on the National Kidney Foundation website and you'll find we compare quite nicely. But let me be a totally transparent. You could die."

Lucas had read that this was a possibility but hearing it aloud made it real. This must be the part scaring the hell out of his wife. He thought about Riley and Mason's glorious wedding. What if he missed Aspen's? Being a grandfather? Celebrating his 30th wedding anniversary?

"Has anyone on your staff ever donated a kidney?"

Rah looked surprised by the question.

"This is the first time a patient has asked me that. Yes. We have one donor. Vera, one of our nurses, donated three years ago to her mother."

He wasn't sure if that was comforting or not, but at least there was one.

"Compared to other surgeries, where would you rate this one?"

She admired his tenacity. She wrote the last two questions down for future classes.

"Let's put it this way. Every transplant team in the country is a veteran team. You don't get on the team without years of training. All the information is shared with other transplant teams, so there are rarely any surprises. You could argue a kidney transplant is one of the safest operations out there. We're loaded with veteran medical professionals."

That felt highly reassuring. "So, if I decide to go through testing, what's next?"

"Just give us a call. We would start you with a blood pressure diary, order blood work and take a more complete medical history. Let's call that phase one. If those go well, we continue with more tests in phase two. One step at a time. But know this. If we feel there is too high a risk to your future health, we won't approve you."

Lucas was not worried. He stayed fit. He was healthy. Of course, he'd be approved.

"Can you tell me... what type of person normally does this? I'm sure you have a lot of people look into it that don't follow through. Who actually goes all the way to the operating room?"

She thought for long moment. She wrote the question down – another good one.

"That's a hard one. Donors tend to be... people who do their own research... are positive, upbeat people... and can trust other people to do their jobs right."

Lucas pondered her answer. It made sense, and yes, he thought that described him.

"Last question. My brother. He's had so many medical issues over the years. How badly does he need this? I mean – is he hurting more than he's telling us?"

She folded her arms and clenched her teeth, as if a mysterious force was painfully stopping her from answering.

"I'm sorry Lucas. HIPAA laws. I can't divulge any health information on your brother."

Lucas laughed. He could give Reggie a kidney, but they couldn't tell him if Reggie had a cold?

The "class" ended. Lucas found himself reviewing the notes in his head as he drove back to Bloomington. There was so much to consider. His job, wife, family, health for the long term. And for the first time, he asked himself if his brother *deserved* this.

He felt an unexpected anger. Reggie hadn't eaten healthy most of his life like he had. Reggie didn't exercise like he did. Lucas admitted to himself that this last thought felt harsh, but Reggie was able to swim. He could have swum his whole life. Why should he donate to someone who didn't take care of himself the way *he* had?

The Nissan gave him a smooth ride, so smooth that when he pulled into his garage next to Kim's Chevy Equinox, he realized he didn't remember driving down the big hill near Goodfield, taking the ramp off I-55, or even driving through his neighborhood. He was so deep in thought his autopilot had kicked in to get him home safely. As a potential kidney donor, he vowed to be more careful in the future.

The house smelled like Green Gables – their favorite restaurant for chili and burgers. Kim had elected to work from home in support of his trip and had made sweet-potato chili for lunch, one of his favorite vegetarian meals. He petted Bali and Fiji, tails wagging to see him home so early in the day. They pranced after him into the kitchen where Kim was slicing a fresh avocado.

"That smells heavenly," he said. He gave her a customary kiss. But it was a level one kiss. Kim didn't know it, but Lucas could decipher *a lot* from her kisses. Level 10, they were headed to the bedroom. Level 6-9, she was in a great party mood, celebrating, or feeling especially proud. Level 3-5, things were fine, but she had a lot on her mind or was busy and was going through the motions. Level 2, more of a peck with chapped lips, sunburn, or illness. Level 1? It meant she was angry but unsure if she had a right to be. When she knew that for sure it was level zero, when there would be no kiss at all.

She put the chili on the table, setting the bowls down a little harder than normal. She garnished them with sour cream, avocado and shredded cheese. They both sat to eat.

"So, how'd it go?" she asked, with a hint of bitterness.

"I learned a ton. If I decide to go forward, there's a lot of hoops to jump through to get approved. I could end up going to Peoria at least three times, maybe more."

She nodded once. "So... what are you thinking?"

He didn't mean to, but he data dumped. He covered everything he learned. He talked about the testing, X-rays, diet, and the procedure. He showed her a list of previous donors he could talk to for advice. He spent time discussing the pros of donating, like getting expensive medical testing on his body for free, including an MRI. He spent equal time covering the cons, like the harsh recovery and possibly a stint with depression. He had a lot more to say when he noticed she was staring out the window at the garden with her arms crossed. When she noticed he had stopped talking, she ate a few bites in silence. Lucas walked around the table and took away her bowl.

Lucas declared, "This isn't us. We don't *do* this. Tell me what's on your mind."

"You don't get it, do you?! You've already decided. Stop wasting everyone's time. This is your stupid process and I'm such a small part of it!"

"I'm talking to you about it right now. I haven't made up my mind yet."

"Yes, you have. You're going to donate a kidney because it's the right thing to do. This is who you are. Exactly. You are that guy that does this sort of thing."

The anger in her statements confused Lucas.

"I don't understand what's going on here. Do you want me to donate a kidney?"

"NO! OF COURSE NOT! I don't want you to *donate a kidney*! It will disrupt everything. It puts question marks on our future, our livelihood, your health! I will have to live with the build-up! The uncertain timing of the surgery! Consoling the girls! The aftermath!"

She took a breath and grabbed her bowl from him. She tried to take a bite but couldn't. She continued her rant at the same volume.

"But you have to do it! You love your brother, and you will *never* have a chance to do something this generous in your life!"

She stood and hit his shoulders repeatedly with her fists, not hard, but showing frustration. She wasn't crying, but needed to be held, consoled. Bali and Fiji normally snuck out of the room if someone raised their voice but they waddled over and laid on the floor close to where she stood. Lucas held his wife tight.

"Wait. So, you DO want me to donate a kidney?"

"YES! YOU STUPID IDIOT! OF COURSE I DO!"

CHAPTER 24

A Pinch of Love

Reggie's and Anne's blood boiled. Anne hovered over Lincoln and Zoey, who sat motionless at the kitchen table.

"How can you possibly sit there and think you are in the right about this?!"

"We were just trying to get a good deal," Lincoln answered. "Dad always says only suckers pay full price." He was trying to toss some of the blame onto Reggie, but it wasn't working.

Anne got in her son's face. "You told us you were going to Frank's house. I checked my phone twice to make sure you were there, like you knew I would. But you're clever, aren't you? You left your phones at Frank's and drove to Springfield without telling anyone! What if something happened? You didn't have your phone! You couldn't have called us if something did happen!"

Lincoln had hit a highway construction barrel on their way home and had to explain the dent and orange paint on the Enclave's front panel. He fessed up and was honest about it. At least there had been no serious crash.

After Reggie learned he needed a kidney, the entire family signed the state registry to become organ donors in the event of death. Reggie pictured his son in a terrible accident. Another horrific image superimposed itself. Even though he knew Lincoln was the wrong blood type, Reggie saw himself getting a kidney from his *deceased donor son.* He was disgusted he could even think of it.

"What did you end up buying?" Reggie asked, hoping to erase the awful image.

Zoey tried to be helpful. "We didn't buy anything. We only drove there 'cause everything was 80% off. The store was picked over pretty good."

Reggie did the math. They used at least six gallons of gas and didn't get a deal on anything. *What a waste!* He wasn't sure which made him angrier, wasting money or denting his SUV.

Anne continued, "You are grounded, Mister, and from now on..."

Reggie's cell phone rang, interrupting her. The phone sat on the table, and everyone could see "Lucas" on the caller ID. He had gone to Peoria for the class.

"Hey Lucas. What's up?"

"Hey big brother." Lucas sounded calm. Too calm. Reggie immediately felt a big lump in his throat, afraid of what might come next.

"I wanted you to know that I've put a lot of thought into it. I took the class, and I had a... bizarre conversation with Kim and... well... she's on board. I've decided to go through the testing protocol to become a donor."

Reggie locked eyes with his wife, Lincoln, and Zoey. All three were hanging on edge.

"I can't tell you what this means to me. I have no words."

"Well, I have to qualify. There's a bunch of tests and X-rays. I won't be approved for weeks so please, save your *thanks* until we know more. Deal?"

"I'm sorry, Lucas, I can't accept those terms. Thank you, thank you, thank you. And if you want me to help, or drive you, or pay for gas, let me know."

"I'll keep you in the loop – my first appointment is in two weeks. Stay away from the large Chee Zees, they taste terrible."

They hung up. Anne hugged Reggie, both hanging onto this glimmer of hope as much as each other. Suddenly the dent in the SUV meant nothing, and Lincoln was smart enough to realize it.

"We're really sorry. We won't do it again." The two snuck out quickly.

"Let's celebrate," Anne said. "Out of the kitchen – I'll whip something up."

Reggie moved to the living room and sat at the piano. He thought about his brother. Lucas ate healthy, had never smoked, ran marathons for crying out loud. His only vice was beer and rum and cokes, but he rarely over-did it. His kidneys must be in great shape – he would get approved as a donor for sure. Reggie suddenly felt like he was sizing up a used car. *How many miles are on it? How does it run? Any rust? What's the current value on this thing? Can I take it for a test drive?* He realized he had no idea if it was better to get a kidney from a 30-year-old vs. one from his brother who was battling the over-50 club like he was. Then, his negative self-esteem took over. *I might not have much time left. Shouldn't Lucas's kidney go to someone younger than me?*

He moved to the computer and pulled up Facebook, ready to publicize the selfless act of his brother and give him the credit he deserved. But – maybe that would stop someone else from stepping up. He deduced any announcement would be premature, possibly detrimental. He wrote a heartfelt email to Lucas instead, thanking him again and again.

And then he felt useless. There was nothing more he could do to speed along his brother's testing. He wouldn't know anything... for weeks.

Reggie put on his coat and pushed his walker out to the driveway, glancing to the corner of the yard where the hibiscus bloomed in the summer. The yard looked bare without it, the white fence blending into the snow. He inspected the Enclave. As he brushed his hand over the wrinkled metal, he again felt angry at Lincoln and Zoey. At the same time, he couldn't help but feel proud of Lincoln. Reggie believed that every once in a while a teenager should get in a little trouble, test the rules, and make their parents angry. *Who wants a perfect kid?* The dent wasn't really *that* bad. Reggie thought if he could get the orange out, no one would be able to notice it from a distance. He convinced himself it wasn't worth paying the deductible to get it fixed. Lincoln certainly didn't need another blemish on his insurance record.

An old pale blue Volkswagen Beetle drove up the driveway and stopped behind the Enclave. Erica, one of Grace's grade school friends and now one of Alice's nurses in the Alzheimer's unit, rolled down the window. She kept the car running to stay warm.

"Erica. This is a nice surprise. You making house calls now?"

Upon a closer look, Reggie could see Erica was upset. She stared straight ahead. She wore her scrubs, as if she had driven straight from work.

"Your mother-in-law has taken a turn for the worse. You and Anne need to go to Evenglow. Now."

Her voice was stern, and she appeared to be choking back tears. Anne emerged from the back door sporting a huge smile and holding two mugs of deluxe hot chocolate made with eight perfectly measured ingredients. Anne saw her mother's nurse in the driveway. She knew this could only mean one thing. She gasped and dropped the glass mugs onto the icy cement.

*   *   *

As a young girl, Anne had watched the TV series *Room 222* with her mother, learning tolerance lessons from Pete Dixon, the black high school history teacher on the award-winning show. Alice used the episodes as a platform to teach her daughter how important it was to love and care for any living thing God had put on this earth. Anne and Alice had laughed and cried together while watching. Prepared for the worst, Reggie and Anne stood in front of the door to room 222 at Evenglow's Alzheimer's unit. Anne found it highly appropriate her mother would spend her last days here, a powerful reminder of the kindness displayed to all that defined Alice's life.

They entered the dim room. Alice's color was gone, her white hair noticeably thinner. If not for the beeping heart monitor, they would have assumed she had already passed. Once the beeping stopped, her life would be over. Anne remembered how painful it was to sign the DNR order two weeks ago. Holding back tears, Anne sat next to her mother and grabbed her hand. Alice didn't respond. Not even a twitch. Reggie stood in the corner, unsure how involved he should be if this turned out to be the last moment Anne shared with her mother.

"Hi Mom, it's me, Anne. It's cold out there today, are you keeping warm?"

She pulled the blanket up to her mother's neck, hoping for some movement, a sign of life. Reggie could tell Anne had already accepted that she might not hear her mother speak another word in this lifetime. He couldn't be sure, but he felt the beeps were getting slower.

"Oh, I need to tell you about Lincoln's job. He's doing great working as a surgery scheduler. Would you like to see a photo of Lincoln in action?"

She held her phone in front of Alice's eyes hoping she might put forth an effort to see her grandson. Not a blink. Anne looked at Reggie, who saw tears begin to flow down Anne's cheeks.

Reggie watched with admiration as she asked several more questions. How brave she was. To be able to love everyone so deeply, so unconditionally, and courageously let that love grow day after day, year after year, knowing the more she let it grow, the more it would hurt when she eventually had to let go.

And what if he were the next to go? He thought about Anne living through life without her mother and her husband of almost twenty-three years. He needed to fight for more time. A new kidney would give him a longer life *and* a life with quality. With Anne. She had so much to worry about and Reggie had become "one of those things," but if he got better, healthier, he could help her and Lincoln for years to come. He would try harder not to be a burden.

Anne continued. "I know you like the oatmeal here with the raisins. Did you have oatmeal today?"

Still no response. Anne sounded more desperate with each question. Reggie needed to help, somehow. He walked to the other side of the bed and thought hard. What words might he use at this moment? He sat down, put his hand on Alice's shoulder and spoke loudly.

"Alice, your daughter spilled her hot cocoa today! Can you tell Anne how to make hot cocoa?!"

Alice's head slowly turned toward Anne. Her voice was gravelly, yet soft and peaceful.

"You silly girl. Did you spill?"

Anne looked at Reggie, thankful.

"Yes, Mom. I did. I forgot the recipe. Can you tell me?"

"You have to use... half dark chocolate... and half semi-sweet. And cocoa powder. But you know the real secret?"

"No Mom. What's the secret?"

"Cinnamon. It doesn't change the flavor much but..."

Anne said it with her mother.

"It adds just a pinch of love."

Alice closed her eyes. And the beeps stopped.

CHAPTER 25

The Cuff Must Be Broken

Lucas sat in the cluttered office at the Chevy dealership. This buyer was typically his most antagonistic client. He painfully watched his newest hire, Kelly, make mistake after mistake. She had already called the client by the wrong name and had a key page missing from her presentation.

"Since the price of gas has gone up, how are sales going this month for the Explorer?"

Lucas bit his lip. She obviously didn't study what brands *Chevy* sells, as he had suggested.

The marketing director patiently sat through it, feeling Lucas's pain. A fellow manager, he also trained recent college graduates and he knew Lucas had his work cut out for him with this one. Because the client had enjoyed several Illini games and a night on the Odyssey with MediaCast, her blunders were not important enough to spoil the sale. He signed the monthly advertising contract for $20,000 which included Kelly's first sports package sale. This would ensure her a company bonus for the month.

Kelly jumped in the car with Lucas and began dancing in the driver's seat. Lucas then coached her for twenty minutes on the importance of research. He taught her to see the meeting from the dealer's point of view. Once she heard her boss list the mistakes she had made, she vowed to prepare better next time.

She dropped Lucas off at the office. He had only twenty-five minutes before a WebEx, giving him just enough time jump in his company car and zip to Walgreens, get a blood pressure reading, grab take-out from Chipotle, and make it back to his office. As he drove to Walgreens, the March rains began to pound down, washing away the dirty snow on Veterans Parkway. He pulled into the parking lot and waited for the rain to lighten up.

He thought about Alice's funeral, one of the saddest he'd ever attended. She was absolutely loved. How awful Anne and Reggie had to live through that funeral while the kidney issues were ongoing.

And news of his intentions to donate? It was the talk of the wake after the funeral. His entire family knew. They asked questions, discussed it with fervor and flooded social media. The news somehow found its way to MediaCast. He was bombarded with emails, texts and I.M.'s congratulating him. Others, however, questioned the decision and his motive. All this – and he hadn't even been approved yet.

A break in the rain did not look imminent. He lifted his jacket over his head, braced himself and ran inside. He found the blood pressure reading station at the back of the store, slid his arm into the cuff and pressed the button. As the cuff filled with air, he read the blood pressure categories: Under 120/80 -- Healthy. Up to 130/89 – Pre-hypertension. Above 140/90 – High Blood Pressure. He had no idea what his exact past readings had been. He expected the reading to be slightly high, like his doctor had told him during his last couple visits. He was in sales – he rounded numbers anyway.

Air started releasing in the cuff and finally gave him a reading: 152/96.

Lucas paused. *That can't be right.* Maybe the reading was so high because he had just run into the store and his heart was racing. He tried to calm it down. He read the signage around the store. He watched customers. He listened to a lady rage on about the price of her prescription and the evils of the greedy pharmaceutical companies. He took a deep breath and tried again.

It read 150/98.

He exercised regularly. He ran marathons. He was pretty careful with what he ate. *The cuff must be broken.* He checked his watch and remembered he had a few snacks at the office. He could blow off lunch and run to CVS to get a reading from that store.

He did. The readings there were worse. Now he felt concerned; he purchased a blood pressure cuff before he left CVS.

Back at the office, he joined the WebEx. HR explained how to rate employees to determine next year's raises. Luckily, it was the same process as last year so he could listen but didn't need to watch. He opened his new blood pressure cuff. Before he could take a reading, two I.M.s needed answering and Molly needed permission to drop the price on a golf package that was only 20% sold out. He was hungry but would wait until after his reading to eat. Nervous he would get the same numbers, he tried to relax. He took a very deep breath. He finally put his arm in the new cuff.

152/92.

He searched on his phone for the heartfelt email Reggie had sent him the day he announced he would go through the testing. The two key phrases were "it's nice to feel my brother has my back" and "you have no idea what this means to my family." Lucas couldn't let his brother down. Maybe these blood pressure readings don't really matter that much. He wrote today's reading on the diary form. There were six spaces to write in his blood pressure readings over the next two weeks. 152/92 felt crazy high, but maybe the next five readings would be lower.

They were not.

Two weeks later, he found himself handing the completed form to a nurse at the transplant center like he was turning in a test knowing he got all the answers wrong. She was reviewing his past medical history as she took some vitals.

"Wow – your heart rate is 50. You must be a runner."

Lucas took that as a good sign. She was impressed with his health – excellent start here.

Rah came in and they discussed the unusually cold weather expected for the next week. She asked him if he had any questions about post-transplant surgery or if he had reached out to any prior donors yet to hear their personal stories. He hadn't. A few more transplant team members popped in, introduced themselves, and got back to work. Lucas felt somewhat like a celebrity. He thought about the transplant center's collective plight. Without people like him, the only transplants would be from deceased individuals – not nearly as happy a story as with a living donation.

Then a doctor entered the consult room. He was stocky, confident, and by the way the staff responded to him, highly respected. He cleared the room before he spoke.

"Good day, Mr. Nichols. I am Dr. Singh. I am pleased to meet you. I understand you are quite the runner."

"Sort of. I haven't run consistently. I've run two marathons and four half-marathons."

"Excellent, your heart rate shows it. You are in excellent shape. I'm a marathoner myself. I think my next will be my twenty-third. Still trying to hit that three-hour mark."

Lucas's marathon time was about four hours – the doctor was putting him to shame. This guy could walk the walk.

"So, Lucas, let us be on the same page. I need you to be clear what role I play here. I am a nephrologist, and I am *your* doctor. I don't care what anyone else in this transplant center wants or thinks. They want to have a robust transplant center. They want to help as many people as they can, including your brother. They want you to be a donor. My role is to protect *you*. To take care of *you*. Today, and farther down the road. Does this make sense?"

Lucas nodded. This guy has run twenty-two marathons. Who better to have as your guardian angel?

"Onward," he continued. "Let us look at the grand picture. Your brother has stage four kidney disease. This means you have a family history with hypertension and kidney disease. At the moment, you are athletic. You have two kidneys. You are generously willing to give away one kidney. But should you? Even though you have two kidneys today, you have high blood pressure. What if, in twenty years, you are no longer an athlete and you only had one kidney? How high will your blood pressure be then?"

Lucas thought this through. It suddenly sounded like a terrible idea to donate.

"For these reasons, I cannot approve you to be a kidney donor."

CHAPTER 26

All In

Rejected. There was no other way to take the news. Never in his life had Lucas been denied anything because of health. As he drove home he ran the gamut of emotions. Shame. Betrayal. Anger. A sense of unfairness. Concern that his own health wasn't as solid as he had thought. Extreme worry about the disappointment and fear Reggie would feel when Lucas shared the startling news. On top of all that he felt one strong, unexpected emotion. He found it terribly hard to admit to himself that he was feeling-- relief.

He had been given an "out." For himself, it was the best of all worlds, really. The news had gone public. The whole universe knew he was the good guy, willing to step up when it mattered. But... *darn the luck!* He would *not* have to suffer through that grueling surgery and recovery. He would *not* have to disrupt his life to help someone. He wanted to... but *they* wouldn't let him.

He felt sick to his stomach thinking this way. What Dr. Singh had told him was to come back in a month and they would re-test his blood pressure. Lucas felt he already lived a healthy lifestyle – how much more could he do to be *healthier* to lower his blood pressure? If the readings stayed high, and why wouldn't they, the doctor would prescribe medication to see how his body would respond. This could delay everything for months and who knows if it would even work? He hated the idea of taking medication for any reason. Throughout his childhood, his mother had kept one small tin of aspirin in her purse.

One tablet was all he or his siblings ever got and even that was rare. A mother's kiss, a glass of water, a walk, or a dab of baking soda on an insect bite cured almost every boo-boo and illness.

He thought he should probably tell his brother right away but felt stressed about making the call. To calm down, he visualized the most peaceful moment in his life – viewing a sunset over Lake Superior –– right after Reggie's first leg surgery. He recalled his Dad and Reggie arriving a day late to the family vacation because the operation was delayed a full week. Because no one thought to pack a pair of scissors, Reggie had to wear his medical wristband the entire trip and later it stood out like a spooky omen in all the photos. On the last night, his Mom and Dad took Scott, Harper and Ava to find some fresh, local Michigan cherries to garnish bowls of vanilla ice cream. Reggie and Lucas got to stay behind to "protect the cabin," as his Dad put it.

When the family drove off, Reggie cranked up his transistor radio and Elton John's *Philadelphia Freedom* crackled through the lousy AM reception. Lucas and Reggie tried to sing with it but not knowing the real words, they creatively inserted their own goofy phrases, butchering it so badly they laughed for ten minutes. Then, arm in arm, admiring the sunset together, feeling like men with their parents away, Reggie told Lucas, "I'm so happy you're my brother."

I'm so happy you're my brother. That statement changed everything. Six simple words. Lucas felt he was suddenly no longer one of five kids fighting for space and attention, hoping to win, striving to beat his siblings at any cost. Somehow, hearing those words from his older brother converted the family in his mind to a team trying to help each other win. At that moment Lucas also realized he had grown taller than Reggie, whose under-developed leg stunted his height.

Now he was tasked with making a phone call that would let his teammate down.

But... not yet. A view of a lake sounded tempting. He decided to abandon his route home and exited onto I-39 north instead. In ten minutes, he was sitting at his favorite secluded spot at Lake Bloomington, tucked on the water's edge behind a children's play area that looked like it hadn't been used in years. It wasn't Lake Superior, but it would do nicely as a venue to just... think.

The water reflected the deep blues of the Illinois sky. The trees had absorbed a lot of spring rain giving the shoreline a healthy green aura. It was too chilly for boats, leaving the lake peaceful. Lucas watched a family of deer emerge from the trees and sip from a small inlet. Catching his scent, they ducked back into the thicket.

Lucas sighed. He pulled out his phone to call his brother and share the terrible news but, hearing a bobwhite sing, he paused. He hadn't heard this sound in years. In third grade, his father gifted him a record with bird calls and for several weeks he listened to it and practiced imitating the sounds. When his siblings told him he was especially talented mimicking the bobwhite, it became his favorite bird.

To delay calling, he thought more about the past. His father, Herb Nichols, lost a lengthy battle with lung cancer so long ago that he was rarely part of the family dynamic. He was a complicated man, forever tortured by the memories of serving in Korea. Back then, PTSD and manic-depressive disorders were not a "thing" so Lucas reasoned that soldiers hid their undiagnosed issues and dealt with their demons internally as best they could. Filled with this bottled-up chaos, his father used to rant about the massive problems he saw in government, the military, social issues and education. In his rants, he would throw in the one message Lucas truly couldn't understand at a young age – that our country, our community, even ourselves can only be at their best if people constantly work hard to live the "best version of themselves." This always confused Lucas. "Best" in whose opinion? How could he know what the best version of himself is?

He finally gathered his nerve and placed the call to his brother as he pondered what the best version of himself might look like. Bailing on his brother wasn't part of that picture. He hung up before Reggie could answer and decided to call someone else instead.

"Schaeffer Jewelry. How may I help you?"

"Hi. This is Lucas Nichols. Any chance Bexley Schaeffer is in the store today?"

"Please hold."

Lucas heard another bobwhite call. Such a happy sound.

"Hey advertising boy! You calling for dance lessons?"

"Yes. But you're out of my league. Not sure I could keep up with the training."

She laughed.

"Yeah, right. I had a great time on the Odyssey. I'm a different person these days – can't thank you enough. You know my Dad was so thrilled to see me dancing, he reduced his radio buy and doubled his spend on MediaCast. I hope you see some of that."

Lucas winced. He would not benefit at all from it, but you'd think the Chicago rep or the manager would have at least called to inform him. Or thank him.

"That's great news. Don't worry, they take good care of me. Hey, you're the only person I know who's received an organ transplant. Did you ever have someone say they would donate, but then couldn't?"

"I did. My aunt raised her hand but they rejected her as a donor."

"So, how did she break the news to you? Were you devastated?"

"Yes, and no. When she couldn't donate, I kind of felt happy for her. She wasn't real fit to begin with. Why do you ask?"

"I signed up to donate a kidney to my brother. I was rejected as a donor today because my blood pressure's too high."

"You're kidding! I watched you and your wife dance together for hours – you *look* super healthy. If you can't donate, who the hell can? Did he actually use the word, *rejected?*"

Lucas thought... *what were his exact words?*

"Um... actually, I think he said, *I can't approve you.*"

"You dip shit. He's probably testing you. You have high blood pressure – so what? If you're all in, and really want to do this, you'll learn how to lower it and keep it low. If you're not all in, you'll use this as an excuse not to donate. Show the doctor what you're made of. Do you *know* what you're made of?"

Lucas had felt such relief earlier in the day when told he could not donate. Who wouldn't like the idea of avoiding surgery? But his brother needed him. *You don't hesitate. You just... help.* Maybe there was no need to tell Reggie. Not for thirty days, anyway. He could do this.

"I'm all in, Bexley."

"Then send me photos of the surgery. I want all the bloody details."

After hanging up, he enjoyed the peace of the lake for another minute hoping for a bonus deer sighting, but nothing came.

He sped home. He went straight to his computer and researched which natural foods were thought to lower blood pressure. Spinach, bananas, dark chocolate, and olive oil were on the list but were already typical staples in the house. He would need to buy kale, pomegranates, blueberries, and pistachios. Beets were on the list, but he always felt they tasted like dirt. They didn't make the cut.

His brother Scott's wife, Emma, owner of three organic food stores, had strong opinions on supplements. He sent her an email. She replied that his best choices to lower blood pressure were cayenne pepper, cinnamon, turmeric, and magnesium. She incidentally added that reducing alcohol would also help. Lucas vowed to scale back on booze going forward.

Next, he admitted to himself that he needed to reduce stress at work. He wondered... could work be the real reason his BP was so high? It was a never-ending battle of emails, appointments, hiring, training, client service, hitting financial goals and more. He wrote a four-page, highly detailed plan that he felt could be sustained long-term. He would delegate three of his responsibilities, eliminate a weekly report, and hold one-on-one meetings with salespeople bi-weekly instead of weekly, except for his newest hire. This would free up four hours. He moved a weekly training to lunchtime every Tuesday, freeing up another hour. It would have to be approved by his boss Toby, but he was confident he could sell him on it.

He read up on sodium. He spent two hours creating an Excel spreadsheet, listing good and bad meal choices and restaurants that offer guilt-free, healthy options. He rushed to Meijer to purchase his new diet items and when he returned, Kim had a delicious shrimp, broccoli, and sweet potato dinner ready. He chose to forego the high-sodium shrimp and instead heated up leftover baked chicken.

Feeling energized at the end of the day, he discussed his dietary changes with Kim in depth. She agreed to support him with the new meal restrictions. He read the labels on his new supplements that he had already taken and re-read his stress-reducing plan for work. It made him happy. This is what it takes, he thought, to be *all in*. His brother needed help and he would figure this out so he could be there for him. He felt less stress just knowing there was a plan to de-stress.

It was time for bed after an exhausting day. Just for kicks, he opened his work bag and pulled out the new blood pressure cuff. Kim wanted to try it first and she came in at 116/76. Typical – she was usually the healthiest person in the room. Lucas then checked his own blood pressure.

138/90.

Lucas clenched his fist and pumped it with excitement.

This is going to work.

CHAPTER 27

Homer Simpson Lampshade

Reggie struggled to push the vacuum cleaner around the living room, using furniture to brace himself with his right hand while trying to move the Bissel with his left. He spotted a wadded-up Tootsie Roll wrapper in the corner. It must have fallen from someone's pocket. Any ordinary person would simply reach over and pick it up after deciding it was too big for the vacuum cleaner to suck it up. But for Reggie, not so easy. With no furniture on that side of the room, he turned off the vacuum, crawled over to the wrapper, grabbed it, rested, crawled to the couch, painfully hoisted himself up, moved to the kitchen and threw it away.

Though this phase of their life was inevitable and expected, Alice's passing had turned Anne into a sort of sleepwalking roommate. Reggie found himself caring for her as best he could. He cooked dinner, cleaned, and hunted for coupons. He allowed her to space out on the front porch for hours. She had become a wife who responded like a robot in a trance.

Reggie felt especially vulnerable. What if this had happened while he tried to figure out dialysis? Or recovered from a transplant? He would need some serious attention post-surgery, but for now it was his turn to step up.

Lincoln seemed to have grown up a few years in just this past week. He pitched in wherever possible and played almost no video games. When his friends did visit, they left the game room spotless. He and

Zoey even prepared a delicious low-sodium Italian pot roast. Skylar and Grace caught on; both *claimed* they wanted to come over and play video games but brought a fully cooked meal with them. And yet, Anne barely tasted anything lately.

Reggie found this stage harder than expected and it took a toll. His pain and fatigue often screamed at him. He had to hide in different rooms of the house to take short rests. He was digressing. There was no blood in his urine, nor was it "foamy" yet, but he could sense his kidneys getting worse based on his itchier skin and increased fatigue. He would be forced to go on dialysis soon but he didn't dare tell Anne in her current state. All talk about health had come to a halt.

As Reggie finished vacuuming, he wondered why Lucas hadn't been in touch. It was so comforting that his brother agreed to donate a kidney, and even more reassuring that the whole world seemed to know it. Lucas must still be going through the approval process but why was it taking so long? Lucas was healthy. *The doctors would surely approve him.*

Reggie wound the cord onto the handle of the vacuum and set it in the closet just off the front porch. Alice's final belongings had been shoved in there until they could find a better place to store them: a large bag of Depend diapers, a Homer Simpson lampshade she bought when the show debuted in 1989, six photo albums of loved ones, a gold hairbrush, and two boxes of clothes. That was it. Reggie struggled to accept that the possessions of a loving saint like Alice were reduced to a cache that fit inside his front closet.

He peeked out the sidelight window where Anne sat, staring into nothingness on the front steps. He wondered if she should see a psychiatrist. Did she need professional help coping with the loss of her mother? Where would he even go to find someone? It didn't really matter, he thought. Neither of them would ever agree to pay for it. Hopefully, she would just snap out of it soon.

As he watched her motionless on the steps, a sudden realization hit him. What had they become? Their life had evolved into a constant, winless battle about money, health, and now death. *Why are we so glum? What happened to us?* They had struggled for years, but so what? So do most families. They had certainly had some genuine laughs along the way.

He typed a text: "If available, please come to my house ASAP. Meet me in the garage." He sent it to Lincoln, Zoey, Ben, Skylar, Gavin, and Grace, hoping he might get at least two of them to come over.

He checked his iTunes account. He had only purchased fifteen songs over the years to use up a gift card he won at work. Most of the songs were sappy ballads but surely there was an upbeat one in there. He moved to the kitchen and checked under the sink for cleaning supplies, then headed to the garage and waited for his children to arrive.

*   *   *

Pontiac boasted one of only three Gilding Arts museums in the country. A tour through the facility taught visitors the history of the delicate art of gold and silver leafing, how it was manufactured and its various applications over the decades in architecture and decoration. One item displayed in the museum was the door to a fire engine from the 1980's with shiny gold leaf lettering that read "Pontiac Fire Department, RFD." The average eye saw only fancy, shiny letters but once a person took the tour, the gold letters could only be viewed as pure art.

Anne had taken the tour twice. As she sat on her front porch, a Pontiac fire engine rushed by on its way to a kitchen fire on the west side. It featured the glistening gold artwork and the siren blared at Anne as if to ask her to look up and pay attention to the delicate mural. Anne watched it speed by giving neither the visual nor the harsh noise any of her focus.

For eighteen months, she had visited the Alzheimer's ward to help her mother re-live joyful memories. She had felt obligated to ensure her mother would keep *living,* which meant something completely different than just *breathing.* Some days were filled with laughs, others without any recognition of who Anne was or confusion that she was someone else. Only now did Anne realize that though she spent a ton of energy helping her mother dig up happy moments from the foggy craters of her mind, Anne had actually been drawing strength from her -- feeding off Alice's history of love and devotion to strangers as well as family. And now that her mother was gone, Anne was terrified she couldn't go it alone.

She had watched Reggie work hard to clean the house. She was grateful that Zoey, Grace, and Skylar, cooked to help out. She had even caught Lincoln's friends cleaning the windows to the game room after somehow spilling root beer on them. She didn't care. None of it mattered. The house could get filthy. So what?

She looked to the heavens and found a cloud that she thought looked like a frying pan. She spoke to it.

"Mom... there's just so much. Reggie. The kids. The house. Surgeries. Dialysis. I can't do this alone." As if to answer her, the winds morphed the frying pan into a white blob.

Her attention was grabbed away by blaring music from inside the house. *Dude Looks Like a Lady* by Aerosmith was cranked - *really* cranked! *Who the hell turned the volume full blast?* She fumed. Lincoln must have friends over. She would stop this.

She burst through the front door. The volume was deafening.

"Why is the music so damn loud?!"

But within three seconds, the scene before her made her laugh harder than she had in years. Eight people danced with their back to her as they pretended to dust the place with fuzzy pink dusters. Each wore one of Alice's ill-fitting Depend diapers over their pants. Ben wore a welder's helmet. Gavin wore a colander on his head. Lincoln and Zoey -- green knitted Shrek hats, complete with horns. Grace wore a cheese hat and Skylar sported a birthday cake hat with six fluffy candles. Reggie outdid them all in a Homer Simpson lampshade. Their stupid hats and hokey dance moves were utterly ridiculous and shocked Anne to her core. The song reminded her of the famous *Mrs. Doubtfire* vacuuming scene -- yet this was even funnier.

The crew was thrilled to have made Anne lose it, especially so quickly. They high fived and pumped their fists. Reggie turned down the music while Anne continued laughing and snorting out of control -- fully appreciating the funny hats and how poorly the diapers fit. She hugged the kids one by one, thanking them for having no shame. Throughout these hugs, she kept eye contact with Reggie. What an amazing thing to do for your grieving wife. What great timing. What a team they made.

And then she asked herself... *what was I thinking?*

It was obvious she had support. She would not have to do this, or anything, *alone.*

She closed her eyes. Silently, and with a jubilant heart, she finally muttered the words she had denied herself for what seemed like an exhausting decade:

"Goodbye Mom."

CHAPTER 28

The Guardrail

It had been two weeks since Lucas and Molly's last one-on-one meeting and it was flying by fast. Molly didn't once glance out the window even though it was April – a very active month for the animal kingdom. There had been no sass. She seemed distracted yet still able to ask her questions. They reviewed their key decisions and action plans, the usual last step to the meeting.

"I have one more problem," she said. "These Cardinal tickets have to get to Carpet Spinners today. The game is tomorrow but I'm heading to Jacksonville today."

Lucas hated the one downside of giving premium tickets to clients. So many of them wouldn't decide if they could go until the last minute. There was often a rush to get tickets into their hands and his promotions department hadn't embraced the email option for tickets yet.

"If no one else is headed that way, I'll drop them off on my way home."

"Thank you!" She gladly handed him four St. Louis Cardinal tickets, knowing it would take her boss out of his way to deliver them. The meeting was over. She stood but did not move to exit his office.

"Lucas, you know I love you as my boss. And as a person. It's really hard for me to say this but I know what you're up to. No matter what you're going through, there's a better way. I'm here to help."

Lucas thought hard about the job, his life, his family. He was clueless.

"I have absolutely no idea what you're talking about."

She nodded kindly, as if she knew all his secrets and his pain would soon be over.

"I saw you. Friday. You went into the bathroom three times. With that."

She pointed to a blue backpack on his coat hook that Lucas had indeed brought to the office last Friday. She grabbed the backpack and dropped it in front of him, then walked around the desk and put her hand on his shoulder. With intense sincerity, she continued:

"This is a safe space. You're doing drugs in the bathroom, I know it. I am not here to judge. I'm here to help."

He tried to prevent it but he burst out laughing. She looked miffed. He tried to compose himself, feeling bad for Molly. He needed to do some damage control here – to make her feel valued. He ushered her back to her seat. Through his sidelight window he saw two reps peek in, curious what was so funny.

"I'm sorry, Molly. Please tell me what else you've noticed."

"Well, you've been bringing your lunch every day and locking yourself in your office. And you only drink water. I assumed whatever drugs you are taking make you thirsty."

Lucas had never had a drug discussion with a co-worker but this was proving to be highly entertaining. He and his reps had a bond -- discussing health was not taboo in the office. Molly had shared everything about her cancer and projected an innocence. It was as if he were talking to his sister.

"You are quite observant. I greatly appreciate your concern, I really do, and I apologize that my actions led you to a false conclusion. I bring lunches from home so I can control my sodium, and I'm drinking water to keep my kidneys healthy. Please don't share this next tidbit with the team but I was using the backpack to hide... well, it's a container that holds a day's worth of urine. The transplant center needed an accurate reading of my kidney function so they asked that I collect my urine for twenty-four hours."

She showed no hint of embarrassment over her error. Only relief.

"Thank God! I was stewing over this the whole weekend. Guess you don't need *this*."

She pulled a notecard from her bra with the MediaCast drug abuse hotline on it. She had added the national number for SAMHSA just in case he didn't trust the company with his drug problem. She ripped it up. Lucas chuckled. *How could she even think it?*

She looked at him with a quick thought. "Wait a minute. We thought you were already in line to donate a kidney. Are you... not?"

"People assumed I was approved. My BP was high but I got that under control. I'm actually waiting to hear if I've been approved. Keep it quiet, OK?"

She nodded. She wasn't good at keeping secrets but she knew she'd keep this one. "So, how bad did your urine smell after twenty-four hours?"

He laughed. "Get out of my office."

He checked his phone. Though several recent emails looked urgent, he ignored them and pulled up his Notes app. He read the last ten readings for his blood pressure, which he had recorded twice a day now for four weeks. Every reading was below 124/82. Dr. Singh had been skeptical when Lucas submitted the new readings, but when he personally took Lucas's blood pressure and it came in at 116/78, he was impressed, congratulated him for achieving this without meds, and approved him for the next phase.

He had gone through all the testing in the past two weeks. Labs. Chest X-rays. EKG. Psych exam. Finance and Dietician consults. Urine samples – including the now comical 24-hour urine collection. The CT scan and ultrasound gave him the best news yet. Lucas's left kidney was a great anatomical fit so his surgery could be done laparoscopically. Smaller incisions. Easier recovery. Though it sounded exhausting to sit through all the tests, the good results from them were quite reassuring.

He thought about the seriousness of this decision. The dietician, the finance gal, the doctors and nurses, almost every member of the transplant team had told Lucas that if he changed his mind at any time, they could come up with a medical reason why he could not donate. He wouldn't have to be the bad guy that backed out. It would never look as if he was letting his brother down. Lucas had not considered changing his mind, not yet anyway. He wondered how many potential donors got scared and backed out. There was certainly plenty of time for it.

Rah had also told him that if he was approved, the results would only be good for one year. If Reggie went twelve months without needing a kidney, Lucas would be right back in Peoria taking most of these tests over again. He had already used four vacation days. *Could this be a yearly thing for a while?*

As a lifelong Cubs fan, he felt it would be bad luck to keep the Cardinals tickets Molly had given him on his person. He put them in his computer bag's zipper pocket. Delivering them would mean twenty extra minutes to get home tonight. He texted Kim to let her know he'd be late for dinner.

The next six hours were packed: employee meetings, lunch in the office, emails, and client meetings in the field. After his last meeting, he stepped into the company Ford Escape. His phone rang -- the Transplant Center was calling.

"Hello Rah. I'm hoping you've got news. Please tell me I don't have to re-do any more tests."

"Hi Lucas. Thank you for being patient with us. I saw you had to come back for two extra visits. This did take a bit longer than normal but that's only because we take your health seriously."

"Well, I don't care how long it took, as long as we got it right."

"I would say we did. Lucas, I'm pleased to tell you all your tests are in and you have been cleared to be a kidney donor for your brother. Even better, you are not just a match, you are six-antigen match -- the closest genetic pairing you can have without being identical twins, which means Reggie may get to take less anti-rejection medications in the years ahead. Approval to donate is usually news we let the donor share with their recipient. Would you like to be the one to share the news with Reggie?"

Share the news with Reggie? Nothing had made this more real than those exact words. A small part of him didn't want to share it. There would be no going back.

"Of course. He's been suffering more than I have through this process... I'm sure he expected to hear this news weeks ago. I'll tell him tonight."

"I've talked with him often. Yes, he's quite anxious. Don't forget – you are giving the gift of life. This is a tremendously admirable thing you are doing. We will speak soon, I'm sure, but you can always call us with any questions." Lucas wanted to call Reggie right away but telling his wife first seemed appropriate. He'd tell her when he got home and call Reggie after that.

He wasn't used to driving west of Springfield on I-72 but he finally made it to Spinner's and delivered the complimentary baseball tickets just as it began to sprinkle. When he started up the Escape, it took three tries – that was odd, he thought. Lucas checked the mileage: 106,224 miles. He had always driven a company clunker. For the last five years, he had asked for a *new* company vehicle on his capital request form, but no dice. So unfair. When the Chicago managers hit fifty-thousand miles they would usually receive a new car and the smaller offices got their hand-me-downs.

He pulled onto the highway, eager to get home and share his news. Classic rock filled the vehicle. Illinois had entered its usual construction season and the rain fell harder, intensifying the traffic. He merged onto I-55. The left lane was closed and lined with orange barrels, squishing all traffic into three packed lanes.

Lucas drove exactly 50 mph, the speed limit through the zone. The Illinois Department of Transportation was one of his clients. He'd feel highly embarrassed if he ever got a ticket in a construction zone when every year his team placed ads on TV begging drivers to slow down when they see orange signs and barrels. He approached a semi going about 48 mph, and the spray it kicked up off the wet pavement made it hard to see. Lucas decided to pass it but he'd stay at 50 mph. Several cars filed in behind him, probably wishing Lucas would speed up and get out of their way. He stuck to the speed limit. When he was just far enough in front of the semi to cross in front of it and swing back to the middle lane, the Escape died. He had no engine power.

His heart raced immediately as the car started to coast and slow down. His transmission had blown. He checked his mirror – there was a line of maybe seven vans, pickups, and cars behind him also trying to pass the semi. 46 mph. He turned off the radio and tried to turn on his hazard blinkers, but he didn't know where the damn button was and he needed to keep his eyes on the road. He put his right blinker on instead, still slowing down. 40 mph. The pickup truck behind wailed on his horn. Two more vehicles sounded their horns.

The semi seemed to take forever, but it finally passed him. 35 mph. Lucas couldn't get over. One by one, the cars behind him zipped around him, honking. It was difficult to see anything through the wet windows – he did see one driver flip him the finger. Not one car let him slide over. Lucas sweated, trying to gauge his next move. 30 mph.

He couldn't stop in this lane or he'd be in a crash for sure. He could either plow into the barrels on his left or find a moment to swerve over two lanes to the shoulder. 28 mph. He was able to swing over one lane, but some asshole in a BMW flew by him on the right – must have been going 70. A minivan zoomed up behind it in the same lane – no room to slide over. More cars wailed on their horns. No one slowed down.

A Honda Accord was zooming up fast in the right lane, but Lucas thought he could beat it. He cranked the wheel and the Escape swerved in front of the Accord, which blew its horn, braked, and swerve to the left. Lucas had done it. He was on the shoulder going only 25 mph. It was close, but he had avoided an accident. His heart pounded and his knuckles ached from gripping the wheel tightly!

He coasted on the shoulder still going 25 mph, a long guardrail on his right. He checked the rearview mirror. A large cargo van approached in the lane closest to him. All three lanes were jammed full of traffic. The van had no wiggle room. Lucas inched as far to the right as he could, careful not to hit the long guardrail along the edge of the shoulder.

He went one inch too far.

His right wheel slipped off the asphalt and crunched into a guardrail post. The post seemed to grab his front right tire, jolting the car and forcing its back end to swing left. The vehicle rolled, slamming the driver's side door into the asphalt. It completed two full rotations on the shoulder of the highway. Rearview mirrors were crushed. Glass shattered. Bumpers ripped off.

But the car kept going. It rolled four more times before it finally stopped thirty feet into the ditch. Upside down.

CHAPTER 29

Let's Go

Reggie tapped the F key on his piano repeatedly. Nothing. He had shone flashlights into the cracks, used a nail file to find anything that might be wedged between the keys, and wiggled the hammers and strings to fix it. He was angry at Lincoln who often ate cookies, chips, or toast at the piano, probably dropping crumbs between the keys. Reggie wanted to play. He needed to play. He should have heard from Lucas a long time ago that he was officially in line to be his donor, but the call had never come. A little Elton John would go a long way right now.

Anne had pulled up a piano maintenance website and started reading a section to Reggie on *Stuck or Sticky Keys* when Reggie's cell phone rang. It was Kim. The unwritten rule seemed to be that siblings always called siblings and the in-laws listened in the background. The in-laws got along well, but it was rare Kim would call instead of Lucas. He answered, hoping it was somehow related to Lucas's testing.

"Hello, this is Reggie."

There was breathing, almost hyperventilating on the other end. Kim was trying to say something but struggled to get any words out between sobs.

"They... called... Police."

Reggie waved Anne over and put the phone on speaker. More sniffling, but no words came forward.

Anne pried. "Kim, are you OK? Try to calm down. What's happened?"

"Lucas had... bad... accident. He's... he's.... E.R."

Anne guessed, "Lucas is in the E.R.? In Bloomington?"

"Springfield. They wouldn't... say... Just, come to hospital. You know... what that means? I can't lose him! What if he's... gone?!" She bawled uncontrollably. She got angry and managed to yell:

"The police don't tell you anything when they die – they just say come to the hospital!"

Reggie took control. "Kim, stop it. You don't know anything yet. Do NOT assume that! We need to get you to Springfield so here's what you're going to do. You need to pack an overnight bag. You need to ask your neighbors to watch Bali and Fiji. Then you stand by your front door with your suitcase and wait for us to pick you up. Got it?"

There was silence. Having overheard the instructions, Lincoln entered the room wide-eyed. He listened as Reggie continued.

"Kim, it's a bad idea for you to drive right now. Say it out loud. I want to hear you say it."

Kim was able to choke out the words, "Bad idea... to drive."

"We're going to hang up now so you can get packed. Call us back right away if you hear anything. We'll pick you up as soon as we can. OK?"

"OK."

Reggie hung up. As they rushed to the door, Reggie stopped.

"Wait. Let's take a breath. What are we missing?"

Anne grabbed a cooler and threw in some iced teas, water bottles and snacks. Lincoln retrieved their phone chargers. Reggie grabbed an umbrella and the $100 in reserve cash they kept stashed in a coffee mug.

"Anything else?" Anne asked.

Reggie and Anne looked at each other. Both were thinking the same horrendous thoughts. Had Reggie just lost a potential kidney donor? Even worse, had he lost a brother? Under any other circumstances, they might hug and have a good cry together. But Kim needed them. Now.

Reggie battled the heavy rain on the trip to Bloomington, angry that rain slowed down some drivers while others ignored the hazardous road conditions and sped along at crazy speeds. "It's the difference in speeds that makes the roads more dangerous!" Anne had heard it many times. Preaching to the choir. They talked about TV shows, which French fries they missed the most, and their favorite Pixar movies. Anything to pass the time and avoid thinking the worst.

As he pulled into his brother's driveway, Kim sped out of the house, ready to enter the Enclave before it came to a stop. She whipped open the back door, sat, put on her seatbelt, and set her suitcase on her lap. All she could say was, "Let's go."

The heavy rain continued to batter the SUV making it loud inside the vehicle. Reggie and Anne both wished the Berly Factor would kick in but didn't dare mention it. Kim was robotic. She spent the first fifteen minutes of the trip yelling on the phone, trying to get someone at the hospital to tell her anything. She finally got a "your husband's in surgery."

"That's good news," Kim said. "At least he's not dead." She wanted to believe it, but she suspected that might be the hospital's strategy of shutting her up and keeping her safe during her trip to Springfield.

Cycling through rage, fear, and sadness, she elected not to share the news with her daughters until she knew more. She spent the rest of the drive researching safety ratings for Lucas's company car -- the Ford Escape. As they passed McLean, Reggie kept glancing at the barrels on the other side of the highway, wondering which one Lincoln had bashed into months ago.

Two miles from the hospital, Reggie saw bright lights from a police blockade on the other side of the road. A fire truck, several flood lights, and seven cop cars barred traffic from the right lane on the northbound side. With the left lane already blocked for construction, the traffic trickled through the two remaining lanes. He could see yellow police tape marking off a section of the road. Could this be where Lucas crashed? From his vantage point, he couldn't see the white Escape in the ditch but he was sure it was there. He looked at Kim in the rearview mirror, in a stupor and reading on her phone. He pushed his worst fears out of his mind and decided it best not to point out the accident site.

The Memorial Medical campus was huge but the signage was unmistakable. Reggie easily found Emergency and parked. Kim realized this was the first time ever she exited a vehicle that was parked in a handicap spot. Being close to the entrance was especially helpful given the hard rain. They walked to the information desk. Despite the urgency, Kim walked at Reggie's slow pace which actually served to help keep her calm.

Lucas was indeed in surgery. They were led to a waiting room. The wait seemed insufferably long. Kim asked every nurse, doctor and volunteer who walked through if they had any information. Finally, a policeman walked in with a hospital administrator, who pointed at Kim. The cop was shorter than Kim, making his shiny badge and gun look larger against his small frame. He carried a white garbage bag.

"Good evening ma'am. Are you Kimberly Nichols?"

She nodded, fearful of what was coming. She hadn't been this close to a police officer in uniform since sixth grade's Public Safety night.

"Ma'am, these items were recovered from the scene. We hoped to prevent the electronics from getting ruined by the downpour. At this time, I can tell you your husband was in a single vehicle accident. He was wearing his seat belt and his cell phone was not a factor when he lost control of the vehicle."

He handed her the bag.

Kim asked, "What happened? Were there any witnesses?"

"His vehicle rolled multiple times and landed in the embankment adjacent to the interstate. That's all I can reveal for now. We are still completing our report."

That wasn't helpful. She knew Lucas never texted while driving and always wore a seatbelt. She checked the white bag. His personal and company cell phones looked dry. His computer bag was damp – no telling how wet it had gotten but she didn't care.

A veteran surgeon with scraggly, curly hair finally emerged, introduced himself as Dr. Pendergrass, and ushered Kim into a private lounge designed for moments just like this. Kim thought he could easily be mistaken for a patient. He definitely needed a shower and a hairbrush.

"Your husband is a trooper. We think he's going to be OK. His radius, the lower left arm bone was broken in two places but the surgery went well. He suffered a broken rib but it didn't puncture the lung. That will have to heal on its own. He has a concussion and two black eyes, most likely from the deployment of the air bag. There were five lacerations on the right side of his neck, where we removed four pieces of shrapnel - glass. We want to keep him here for a couple days for observation. After that, we expect he will be released. He's looking at a good six weeks before he's fully recovered."

She exhaled. Tears of relief clouded her eyes. Harsh news, but it was much better than she had feared.

"Once the anesthesia wears off, you can see him. Any questions?"

She couldn't think of any.

"Rollover accidents can be nasty. In this case, there's no indication of neck or head trauma, or spinal issues."

Through more tears, she managed to squeak out, "Thank you Doctor."

He gave her a reassuring nod and started to walk out but stopped.

"Mrs. Nichols, one more thing. A broken rib sometimes tricks people. Lucas had difficulty breathing and may have thought he had some internal organ damage. By any chance, is he going to donate a kidney?"

How could he possibly know this? She had forgotten to ask if he had any internal issues. *Could he still donate after this?*

"He's thinking about it. How did you know?"

"He came to as they wheeled him into the O.R. He told the surgical team, *Save my kidneys first.* Never heard that from a patient before. His injuries should not restrict him from donating down the road."

185

He left. She imagined her husband with two perfect kidneys but with a prosthetic arm because of the instruction he gave to his doctors. In her mind, he looked ridiculous with a fake arm and she got mad at him for saying what he did.

Her stomach growled loudly – reminding her she hadn't eaten since lunch. She searched for Reggie and Anne to give them the update. She found them in Lucas's recovery room despite not having permission yet to be there. They sat quietly, waiting for him to wake up. Anne offered Kim snacks but all she wanted was plain toast. Reggie insisted Anne take Kim to find some sustenance -- he would sit with Lucas until they returned.

A few minutes later, Lucas awoke. He looked around the room completely dazed.

"You've been in a car accident," Reggie explained. "This is Memorial Hospital in Springfield. Kim and Anne are getting a bite to eat but will be right back."

He stared at Reggie, trying to comprehend it all.

"Water?"

It was raspy and barely audible, but Reggie understood. He picked up the Styrofoam cup and held the straw to Lucas's lips. He took a long sip.

Reggie had trouble looking at him. Though covered in blankets from mid-chest down, the neck bandages, big cast, and two black eyes were the epitome of gruesome. Lucas spoke – a bit more audible this time.

"Are my kidneys OK?"

Knowing his brother was truly lucid, Reggie breathed a sigh of relief. He nodded.

"I was approved today to give you my left one."

The irony struck Reggie like a baseball bat to the throat. Of all the times he had received great news in his life, this by far came with the most amount of irony. His brother looked as if he were savagely beaten and on the brink of death. Yet he felt compelled to share news of what he could still offer.

Lucas continued. "One rule. You can never forget this was my decision. Not yours. If anything ever happens to me during surgery or down the road, you had nothing to do with it. I made this choice."

That helped reduce some of Reggie's worries. He needed Lucas to realize just how thankful he was for his decision to donate and for not changing his mind.

Reggie spoke slowly. "Do you have any idea how hard it is for me to see you in pain like this, knowing that I've asked you to help me by giving me a kidney?"

Lucas decided to answer it with his own question. Through his pain, he also spoke slowly.

"Do you have any idea how hard it has been for me to see you in pain *every single day of your life,* and NOT be able to help?"

CHAPTER 30

Driving for Dummies

Drugged, bruised, and achy, Lucas rested in the hospital bed with his eyes closed. He pictured a client meeting from four years ago. His traffic department had aired $18,000 worth of the wrong Chevy Silverado commercial and the manufacturer had denied co-op reimbursement. An apology from MediaCast to Lucas's most difficult client was warranted. To restore the trust, Lucas sat in that office, ready to eat crow and offer $19,000 in bonus advertising. The client made Lucas wait. And wait. Lucas could see the marketing director for the entire hour through the glass wall, taking calls, laughing, even pouring a second and third cup of coffee. Lucas was being punished for his company's mistake but he refused to let his time be wasted.

He answered emails and texts. He hunted for new prospects for his team. When out of things to do, he found a newsletter buried among their industry magazines. One article instructed what one should do if inside a vehicle about to be in an accident. Always wear a seatbelt. When to duck. What to do with your arms. How to cover yourself. Front seat vs. back seat. Pick-up vs. sedan. The last line of the script read, "If your vehicle is going to roll over – good luck. There is nothing you can do except *brace yourself.*"

Those words flashed into Lucas's head the instant his wheel got caught on the guardrail post. Knowing the airbag might deploy, he had removed his hands off the steering wheel and braced himself. He pressed his left hand hard against the dashboard and his right hand against the passenger seat headrest. He remembered closing his eyes tight and fiercely pushing outward with both hands. As the car rolled, he moved with the vehicle, as if he were solidly attached to it instead of a free-floating object to be tossed around inside. The seatbelt helped tremendously, especially when he flipped upside down.

Who could have predicted that a vindictive client trying to punish him years ago had actually helped prepare Lucas to save his own life?

Lucas opened his eyes. A dozen flower vases peppered the room, each with small envelopes attached. He smelled mashed potatoes. A cast immobilized his left arm, reminding him of the pain he felt when his arm popped. He could barely turn his heavily bandaged neck, but looking as far left as he could, he saw Kim reading a book in the chair next to him.

He asked, "So – is this where you go to pick up helpless guys?"

She smiled, not because she thought it was funny but because Lucas often joked to let people know he was OK.

"Yes. I found a nice man with leprosy last night. Very generous. He gave me his hand. Literally."

Lucas laughed, but it put his lungs on fire.

"Stop. That hurts."

"Gavin got you this." She showed him the book she had been reading: *Driving for Dummies.*

He stifled a laugh. That also hurt.

With his left hand fully covered by the cast, she moved to the other side of the bed and held his right hand.

"Reggie said you told him last night you were approved to donate a kidney. Is that real, or was that the pain killers talking?"

He had to think. Yes, he had awakened for a bit and talked with Reggie. It was great talk. Unable to nod, he winked at her. They contemplated the difficulty and uncertainty of adding a kidney surgery to their overall plan, especially at a time when neither knew how he might recover from this.

Lucas explained, "The surgery is always on the *donor's* schedule. It's never an emergency. It has to be planned for weeks -- I'll have time to recover. Once Reggie is ready, we'll get on the calendar."

She remembered a life lesson that Lucas had voiced long ago. They had repeated it often during their marriage. She recited: "Always have a plan. And a plan B. And a plan C..."

He finished it. "Then throw them all out the window."

She smiled, both proud of and scared for him.

"Riley and Aspen want to see their father. They are on the way. Several people have stopped by already. My phone is blowing up."

A tall Illinois State policeman with a notebook interrupted them. He looked angry but professionally held it in check.

"Mr. Nichols. I'm officer Goodwin. Are you feeling well enough for a few questions for our police report?" He eyed Lucas with an accusatory look.

"Sure."

"First, may we have permission to access results of your blood work?"

Lucas and Kim thought that was odd.

Kim asked, "Why do you want the bloodwork?"

"We have an eyewitness who claims he saw you cutting off other drivers and then," he checked the notebook for the exact words, "Seemed to take his vehicle into the guardrail on purpose."

"That's ridiculous," Lucas answered. "The transmission blew while I was in the left lane, and..."

The cop interrupted, "How do you know the transmission blew?"

"The radio and windshield wipers still worked but there was no engine power. It was a construction zone, heavy traffic, the car was slowing down on its own. I was just trying to save my life by getting to the shoulder as fast as possible. You can have all the bloodwork you want."

Kim was irate. She pictured her husband unable to give a kidney because he was in jail on some destruction of property charge.

The cop thought hard on Lucas's words. "Left lane, rush hour, heavy rain, in a construction zone, with no engine?"

Lucas tried to nod but couldn't move his head up or down. The cop closed his notebook realizing he had the story all wrong.

"That makes more sense. Hm. Just so you know, only three percent of the nation's accidents are rollovers, yet they account for one-third of all vehicle occupant deaths. Glad to see you're going to recover. The insurance company will want to inspect that transmission. Have a nice day."

As he walked out he stopped, almost as if thinking aloud.

"Company vehicle? A hundred and ten thousand miles? And the transmission blew?"

He stared as if he expected to see them jump up and yell, "We'll sue the bastards!" Getting no reaction, he tipped his hat and walked away.

Lucas and Kim read each other thoughts. *Could they sue? Should they sue? At the very least, they should get the medical bills covered, right?*

They let it go for now. Lucas started to gain strength as the drugs made their way through his system. His daughters, co-workers, and team members dropped by for the rest of the day with well wishes, food, and a couple of hard-to-find bottles of Flor de Caña Rum. The attached note read, "Take this instead of any painkillers they give you."

That night, Reggie and Anne returned to the hospital. They announced they would only visit a short while and had brought a cooler of healthy foods to share. Before leaving, Kim walked Anne down the hall to help her find the *good* bathroom, giving Lucas and Reggie a moment.

Reggie read the critical notes about the patient and staff on the room's whiteboard.

"You realize you have two doctors and three nurses on this shift alone?"

He glanced around the room, awed by the equipment.

"Don't you wonder how much all this costs?"

Lucas saw a desperation in Reggie he'd never noticed before. The Nichols never discussed money because their father had taught them it was impolite. He did share one valuable lesson: "All one can really see in people is how much they *spend,* not how much they *have.*" Lucas had witnessed it firsthand. One of his neighbors flaunted a membership to the country club, took lavish vacations and upgraded to the newest Mercedes annually. When he asked Lucas to collect his mail while he traveled in Europe, Lucas saw several past due notices. The neighbor fled in the middle of the night last January -- everyone assumed to avoid creditors and possibly the law. Lucas's other neighbor wore clothes from the '80's and drove a beat-up Dodge Caravan. He let it slip after a few Miller Lites at a backyard barbecue that he had sold some shares of Google stock. "He only had four thousand shares left." Lucas did the math. Though no one would suspect it, that put his neighbor's net worth at a minimum four million dollars.

Wealth was an illusion. Lucas decided to break the family taboo.

"Reggie, are you worried about money? About the costs of having this surgery?"

"Well... yes. It's all just so much. I pay this crazy deductible, but there's always so much more we have to pay for. The gas and tolls to see Chicago doctors. The walkers for me and Lincoln. Fixing the walkers. Leg braces. New leg braces. Medicine. Throw in the mortgage, out of control property taxes, car repairs. I'll miss at least a month of work. What if my wife gets sick? You know, Anne wanted to buy a small bag of cashews. We about flipped out – it was $9.99! We stuck with generic peanuts, thank you!"

They heard Kim and Anne coming back, giggling because a doctor in the hall looked like a star on *Grey's Anatomy.* The room was quiet when they entered and Anne announced, "We better let Lucas rest."

Before leaving, the *Grey's Anatomy* sighting led to the subject of TV. Anne tried to convince Kim to watch the funniest show ever on Netflix. As she described the show, Lucas eyed his brother trying to maneuver his walker to get out of the cramped hospital room. Even with insurance, the medical expenses he must have paid over the years.

How all-consuming the medical issues must be in his household. How difficult it must be to walk through life with a son sharing the same physical ailment. How unfair was it that, going into a transplant surgery, Reggie's fears would be greatly intensified by deductibles, the cost of post-op meds, lost wages and more? *What if there were some way to erase these concerns?* He knew Reggie was proud. He would never accept an outright check.

Once Kim finally agreed to watch Reggie and Anne's favorite comedy, they left. Kim picked up the mess from the parade of visitors and noticed Lucas was quiet. He still looked ghastly -- as if he would need a full year to recover. He appeared as if in a trance.

"Hey. What's on your mind?"

Lucas thought more about Reggie. He was funny. Likeable. Always doing little things for others. His home was filled with so much love it spilled out around the family and into the community. He was quite possibly the most deserving man Lucas knew, yet a huge chunk of his possessions had been purchased at garage sales.

Lucas uttered a statement. Given his beat-up body and his jam-packed calendar, it seemed so ridiculous to Kim that she burst into laughter.

"I'm going to throw a fundraiser for my brother."

She blamed it on his concussion.

CHAPTER 31

Amber Beer

An iconic, brightly painted 3-D mural covered all three stories of the brick building.

"This must be the largest Route 66 sign *in the world*," Lincoln said. He and Reggie slurped on lemon slushies in downtown Pontiac watching tourists drive up and snap pictures. So far, Reggie and Lincoln had observed two Mustangs, a Corvette, and a 1969 GTO. The sign was so big many people fit their cars into their photos. Lincoln sat comfortably next to Reggie in the shade on a city bench, proud that he had paid for both slushies proving he was becoming more responsible. A Japanese Mom asked Lincoln to snap a photo of her family in their open air Jeep. He did, capturing for her a perfect memory.

"They should put this in a video game. It'd be a cool vintage throwback for a bonus round," Lincoln suggested.

Reggie and Lincoln were celebrating the Enclave's repair. Earlier today, they had worked in the garage to remove the orange paint embedded into the front panel by the roadside barrel. A neighbor saw them working on it as he biked past and returned with a glue tab kit. He showed them how to apply glue, stick the tabs onto the massive dent, and use a dent puller to remove them. The dented metal eased back into shape. Then he sprayed on a solution to remove the glue. It wasn't perfect but the dent was hardly noticeable. Reggie thanked him, adding that he would feel proud to drive it again.

Reggie's melting slushie dripped through the cheap paper cup onto his untucked shirt. When he wiped it with a napkin, he realized it was right on the spot where the incision for a new kidney would go. It triggered thoughts about his health. Two weeks ago when Lucas had his car accident, Reggie's body reacted magically – as if it healed itself temporarily to give Lucas time to recover before the eventual transplant. His back and leg pain were barely noticeable. Surprisingly, he didn't itch at all. Work had been a breeze and he had the energy to clean out the entire garage. He began to think the connection with his brother acted on some advanced plane – like twins who report feeling each other's emotions from miles away.

As if to confirm his theory, his cell phone rang. It was Lucas. To free his hands, he gave the paper cup to Lincoln who started a trek to the garbage can.

"Hello, this is Reggie."

"Hey, it's me. I need your help with something."

"You want me to teach you how to drive safely? Easy. Stay between the lines, knucklehead!"

Lucas laughed.

Reggie asked, "How's the recovery coming? Are you still ugly? Will Kim even kiss you?"

"Yes, for a fee. No, they want me to take six more weeks 'cause of the broken arm, and even then, I might have restrictions. I'm feeling good, though. I tried toying around on the computer today. If I sit at the right angle above my keyboard, I can actually type an email."

"Stop it, you moron. Rest. Get better. You're healing for two, if you catch my drift."

"That's kind of why I'm calling. I just can't let you go into a transplant surgery worried about the *cost* of it. I have a way to make that anxiety go away. I can throw a fundraiser for you."

Reggie was silent. The center of attention? He didn't want any favors, pity, or charity.

"Well... I don't feel comfortable with that."

"It's just a party, Reggie. Music, food, maybe dancing. We can get some silent auction items donated and the money we raise will go toward your family's medical expenses."

"But everybody has medical expenses. Why should I get special treatment?"

"It's not special treatment. Can't I just do something nice for my brother?"

"You're already doing more than enough, don't you think?"

Lucas sighed. If Reggie could see him, still so beat-up, he'd never agree to his plan. That's why Lucas chose to ask over the phone. There would be no winning an argument with Reggie, so Lucas simply avoided having one.

"I need you to sit back and just let this happen. It's not just for you. It's also for Anne and Lincoln -- to pay for any medical expense in the future. You won't have to do anything except show up. I have all this free time now anyway to start organizing - I need something to do. Help me out."

Reggie glanced at Lincoln, who had taken the roundabout route to throw the paper cups away but cut across the parking lot for a shorter trip back. He was struggling to lift his walker over the cement wheel stops because it wouldn't fit between them. He winced. *Why was it so painful to watch Lincoln struggle?* Perhaps a fundraiser could benefit Lincoln. Maybe it'd be OK. Reggie thought about the small donations he had made to dozens of charities and school fundraisers over the years. Maybe it was his turn. He could certainly use a financial boost.

Lucas kept on. "If I understand the scheduling, your body basically decides when it's time for surgery. When you feel you're ready, I'd like to schedule the transplant three months out. That would give me time to plan and execute the fundraiser. We could hold it a week or two before the surgery. Sound good?"

He wasn't worth a fundraiser! He felt like arguing about it but Lucas had been convincing. How much could Lucas possibly raise anyway? Six grand? Nine grand tops? Perhaps there wouldn't even be a need for a fundraiser. These last two weeks had been mostly pain-free and his last score was 19% kidney function. Perhaps he could go years without needing any help. He remembered that just a few weeks ago, he felt his kidneys were getting *worse*. It was so confusing.

"I like to think I could go years without needing surgery. But... OK." Reggie couldn't help but feel special – his brother was really fighting for him and his family.

After hanging up, Reggie and Lincoln stayed to enjoy another lemon slushie. They were rewarded with a procession of Harley Davidsons, a busload of Chicago ladies in purple hats and three vintage Volkswagens stopping for group photos in front of the mural. When the novelty wore off, Reggie and Lincoln climbed into the newly refurbished Enclave and headed home.

Anne had a pot roast and vegetables simmering in the slow cooker. A fresh strawberry cake with buttercream frosting waited on the counter. As they sat for a delicious meal, Lincoln blurted out, "Uncle Lucas is going to throw Dad a fundraiser."

She stopped serving food and looked at Reggie, concerned.

"With what army? You know how much work goes into that?"

Reggie tried to calm her, "He said I don't have to do a thing. He'll take care of it."

Anne had attended a couple of embarrassing fundraisers. Duds.

"I don't know if I like this. Did he say where? Or when?"

"He throws a fun Christmas party," Lincoln added.

Reggie suddenly felt incredibly thirsty He took a big sip of water, then used the table and kitchen counters to help him move to the bathroom. As he got to the door, a searing pain in his back forced him to his knees. This was new – he had never had a *sharp* pain there before. He resisted the urge to cry out, pulled himself up, and checked to make sure Anne and Lincoln hadn't seen him. He took a deep breath and slid into the bathroom.

After peeing, he glanced into the toilet. He stopped himself from flushing.

It looked like amber beer. Dark... and foamy.

I'm running out of time.

CHAPTER 32

Four Weeks

Lucas stared at his face in the mirror. The black eyes were almost healed, just a trace of purple and gray remained around his right eye. The sores and scars were fading thanks to Kim who smeared Vitamin E on his neck twice a day. The headaches and "fogginess" from the concussion had stopped a week ago. His arm felt like it didn't need the cast anymore though he was stuck with it for two more weeks.

The broken rib had been the hardest to deal with, causing debilitating pain at times when he breathed. The doctors seemed particularly concerned about the potential for pneumonia but insisted the best course of action was to let it heal on its own. The worst moment of recovery had been a case of the hiccups, each spasm sending shockwaves of discomfort through his chest. He was forced to absorb the pain while trying to both brace for and stifle the next one. He held his breath, drank water, and pulled on his tongue. After a while, they finally went away. Today was the first day he felt he could breathe normally.

Lucas thought about his past involvement with the local St. Jude's men's and women's golf tournaments. He served on the committee for a stretch of nine years. He wasn't involved in any high-level planning – his position could best be described as a grunt. He worked like a dog the day of the tournament, hanging banners, filling and delivering coolers to the tee boxes, taking photos, and fulfilling any number of outlandish requests to make the players, some of them drunk by the end the day, feel pampered. He handed out awards during the late-night presentation and cleaned up afterwards.

Leading up to the event, however, he offered sponsorships to businesses -- a task smack dab in his wheelhouse. Having read between the lines for nine years, Lucas was convinced the golf tournament was about so much more than raising money.

He could still picture the faces of the St. Jude's kids. These children had been to hell and back, suffering from all kinds of tumors, sarcomas, carcinomas, leukemia – the website listed almost a hundred ailments. The tournament brought out a handful of these young cancer survivors to speak or perform in front of the golfers. They sparkled. Their stories, songs, and skits were so compelling they inspired the golfers to open their checkbooks nice and wide to donate.

Of course, the real purpose *was* to raise funds, but Lucas saw so much more than the money side of it. This event was the Super Bowl for these kids and each one was a star quarterback. They were the center of the universe for the day. At the end of the awards ceremony, they felt vindicated, successful, and needed. He could see that they left the tournament the princes and princesses of their own world.

What if he could give even a hint of that feeling to his brother?

He had met dozens of business owners during those tournaments. Combined with his client list, he hoped he could secure enough auction items for an effective fundraiser. His long history in Bloomington and having been raised in Pontiac convinced him he could pull this off. At the same time, he admitted to himself that he'd never *organized* something like this. He was winging it.

His managerial instincts kicked in. He started with a spreadsheet. He listed the elements necessary to host a fundraiser: venue, decorations, music (DJ or band?), T-shirts, food, games, programs, signage, publicity, and auction items. He thought of possible expenses and made a budget. He set a goal to raise fifteen thousand dollars and a stretch goal of twenty thousand. He reminded himself the occasion would be held in Pontiac, a town much smaller than Bloomington.

Reggie didn't hang with an upper crust crowd and *substantial* donations might be scarce. He lowered the goals to twelve and eighteen thousand.

He listed a friend or family member next to each task who might be a good fit to assist or take ownership of it. MediaCast had a program where employees could personally star in a commercial to push a charity event – maybe they'd allow him to promote his brother's fundraiser. Perhaps he could set up a GoFundMe page. He typed an asterisk next to items that could be completed before the date of surgery was even announced, like T-shirt and program design and getting bids for a DJ and a venue. On paper, it was coming together.

The last detail was the timeline for his little project. His St. Jude's committee had started meeting four months before each year's tournament, but they had to sign up a hundred and forty golfers. Like he told Reggie, he felt he could pull this off in only three months. It would be tight.

He stepped back from the computer, happy to be working on a project that kept his mind off the actual transplant and his own recent accident. A text popped up on his personal cell phone from his boss, Toby. Years ago, the MediaCast managers exchanged their personal phone numbers in case of an emergency. This was the first time his boss had used it.

It read, "Driving through Bloomington in 90 minutes. Up for a beer?"

Lucas hadn't had a beer or a rum and coke in... forever. It sounded tasty. He figured he could get caught up on all the employees and company news in one meeting. Plus, he could brag to Toby how MediaCast had paid his entire medical deductible and the time off he was using to recover would *not* count against any sick or vacation days. It was the company's way of saying, "Please don't sue us."

Even though Toby was a major Bud Lite fan, Lucas suggested a local craft brewery. It was close to the highway, easy access for his boss, and there were outdoor picnic tables to enjoy the nice June breeze. Lucas found himself at the brewery with a delicious pilsner for his boss and an IPA for himself when Toby strolled up. He pointed at Lucas's cast.

"Look at you all beat up. You look like a typical sales manager."

As he sat, Lucas noticed Toby hadn't shaved in a couple days. Toby worked in the Naperville office and Lucas sometimes went several weeks without seeing him. Over the years, Toby gained weight when stressed. Lucas noticed he was packing several more pounds than usual.

"A *typical* sales manager would be sitting here with a *case* of beer, am I right?"

They laughed, chatted about other employees, the remodel planned for the Chicago office, and how fast the company was changing. That segued into the real reason Toby wanted to see him.

"I wanted you to hear it from me. MediaCast is restructuring. The Bloomington accounts will be managed by Peoria, the Springfield accounts managed by Champaign. We put together the largest sales list downstate, lots of auto, and we're going to offer that to you the day you come back. I personally put the list together... it matches your current salary almost to the penny. I felt you deserved a heads up."

Lucas was grateful for Toby's candor, but he wasn't shocked by the news. He had thought of this cost-savings plan himself two years ago. It made good business sense for MediaCast as they faced more and more streaming video competitors. But it was still hard to hear his job was being eliminated and he would no longer be leading his team. He needed to think -- his head was jumbled up.

"Toby, is your role changing?"

"I won't have one. Putting your comp plan together will be my last project at MediaCast. Now, if you'll excuse me, I need to work on my resume."

"That bites! Sorry Toby. I don't think this company deserves you anymore."

Toby nodded. He chugged the last of his beer and stood to leave. He remembered Lucas's transplant.

"Haven't heard about the kidney in a while. You still on board to do that after all... this?"

Lucas nodded. They shook hands, as much friends as co-workers, shrouded in uncertainty. Lucas watched him walk away, taking his vast leadership skillset with him.

The news was highly taxing. For Lucas to step back from management and accept a sales position meant he'd be on the road three or four days a week. Without his favorite boss. He would have to deal almost exclusively with car dealers who faced a huge set of challenges and new competitors, just like MediaCast. He'd have to pour his heart and soul into it with unabandoned passion for at least six months to make it work – the last thing he'd need coming off a kidney donation. Did he have the energy for that? Did he *want* to do that? *Was he still on board to donate?*

He thought of the question he had posed months earlier: How many people backed out of a transplant donation at the last minute? Could this be the reason many did? A tremendous bucket of doubt gets dumped on a person and their thoughts start swirling like a tornado inside their minds? Or, more simply... *life happens?*

He left half a beer on the table, the first time he'd done that since Kim was pregnant. A few years back they switched to her company's health insurance plan so that was not an issue. He drove home to discuss his options with his wife. She was his rock. Together they made better decisions.

He found her at home on the patio drinking her favorite hefeweizen, laughing at videos on her phone. She was beaming. She had discovered a twenty-five-million-dollar error in her company's favor as they drafted a quarterly report – a mistake missed by several folks up the ladder. Her VP had sent a special email to the department praising her efforts. She was giddy.

She kissed him – a level seven kiss. He sat next to her, ready to spoil her predominant mood for the day. This was going to be difficult. As he began to explain his meeting with Toby, his cell phone rang. It was Rah from the Transplant Center. Odd – it was almost 7pm.

"Hello?"

"Lucas, this is Rah. Reggie was here today to have some tests done in our office. He's decided it's time. He'd like to get the transplant on the schedule. I'd like us to pick a date for the surgery and give you the honor of informing him."

"Really?" *What terrible timing.* Lucas thought about his job, his future, the cast on his arm. Maybe he should postpone this conversation for a week or two. He was surprised where his mind went. This suddenly seemed highly inconvenient and worrisome. Maybe he shouldn't donate a kidney at all. He glanced at Kim. No... backing out was not in his nature. He remembered his spreadsheet. He needed three months, minimum.

"OK. How about we look at something a few months out?"

"Um... let me rephrase this. As promised, the surgery is on *your* timetable. We told you this would never be an emergency type of situation, but... how can I say this? Your brother has an especially high tolerance for pain. He may have waited longer than our average patient to make this decision. If you want to keep him from dialysis, his health would be best served if he received a transplant as soon as possible. We have an opening in four weeks."

CHAPTER 33

The Best in People

Lucas and Kim went back and forth for two hotly debated hours on the pros and cons of trying to throw a fundraiser before the surgery. They agreed on only two things: if they did host one, it had to be held on a weekend, and it shouldn't be scheduled one or two days before surgery for fear Reggie or Lucas could catch a cold or the flu, postponing the transplant. That gave Lucas just three weeks. Kim reminded him he'd be in a cast for two of them and that he was still healing. He should be *resting.* Lucas was just about to admit defeat and forego the idea, but he thought about the beaming faces of the St. Jude's kids.

"I think Reggie could greatly benefit from a boost of... a sense of belonging and community."

Kim finally caught on. Lucas thought that the *event* was more important than the *money.*

"All right. I think you're crazy, but... tell me what I can do to help."

He stayed up until 2am choosing graphics and putting together a flyer and T-shirt design. He found a recent photo of Reggie and Lincoln on Facebook and used it to set up a GoFundMe page. In the morning, he learned the Pontiac VFW had space available. Though Saturday would have been his first choice, only Sunday was open. The venue didn't charge for their space for local fundraisers – they were content with revenue from beer sales. Score one for small town living.

The DJ was tricky. All the recommended ones were booked, but he was referred to a guy who did a handful of events a year. He had his own sound system, music, and his humor would match Reggie's kind of crowd. After hearing Lucas's story, he cut his normal fee in half.

The big "aha moment" came from his sister Harper in North Carolina. She had worked on an annual benefit at her church and gave Lucas a stern lesson in fundraising 101. If the event could somehow be tied to a charity, like St. Jude's or a church, there would be a tax-exempt ID number. Donors could then write off contributions on their taxes. Larger businesses would most likely demand a tax ID number to contribute. Within twenty-four hours, St. Mary's church in Pontiac, where Ruth had been active for fifty years, agreed to be the charitable entity. A secretary at the church opened a special checking account for donations. Lucas printed out special information sheets for donor businesses.

Now for the real test. He dressed in one of his best work shirts, collected his flyers, snacks and three bottles of water. He hit the road. Kim had heard from a co-worker that Auto Zone was quite friendly with fundraisers; he would start there. He had learned years ago how *not* to look like a salesperson so he carried only a pen and three folded flyers. He stopped at the auto supply store doorway. Apprehension set in.

For years, his clients had shared with him the charitable demands on local businesses. An owner of the local Subway restaurants claimed he got eight requests *per day* for food, cash donations, or gift cards. St. Jude's was easy – it was nationally known and the event was annual so after nine years on the committee, Lucas's pitch was a reflex. This event, however, was a one-time hit benefitting his family. Asking for money for his brother felt so... self-serving.

What would he say? He forced himself to go in.

The clerk was busy with a customer. A teenager stocked motor oil against the back wall. The manager, a woman with a rough demeanor, instructed another employee how she wanted an air freshener display built. Lucas waited, still feeling greedy. Finally, the manager realized Lucas was standing unattended.

"Can I help you?"

Lucas felt like he did on his first day in sales. He had to take a deep breath but pressed on.

"Hi. I'm Lucas Nichols. In four weeks, I'm going to donate a kidney to my brother."

He handed her a flyer. He was nervous, his voice cracked, and he felt ridiculous with his cast.

"We're throwing a fundraiser to help offset medical expenses for the family. I was hoping your company has it in their budget to support local efforts like this. Could Auto Zone donate a gift card or maybe some merchandise for the event?"

She glanced at the flyer for only a second and looked at him as if he were an angel who needed help getting his wings. "Oh my! Of course! Hold on a minute, I'll put something together for you."

It was the easiest sale in his life.

Having heard his own pitch aloud, he knew he had a compelling story. And with this cast? It added some drama, for sure. He suddenly liked the overbearing accessory on his arm. He thought of the list he compiled before he left -- over a hundred businesses to visit. This was going to work. He felt giddy.

"My aunt needed a kidney."

He turned and saw the teenage stock boy had walked over. He looked sickly and solemn, and when he spoke it looked grueling, as if he were terrified to speak to a stranger. His voice trembled as he spoke.

"She waited five years, but when they finally found a match, it was too late. She died last summer. I just wanted to say it's a great thing you're doing."

Lucas guessed this teen was a textbook introvert. Yet he overcame his fear to unload a very personal story. Lucas was humbled.

"I'm sorry to hear that. Five years sounds like a long time to feel... anxious."

The stock boy nodded and went back to work. Lucas hadn't thought it through before but had he *not* been a genetic match for Reggie, would anyone else have stepped up? Reggie could still be in line with almost a hundred thousand others waiting for a kidney. *Would he have died on the waiting list?*

The manager returned with a big bucket filled with wax, soaps, sponges, and other car cleaning items. Lucas estimated forty dollars in value – not bad for his first stop. He thanked the manager, but the employees were more intent on thanking *him* for his sacrifice.

His next stop was Starpoint Cleaners where he'd taken his work shirts for years. The owner came out from the back to authorize gift certificates. While signing them, he regaled Lucas with hilarious stories on how loopy his father got while on the waiting list for a kidney. He peed in the Wal Mart parking lot to protest the cost of butterscotch candy. He hid in a furniture store at closing time so he could sleep on a $20,000 mattress and tell the world about it. He took out a loan for ten grand so he could buy drinks all night at a local college bar. Lucas's gut hurt from laughing so hard with the owner. In the end, the spunky senior did get a kidney, but his body rejected it and he died three years ago. When Lucas got to the car he looked at the packet -- $200 in free dry cleaning.

The day continued with fundraising triumphs. His car dealers, furniture and jewelry stores, contractors, restaurants, even Illinois State University Athletic Department made contributions. Three weeks wasn't much time so he pushed through lunch. A 60-inch TV. Dozens of gift cards. A Cartier bracelet. Gift baskets of fancy olive oils.

As the day was winding down, he secured a gift card from a music store – one of his longest running clients. Next door was a wine shop about to close for the day. He'd never been in the store but gave it a shot. He told his story and waited while the owner wrote up gift certificates for free wine tastings. An intimidating customer who looked like he might be the ringleader of a criminal biker gang walked up to Lucas.

"I don't mean to eavesdrop, but I love your story, man. Good luck to you and your brother."

He opened his wallet and gave Lucas $90 -- all the cash he had on him. Lucas was stunned and could only muster a "thank you, kind stranger."

What a roller coaster day. Almost every business had given him something of value, or a "come back when the boss is here." But the success was coupled with dozens of sad tales surrounding the lack of available organs. A friend lost a life waiting for an organ, a cousin still desperately waits for one, a sister rejected a kidney and was in her third year on dialysis, waiting for another one. It was heart-wrenching to hear them back to back for the entire day.

Lucas drove home, excited but tired and hungry. He saw the entrance to the Chevy dealership. *Why not?* he thought. *Let's see if the old son-of-a-bitch has a heart after all.*

The marketing director who had repeatedly made Lucas wait over the years and had treated him like dirt actually listened. Intently. After Lucas finished, he asked for the tax ID number, then went to the back of his office, unlocked a drawer and placed something in a business envelope. He gave it to Lucas and politely sent him on his way.

Sitting in his car, Lucas opened it: a certificate for up to $2,000 in parts or service – his highest value donation yet. He scanned the back seat, packed with merchandise. So was the trunk. He would have to drive the Equinox next time for more room. He sifted through a huge pile of gift cards and certificates in the passenger seat. He had barely scratched the surface here in Bloomington; there were still Springfield and Pontiac businesses to approach.

What he had witnessed today was powerful. Overwhelming. The willingness of people to help and the generosity he'd seen at every turn made him numb. For the entire day, he had observed the best in people. *There is just so much good in the world.*

He drove home and Kim helped him unload the car. They set up a fundraising center in their basement to keep track of it all and Kim started logging everything into a spreadsheet to help him stay organized.

She set up a system where he could quickly compile and print *Thank You* notes to each business after the event.

She was on a roll. "OK, I reviewed your finances like you asked me to. I think you're underestimating expenses. You probably won't get *all* the food for free. The decorations estimate should go up, T-shirts should come in at $800 and if you still want a website for the event, it'll cost you. This looks more realistic to me."

She showed him the new number: $4,100. It was still crazy low for all they wanted to do. She had another question.

"Are we fronting the cash on this? I know you had a great first day but I feel strange paying for stuff up front. I really wish we had some guaranteed cash to start with."

That reminded him of the GoFundMe page. He hadn't checked since it went live twenty hours ago. He pulled up the site and saw only one donation so far: Bexley S. $5,000.

The comment she wrote: "Thanks for the dance lessons. Worth every penny!"

He showed it to Kim, who laughed.

"Yeah right. Let's see if you're really worth five grand."

She picked up her phone and played *Wonderful Tonight* by Eric Clapton. She grabbed him carefully so she wouldn't hurt his arm and they swayed slowly like high school sweethearts.

She whispered, "I still think you're crazy."

"Me too," he whispered back. "There's so much, but it's going to come together. It has to. I have this feeling it could be..." He couldn't think of the right word, so he just stopped talking.

For the next four minutes, he was able to put all the concerns of a fundraiser, a surgery, and his career out of his mind. He simply felt the music and danced with his wife.

CHAPTER 34

Doors

Reggie wore a new "Be Hip, Be Edgy! Donate to Reggie!" t-shirt. It was shamrock green and featured a leprechaun dancing with a smiling cartoon kidney. He set his walker to the side and sat down in what he thought must be a 50-year-old wooden chair. He scanned the massive VFW banquet room. The space was dominated with outdated wood paneling, long brown tables, and a dingy tile floor. Flags and pictures of past quartermasters lined the walls and the stage in front was cluttered with broken furniture. One could argue it was dark and depressing, if not for the open bar on the far end.

Reggie saw Lucas positioning tables near the front wearing an identical shamrock green t-shirt. His cast was gone. His left arm was less tan than his right. He waved at Lucas, who ran over to him with urgency.

"It's going to be a long day, Reggie. You need to stay there and save your strength."

Reggie was grateful. His latest test results came in two days ago showing his kidney function had dropped to 12% -- the shocking score made it hard for him to sleep. He braved a smile to hide his fatigue but was happy to have been told to just sit. The star of much publicity, Reggie had felt famous for three weeks running. Lucas had posted the fundraiser notice on Facebook and Twitter, and the news of one brother donating a kidney to another was obviously eye-catching. Over five-hundred people had liked it and over two hundred had *shared* it.

TV commercials ran in the Pontiac area announcing the event, courtesy of MediaCast. Over a hundred flyers hung in local businesses.

This publicity stirred up a constant stream of well-wishers who were unable to attend today to go directly to Reggie's house and drop off gifts and checks in his mailbox. Willow led the way, dropping off $400, twice what he gave her a year ago after she twisted her knee. The flu started ripping through town prompting many to mail their checks to avoid any risk of getting Reggie sick. Reggie had received $4,300 already. The GoFundMe page had raised $26,000. Reggie was thrilled with the numbers, but also conflicted. *Was all this just "pity" money? He needed the cash, but shouldn't he just give it back?*

The side door opened and light flooded in. He watched a crew of forty people – family, friends, co-workers, neighbors, even Lucas's friends haul in six vanloads of gear, merchandise, coolers, and food. Most had pre-purchased the leprechaun t-shirts; they greened up the room. Reggie watched them work diligently like a colony of ants hurrying to prepare the space in only two hours.

Skylar and Jack unloaded and filled coolers. Gavin set up a display of over eighty bottles of wine donated from a collector in Bloomington. Kim and Zoey organized the silent auction sheets and helped set up the registration area. For an hour, Grace, Lincoln and friends hauled in the auction items as more gift baskets arrived.

"Reggie, are you watching this?" Anne asked. "Lucas got ninety silent auction items. Drucker's employees have added at least twenty gift baskets today. And some lady named Molly from MediaCast dropped off five more. I'm excited!"

At times, it was chaos. Tables were set. Then re-set. Then moved back to where they started. Each last-minute gift had to be logged into the computer, a new description sheet and bid page had to be created and printed, and then someone had to find space for it. Reggie watched Lucas field questions as if this were his full-time job. He formulated answers as best he could. To be helpful, Reggie did his best to keep track of where people set down the tape, stapler, folders, even their water bottles – people seemed to be losing track of everything. It was a tough assignment for him. As the guest of honor, anyone who passed Reggie distracted him with questions about his health and the surgery.

The big surprise was that Reggie's sister Ava flew in from Seattle. Using the below-freezing temperatures of the Midwest winters as an excuse to rarely visit Illinois, this was the first time in years she came for anything except the Fourth of July party. She was all business and her computer expertise proved to be vital to the set up. She networked four laptops and a printer to the VFW Wi-Fi. Guests would now be able to pay by check, PayPal, credit card, or cash and would walk away with a receipt. This made checking guests in, tallying their purchases, and checking them out a breeze. Ava said it would prevent an insufferably long line at the close of the event, unlike some poorly run events she had attended on the West Coast.

Lucas admitted to Reggie he had completely overlooked the speed of checkout. They agreed having siblings who had their back was a real blessing. Reggie wished he had those types of computer skills, but... *he just didn't.*

Reggie ended a long conversation with two VFW employees who had begged to hear his story and wish him luck. He looked up. Every table now had a green tablecloth. Signage and posters covered the walls. Green cups, napkins, and balloons peppered the room. Each auction item was displayed neatly with accompanying description and bid sheets. The space had transformed into a festive, happy "Luck of the Irish" party room.

At 1:50pm, Reggie watched Anne and her friends set up "Home Cookin' Corner." Nine crockpots filled with homemade soups, stews and pastas lined the kitchenette area; Anne had run home to grab an extra power cord to handle it all. The crew paraded in thirty homemade cakes, pies, and cookie plates – each one looking yummier than the last. Dairy Queen arrived with donated BBQ and buns for up to two-hundred people and Avanti's matched them with two-hundred sandwiches and chips. Thirty Mario's pizzas would arrive at 6pm just in case the party was worth extending. Lucas had assigned a dozen friends to donate cases of soda or water. All day, the VFW's ice machine cranked out enough ice to keep up with demand.

At 2pm, the work was done. The DJ played dance music and the room's vibe shifted into party mode. Reggie wished there was some way of knowing how many people would show up, if any. Lucas had told Reggie his ideal crowd would be two hundred but thought there would be enough food for four hundred. He priced admission to bring people in -- only fifteen bucks, food and drink included.

In the first ten minutes, when only five people strolled up to be checked in, Reggie felt increasingly nervous. Unloved, even. *Where was everybody?* The presentation was scheduled for 4:30pm. He knew Lucas had a speech and a Power Point planned, and then Reggie would speak. He had practiced, just like he had taught Lincoln, but he wasn't sure he'd remember all of it. *What if there were only a handful of people in the crowd?*

Fifteen minutes later, sixty people were in line. At the one-hour mark, three hundred people shopped through the auction items, danced, ate, laughed, and reminisced. Reggie's head spun with delight as former teachers, co-workers, friends, neighbors, even store owners where he shopped fought for his time and attention. They shared stories, pictures, and laughs. A few handed him envelopes with cards or checks inside.

Two kidney recipients from Wisconsin showed up to support another transplant patient. Reggie thought enough love to last a whole year was jammed into one afternoon. He wished every conversation could have been recorded.

He looked up from chatting to glance at the clock. 5pm already. Lucas must have decided it was OK to delay the presentation, and why not? It was taking a long time for people to get through rows of auction items. Reggie scanned the room for Lucas, caught his eye and tapped his watch. Lucas headed to the stage to alert the DJ. Reggie watched Lucas take the microphone and wait for the current song to end so as not to disappoint the kids on the dance floor.

Skylar and her daughter Hope, who had just turned five, walked up to him.

"Isn't this day just lovely?" Skylar asked. "Great to see you being honored for what you've done, Dad. You've opened so many doors for people."

Reggie was confused by her comment. Before he could say anything, Skylar saw Hope getting into the Pepsi cooler.

"Hope! No Pepsi!" She ran to the cooler to stop her daughter from drinking caffeine.

He watched Skylar lift her daughter high in the air to distract her attention, getting her to giggle. He recalled his conversations with Skylar after her miscarriage years ago. He reasoned, in a way, he did open the door for her to consider trying to have another child. *Is that what she meant?*

The song ended. Lucas quickly got the program rolling, demonstrating his corporate experience speaking to large groups. In less than two minutes, he had calmed the room, welcomed everyone, thanked all the key contributors, and got a round of applause for his 88-year-old mother. He shared a couple anecdotes, one touching and one hysterically funny. He then convinced the audience to sing the refrain as he belted out a festive Irish drinking song. The lyrics jokingly described key points in life when Lucas felt jealous of Reggie. He also projected ridiculous Power Point pictures onto the stage wall making the audience laugh throughout.

Reggie worried about his own speech, making it hard for him to focus on the lyrics and sing with the crowd. He couldn't get Skylar's words out of his head. *You've opened so many doors for people.*

The DJ blasted the rousing opening to *Chelsea Dagger*, which the crowd knew as the Chicago Black Hawks rally cry. Lucas introduced Reggie, the man of the hour. Children jumped up and danced to the fanfare while the crowd gave Reggie a galvanizing standing ovation. Reggie humbly pushed his walker in front of the small stage where Lucas handed him the microphone. The crowd continued clapping and screaming until Lucas cued the DJ to fade out the upbeat tune. The crowd sat down, expectant.

Reggie looked at his enormous audience, a bit panicked on the inside. This was the first time since his solo in eighth-grade, 42 years ago, that he had stood with a microphone in front of a packed room. They were here to support *him*.

You've opened so many doors for people. Had he?

He started his prepared remarks. "I am so humbled to be standing in front of you today. Thank you all for coming to support me and my family."

He saw Ben and Samantha at the front table – looking happy as ever. Was it *his* advice to Ben at the Fourth of July party that kept them from separating when they were on the verge of a breakup? He noticed Gavin, who now lived in a house he loved due to Reggie's help. He saw his sister Ava at the registration table with four laptops. Decades ago, it was Reggie who had noticed her knack for computer languages. He pushed her to study computer science, thinking it best she work toward a career dealing with buttons instead of people. Her career thrived.

"I look out at all of you, and I see so many friends and family members, and also many people I don't even know."

He spotted a table of Drucker's employees. He had trained every one of them. He saw Willow, who had filled a table with family and friends. He saw his brother Scott, remembering the dozens of grueling nights he brought Scott meals and helped him study for his LSATs to get into law school. Mr. Carvell sat in the back -- Reggie had organized the get-together. The more he scanned the crowd, the more people he spotted that he had helped.

It hit Reggie right there in front of this gigantic crowd. He had dismissed Mr. Carvell's book because he couldn't *physically* open doors for people, but now he understood – the book was written for *him*. He was the guy that had forgotten all the doors he had opened for people.

The crowd was waiting, hanging on his next word. His practiced speech was no longer relevant, and he decided not to use it. He improvised from the heart.

"The main thought that ran through my mind when Lucas said he would donate a kidney, was.... Am... I... worth it?"

Having finally said those words aloud, a flood of emotion gushed down on him. He knew the answer to his own question now and it freed him. For his entire childhood up until now, he had been wrong! All those decades he believed that he was damaged because of his feet and legs. That he didn't make a difference. That he couldn't *do* for others. His place had been to let others *do* for him. *How could he have not realized just how much he was giving back all this time?*

He glanced at the auction items and thought of the considerable monetary donations. They were *not* pity gifts. This VFW was packed, but not because people felt sorry for some guy forced to use a walker. It was because of who he was, *how* he was, and for what he had *done for them.*

He looked at Anne who had shed a tear after his last words. She was beautiful. She had loved him through his self-doubt and lack of confidence. He got choked up and for a moment couldn't speak.

He glanced at Lucas. The effort he must have put forth to make this a success. He saw his mother and wished he could call out to her right then and there that he finally understood what she had so often tried to teach him -- that he had value.

He repeated, "Am I... worth it?"

The room was silent. Even the children listened intently. A tear streamed down Reggie's face, but with a renewed confidence, he fought right through it.

"Just by being here today, you have helped me answer that question. Lucas is giving me the gift of life, but he reminded me, it's not *my* kidney, it's his, and he wants me to take care of it for him. All Lucas wants in return is for me to live a good life. In front of all of you, I promise to do my best to honor his request."

He looked at Anne. "Because I have so much to live for."

He wiped his tear away. "Thanks again for being here for my family. It means the world to us."

He handed the microphone back to Lucas, who hugged him. The crowd applauded.

The DJ fired up the music and people scrambled to the dance floor.

CHAPTER 35

Where's Yer Fundraiser?

Lucas was spent. He slouched in his chair staring at the long tablecloth covered in crumbs and a small puddle of Sprite. The DJ had left two hours ago but Grace brought in a Bose speaker and blared her favorite playlist to keep the party going. The fundraiser was finally winding down at 9pm.

Lucas observed the table by the bar where Reggie chatted with a former co-worker. Her family had driven five hours from Louisville to support him. Reggie was laughing, sharing stories, more in his element than Lucas had ever seen him. Kim hustled over to his table right as the bartender, who looked like she had been to war and back, strolled up with a bottle of Modelo and set it in front of Lucas. Her nametag read *Jin*.

"Hey hon. We git 'bout twenty fundraisers a year here. Nuttin' like this though. You deserve one on the house."

She winked at him and headed back to the bar. Kim picked up the beer.

"What am I, chopped liver?"

She took a sip, then slid it over to the man who was responsible for the whole shebang.

"You want the total?" She was dying to tell him. Her corporate financial instincts were to celebrate the numbers. Over the last hour, she helped tally the receipts so she could be the first to see the results. Lucas kept his eye on Reggie. He looked *immensely* happy.

"Doesn't really matter," he said. "Sure."

"All in, websites, one-offs, plus today, we're at sixty-eight thousand, net."

Lucas chuckled. That was much higher than he thought possible and proved he didn't know diddly about how to forecast revenue for a fundraiser. His brother could now go into surgery relaxed about costs. He watched Reggie laughing boisterously. All this effort was well worth it. Lucas yawned.

Kim continued. "You know why you're so tired, right? You can run a marathon in four hours but today's marathon lasted nine. All this, after you've already been running for three weeks."

She grinned hoping for a laugh, but he was too fatigued.

Instead he said, "I'm not going to take the sales job. I think I want to use my energy for something else."

He expected a lengthy discussion and immediately regretted saying it at this moment. She liked structure. She was comfortable knowing exactly what was going to happen. Schedules and spreadsheets defined her world and uncertainty was a demon. She grabbed a random pencil from the next table and wrote "$68,000" on a used napkin. She showed it to him as if to say, *You can do anything.*

"I'm not worried," was all she said.

She left to help with the cleanup. Lucas watched two dozen family members clean tables, retrieve decorations, and pack up supplies, signage, and computers. Ten leftover pizzas were given to workers who wanted them. Twelve auction items remained, won by people who left the event before the bidding closed. Lucas would have to take four to Bloomington to deliver them in person.

Lucas sipped his beer and turned his eyes back to his brother. His beaming smile was infectious. He was now laughing it up with his former co-worker Harry Schott while Anne hinted it was time to get Reggie home. Harry finally said good-bye and Anne whisked him away before any more conversations could get started.

Reggie, Anne, and Lincoln strolled over to say goodnight. Lucas chuckled at the sight. All they were carrying out were Anne's crockpot and power cord. He felt like offering $68,000 for both.

Lincoln spoke first. "Uncle Lucas, this party was really fun. Thanks for all your work and for saving my Dad's life."

Anne added, "I'm sorry we ran out of desserts. We could have raised more if we had brought..."

"Wait. Stop," Lucas said. "We did *really* well. What a team effort. Kim and Ava will have a final number for you tomorrow."

Reggie said a million thanks with just one long look. Lucas thought Reggie stood taller. More confident.

Lucas broke the silence, "One week, Reggie. See you at the hospital."

Reggie felt strong, even after this strenuous day. He thought about the required last-minute blood tests before surgery. The momentum was crazy high after this party. *What could possibly go wrong at this point?*

Anne replied, "Don't get sick. How awful if someone caught the flu and delayed surgery, right?"

They hugged Lucas and headed for the exit. The bartender noticed when Lucas finished his Modelo and returned.

"Hey hon, another brewski?"

He shook his head. She took his empty bottle but she had to get something off her chest.

"You know, I been watchin' y'all. Yer the one givin' up a kidney. Where's yer fundraiser?"

Lucas studied her. She was confused why his brother wasn't the one throwing a fundraiser for him. He thought about explaining how Reggie's insurance paid for both surgeries and that his only expense was fuel to Peoria, but he had a better answer. He looked at her nametag.

"Jin, I will donate a kidney, my recovery will be painful and I won't get a dime for my troubles. But I am getting more out of this than you could possibly imagine."

She read him and could tell he meant every word – a learned talent of good bartenders. She nodded as if they suddenly shared a secret.

Kim drove Lucas home. They discussed the success of the fundraiser, focusing on the numbers and revenue streams. They reviewed the good decisions they had made and where they might have handled things better. Lucas decided not to talk about the change he had seen in his brother. Lucas hoped it would be permanent but there was no way to know.

They agreed to empty the Equinox in the morning and went straight to bed. For the first time since his eighth-grade bout with pneumonia, Lucas slept for twelve hours.

CHAPTER 36

Comedy Hour

Reggie felt the precautions were outlandish, even comedic, but he was on board with all suggestions to keep him safe for the last-minute drive to Peoria. Anne insisted they leave the house a full hour earlier than necessary, just in case. Lincoln didn't think a seatbelt alone was satisfactory so Reggie wrapped himself in a sleeping bag and wore a helmet for extra protection. Two vehicles escorted the Enclave across route 116 and two more trailed it – his own personal motorcade for additional safety. There was no traffic at 4:30am but Reggie had to admit the convoy gave him extra peace of mind. He felt important.

Reggie had HR start his short-term disability status at work the day after the fundraiser. He had been home all week completely focused on avoiding illness or injury. It was nerve-racking. Germs were the new enemy so Anne disinfected half the surfaces in the house daily. He washed his hands almost every hour and even hid in the basement when a plumber came to fix a kitchen pipe. Reggie would not be the reason for a delayed surgery so he went nowhere. He would stay healthy at all costs, though the fanatical effort was making him an anxious mess. The pressure was greater knowing family members were travelling from out-of-state to show support. How disconcerting if they paid to travel only to have the surgery cancelled.

Reggie arrived in Peoria with sixteen friends and family members, impressing the employees at the registration desk. The crew settled in for a long day with books, puzzles and games. Lucas and Kim arrived from Bloomington – Riley, Mason, Aspen and Carter were on the way. After being admitted and getting ID tags on their wrists, Reggie was whisked away to get a battery of tests. Lucas was sent upstairs to check into the surgery center.

Within an hour, Reggie lay on a hospital gurney wearing a gown. He told himself to stay confident. All would go well today. But thoughts of what *could* go wrong still popped into his head. Anne walked behind him as the nurse pushed his gurney toward the pre-op room. Reggie knew Lucas and Kim would already be in pre-op. He had often thought about what he was going to say to his brother just before surgery. He had planned a serious, heart-felt story and would follow it up with a sincere thank you.

They entered the pre-op room and the nurse positioned his bed on the other side of a curtain from Lucas, who was joking with every medical professional in the room. Reggie instantly knew he wouldn't get a chance to get sentimental – Lucas had turned this moment into a comedy hour.

"Lucas, would you like some Tylenol?"

"No thanks – that's obviously a gateway drug. That's how they get ya."

"Lucas, who's your doctor?"

"Zhivago? No, wait, Doolittle? Oh, sorry, it's Dr. Who."

"Lucas, you understand this surgery will be done laparoscopically?"

"Yes, and while you're in there, could you do a little lipo on my love handles. Thanks... that'd be great!"

Kim stood in the corner shaking her head, a little embarrassed that the jokes might be inappropriate, but the medical staff laughed consistently throughout. She knew it was Lucas's way of letting her know he was doing OK and she figured it would also help Reggie and Anne relax.

Reggie wanted to join the fun. He heard a nurse ask Lucas to state his name and report who was with him today.

"My name is Lucas Nichols. I am here with my wife, Kim."

Later, they asked Reggie the same question.

"My name is Reggie Nichols. I am here with Lucas's wife, Kim."

Anne slapped him playfully and the nurses cracked up.

The jokes were easing Reggie's tension considerably. He was asked dozens of questions as Lucas answered the same queries on the other side of the curtain.

In total, Reggie met four nurses. He got an IV started. An anesthesiologist stopped in -- more questions. Dr. Sahill entered and confirmed what was going to happen today. He reminded Reggie that Lucas's surgery might take longer than usual because Lucas's kidney had an extra renal artery, common to about twenty-five percent of transplants. Dr. Singh would have to remove Lucas's kidney and operate on it before it could be transplanted. *An extra artery -- another thing that could go wrong.* Reggie pushed that thought away - *Everything was going to be fine!*

Before Reggie was ready for it, they were wheeling his brother out for surgery. Lucas joked, "Don't say I never gave ya nuthin." Reggie laughed, and followed it with the only rehearsed words he could squeeze in, "Thanks for the kidney. Love you."

The next three hours were grueling. All Reggie and Anne could do was wait. Scared of the worst-case scenario and reminded of her mother's recent passing, Anne cried intermittently. To help distract her, Reggie told her to get on her phone and update family and friends. After a minute, she laughed and read aloud Lucas's last post:

Just checked into the all-inclusive OSF 5-star resort overlooking stunning waterway.

Isle de Peoria. 3 days, 2 nights of pampering and constant attention.

Concierge services, free parking, stellar medical staff, and an afternoon nap planned.

All this can be yours FREE - contact your local Organ Donation hospital to sign up!

There were already ninety-two comments on it.

A nurse eventually entered and announced that Lucas's surgery was almost complete. Reggie held his wife's hand as they rolled his gurney down the hall to the double doors. Anne kissed his cheek.

"You'll do great. I love you."

"Love you too."

They pushed him down a long hallway into the sterile operating room. He saw massive trays filled with chrome utensils, computer monitors, lights, and lots of strange looking equipment. There were six people decked out in masks and blue scrubs busy at their individual prepping task. They came together to move Reggie off the gurney onto the operating table. Two nurses started draping his body with cloth and sticking all kinds of things on his chest. Dr. Sahill gave orders to move this and that – he had specific demands on his preferred setup and would not start until they were met.

This was suddenly scary. His heartbeat quickened. Reggie remembered the doctors had informed him that later tonight they would expect them both to walk a few steps to help prevent blood clots. Lucas had promised he would walk to Reggie's room.

He took one more glance around the room at the equipment and the team of people working to extend his life -- to *save* him. What massive costs, efforts, and planning that had gone into this day! He thought fondly of the sacrifice of his younger brother.

As the anesthesiologist lowered the silicone mask and Reggie breathed in the sleep-inducing gas, four significant words resounded in his mind.

I am worth it.

CHAPTER 37

Like Brad Pitt

Lucas opened his eyes. In his vision was a blank white wall with a clock that read 2:15. He had expected to wake up in a recovery room around 1pm. Did something happen? How was his brother doing? He was so tired he could barely keep his eyes open. He remembered a joke he had prepared. He was going to ask, "Hey, do I look like Brad Pitt?" When the nurse said "no," he was going to say, "Then wheel me back in there, let's do it right this time." But no nurse came forward. He drifted back to sleep.

Lucas woke again. He saw a blank white wall and a clock. He was nauseated. His abdomen felt like someone ripped it open with a knife. Then he remembered, *oh... someone did.*

Lucas woke again. He noticed the white wall and a clock: 2:45. He wondered if he had been awake prior to this. He remembered a joke he wanted to tell. Telling a joke would let the nurses know he was all right. On cue, a nurse came into view and peered down at him.

"Hey, do I look like Brad Pitt?" He could tell she was more annoyed than amused. She continued to stare. He was drifting back to sleep. His eyes were so heavy – he couldn't stop it. He wouldn't get to say the next line. Just before he fell asleep, he heard a nurse behind him yell.

"Why the *hell* does this guy keep asking if he looks like Brad Pitt?!!"

She would never get to hear the punchline.

The next time Lucas woke, he was in a different room. He could hear his family talking. Kim, Riley, Mason, Aspen, and Carter were crammed into the small space. He heard them debating from which restaurant they should order sandwiches.

"I want Jimmy Johns," Lucas offered. Everyone turned to look.

Kim sidled up to him, happy he was awake. She took his hand. "Hold on there, Slugger. No food for you for a while. How you feeling?"

"Like shit. How's Reggie?"

"Amazing," Kim said.

She shared a happy glance with the rest of the room. Lucas managed to lift his hand and wave hello, happy to see loved ones around him.

"Dr. Sahill said they could see the kidney working before they sewed him back up. They're calling it a Super Kidney. It's pumping out urine and toxins like the Alaskan Pipeline. Reggie should be able to tell the difference right away."

Lucas felt an overwhelming wave of relief. It may have been the drugs, but he shed a tear and fell back asleep.

He opened his eyes again, remembering how annoying the heart rate monitor alarm was after his appendectomy. From running twenty miles a week, his heart rate was too low for the usual setting. The beeping had awakened him every fifteen minutes until the nurses finally made an adjustment.

He asked the room, "Did they lower the heart rate monitor setting? My heart rate is sooooo loooow..."

He saw all five of them look at each other and laugh. It was the third time he had asked and he sounded drunk each time.

The next time he woke, he was in a regular hospital room. It was 8:30pm. Kim had given her blessing for the children to go home because there was nothing more they could do and they had long drives ahead. Lucas remembered that Reggie was doing well and the transplant had worked. He wanted to see his brother. He had promised to walk to his room.

"Can I go see Reggie?"

Kim could tell by his voice he was more lucid than before. She flagged a couple nurses to help him make the trip. When Lucas sat up, he felt too nauseated to stand. He slumped back down, frustrated by his body's betrayal. Kim asked the nurses if any anti-nausea meds were available.

"Yes, we'll get him something. He needs to walk if at all possible."

An hour later, he tried again. He fought through the discomfort and was able to stand. Despite being pumped with pain killers, the four-inch incision in his abdomen triggered relentless pain. He fought the urge to cry out. He thought he might vomit but it wasn't as bad as it had been an hour ago, so he pressed onward. Strategically, Reggie's room was right around the corner. One nurse held him stable while the second nurse pushed the rolling IV stand. Kim could barely watch. He was gray, shaky, and he walked hunched over as if he had aged forty years.

He shuffled into Reggie's room. Propped up in bed, Reggie looked just as gray and shaky as Lucas. They stared at each other with foggy minds. Reggie finally thought of something to say and in his best angry Dustin Hoffman voice...

"Hey, you're walkin' here!"

Lucas laughed. "Barely."

Reggie smiled. "Thanks for the kidney."

"You're welcome. I think I should get back," Lucas said. "Love you bro. I'm out."

He waved and trudged back to his room with his entourage.

The next day was wonderfully enchanting. Visits from family and friends. Rock-star treatment by the nursing staff. Hundreds of social media posts of encouragement and congratulations. More humorous Lucas/Reggie interactions. The only downside for both of them was trying to figure out how to get off the hospital bed without the abdomen feeling as though it were splitting open.

Lucas was astonished that he was released just forty-four hours after surgery. Reggie was expected to be released the next day.

*   *   *

Lucas spent his first day at home on the reclining couch. The pain killers were still in his system so while at rest, he was comfortable. Relaxing with his butt in one place, he hugged the couch pillow and the remote control as if they were family heirlooms. He read the hundreds of social media posts from well-wishers as he anxiously waited for Reggie and Anne's hourly updates. The kidney was working perfectly, and Reggie was getting stronger.

Lucas planned to sleep on the couch until getting in and out of bed would be tolerable. At bedtime Kim placed next to him water, tissues, snacks, his phone, even a broomstick to help Lucas lift himself off the couch in the middle of the night. She put Bali and Fiji to bed in their crate and was just about to walk upstairs when her phone rang. It was Anne, probably with another update and a "thank you so much for everything!" Hopefully, she would confirm that Reggie would get to go home tomorrow.

"Hey Anne," she said. "How's my husband's kidney doing?" Kim put the phone on speaker so Lucas could join in the fun.

Anne spoke in her nurse's voice. She had learned to use it when delivering unwanted news. It was slow and methodical so the news could not be misinterpreted.

"Thirty minutes ago, Reggie suffered a massive heart attack. He went into shock. That's all they told me. Lincoln will drive me to Peoria. Kim, stay there and take care of Lucas. I'll update you when I can."

She hung up.

Lucas and Kim both gasped. Awful! Unexpected! How could this happen?!

Kim trembled with her own diagnosis. "What if... what if that was a widowmaker?"

CHAPTER 38

Vertical Talus

Reggie felt so good about the transplant and his recovery that he sent his family home for a good night's sleep. His post on Facebook read, "Headed home in the morning! New kidney working great! If you ever get angry and tell me to piss off, I will now be able to!" Attached was a video of a dog humorously dancing up and down on one leg as it peed on a statue of a cat. Though he knew it was tacky, the visuals made Reggie laugh. He tagged his brother Lucas. There must be five hundred friends following their transplant story and he couldn't wait to read the replies.

He re-watched the video and chuckled, but his chest started to hurt. Suddenly, he couldn't catch his breath. After several seconds, he felt nauseated and his heart pounded. The chest pain kept getting stronger. Something was terribly wrong. The pain radiated into his arms, legs, back, even his jaw. Half his body felt numb while the other half felt on fire. He reached for the call button to alert a nurse but all he could do was scream into the speaker. He grabbed his chest. Two nurses finally ran in -- thank goodness the transplant patients had rooms closest to the nurse's station!

A moment later, Reggie heard the head nurse shouting orders. Doctors were paged. His IV was changed. Reggie wiped his hands on the blanket; they were sweaty, yet his feet and hands were cold. *Was he having a heart attack? Would he see his wife and children, his brothers and sisters, or his mother ever again?*

He watched the nurses work frantically. He was slipping. A year ago he would have been ready to accept the worst. But not today. He would refuse to die. He closed his eyes and told himself that no matter what was happening he would fight like hell. Lucas had given him a kidney and asked for only one thing in return – *for Reggie to <u>live</u> a good life.*

He felt his body being wheeled out of the room. Someone tried to explain where they were taking him but all sounds were muddled. Before losing consciousness he gritted his teeth and told the universe, *"Bring it on!"*

*   *   *

Why had she agreed to go home for the night?

After three straight days in the hospital, Anne had allowed her husband to talk her into getting a good night's sleep at home. It felt refreshing to take a hot shower and cook a meal for Lincoln and Zoey. After sharing scoops of ice cream with Anne's legendary butterscotch topping for dessert, she got the devastating call from OSF. Anne frantically made a few quick calls and texts to key family members, then hit the road.

Anne was proud of Lincoln for driving so carefully to Peoria yet she still felt numb as he eased the SUV into a parking spot in the OSF parking garage. Her husband had experienced a major cardiac event and lost consciousness, but that's all she knew. She was petrified of what she might learn in the next few minutes. Might his heart be damaged forever with scar tissue? Would he be left with an irregular heartbeat? This could lead to eventual heart failure. She dared to think it... would they tell her he was dead? She thought of Lucas's car accident. How unlucky the family had been lately.

Zoey sat silent in the back seat. The whole trip she had been scared to say anything. Lincoln had been quiet too, but anger got the best of him as he put the gear shift in park.

"I don't see how something like this can happen! How could they do surgery if he was at risk for a heart attack? Didn't they know this could happen?"

Zoey jumped in. "You said they did a stress test."

Anne felt awful. She remembered patients from her nursing days who showed symptoms of lung cancer, who *had* lung cancer, but the chest X-ray showed a clean bill of health. She had seen patients whose tests showed normal thyroid antibody levels but they had thyroid cancer anyway. A forty-year-old Mormon woman who desperately wanted to love a child of her own finally got a positive result on a pregnancy test from her doctor. Later, Anne had to personally inform her that it was a false positive. Anne knew medical tests were just that – tests. Not proof. Sometimes, the results were unexplainably wrong.

Anne was candid. "Reggie did take a stress test. A *chemical* stress test because he can't run on a treadmill. It showed nothing to be alarmed about." She wished she had someone to blame but in her heart, she knew she didn't.

"We can't blame the doctors on this one."

They rushed to the nephrology wing only to learn Reggie had been moved to the cardiac ward. Frustrated, they found the correct waiting room. Within minutes, Rah walked in at a brisk pace. She made it clear that Reggie was stable for now and ushered Anne to a consult room. Anne stopped mid-step and broke down crying. Rah waited. After they finished the walk and sat down, Dr. Sahill entered and began the complicated discussion.

"I'd like you to consider the long list of procedures we have for a transplant patient recovery. Now, over here, imagine there is another list of rules for a patient after a cardiac event. Your husband experienced both only three days apart so we have to throw out everything and collaborate on a new plan."

Then Rah explained, "For example, Reggie is on a strict regimen of anti-rejection medications which, as you know, he needs to take at exactly 9am and 9pm. These meds will weaken his immune system so he'll be more susceptible to infections. Any surgery to repair an arterial blockage is riskier than normal and must be scheduled around the needs of the new kidney."

Dr. Sahill ran his fingers through his thick dark hair, agitated that Rah had taken over the conversation. Anne could tell Rah was comfortable jumping in and probably did so often. Back in the day, Anne had done the same thing when doctors were overly clinical, slow, or not expressing enough empathy for their patients. Dr. Sahill took back control.

"Another challenge. Red dye is normally inserted into the bloodstream to track where the blockage to the heart might be in a cardiac event but red dye can be damaging to kidneys, especially one transplanted this week. In a few moments, the transplant team will meet with Dr. Conway in Cardiac to formulate our plan going forward. This medical scenario is rare, of course, but please note we are prepared for it."

As they left the consult room, Rah put her hand on Anne's shoulder to comfort her.

"You know, it's extremely fortunate Reggie was in the hospital surrounded by medical professionals when he went into shock from cardiac arrest. If he had been at home..." She looked at Anne's ongoing desperation and decided not to finish her thought. She gave her a warm smile and walked out.

In just ten hours, Anne thought, ten quick hours, Reggie would have been at home on his recliner. She closed her eyes. She pictured herself coming out of her kitchen to hand Reggie a plate of fresh fruit and finding him keeled over from a heart attack. She was supposed to be bringing her husband home but instead was ramping up for another surgery. She looked around the consult room, angry at every leather chair and flowery wall hanging. She wasn't sure how much more of this she could take. *How close had she come to being a widow?*

She found Lincoln and Zoey in the waiting room tapping on their phones. Lincoln looked up.

"Mom... look at this." He handed her his phone.

Hundreds of posts. Prayers and comments had come in fast and furious to wish Reggie the best. Dozens of texts showed a parade of visitors on their way: Gavin, Grace and her boyfriend, Skylar and Jack, Ben and Samantha -- all driving over. Reggie's brother Scott was coming down from Chicago and would drive Ruth to the hospital. Drucker's employees. Former classmates. Even a few fundraiser attendees they didn't know well.

It felt like double the response from the kidney surgery. Anne updated Lucas and Kim first, then helped to clarify some questions that were posed on Facebook. It helped take her mind off the uncertainty for now.

Time flew by with the social media distractions and the arrival of family and friends. After a few more hours, Anne was ushered back into the consult room. She met Dr. Conway who appeared young for a cardiac surgeon. Anne figured out she had worked with his father years ago which made trusting him a little easier. The team suspected Reggie had a blockage and would use the bare minimum red dye to confirm. They would most likely insert a stent into his blocked artery by going through his leg. For various reasons, none of this could happen for two days.

Dr. Conway left. As Rah walked out, her final comment was, "Your family has been so lucky through all of this."

Lucky? Who in their right mind would call them *lucky?* Then Anne thought of the fundraiser and the financial cushion it gave them. The way the family bonded together to help. She thought of the fortuitous timing of Reggie's heart attack. That Lucas survived an SUV rollover accident. That he ended up being not just a blood type match, but a six-antigen match. Perhaps they *had* been lucky. Or blessed. Maybe things would be OK.

She looked around the room and took a deep breath, feeling less agitated. For the first time in years, she reasoned that maybe hospitals weren't so bad after all. Everything was going to be all right.

*　　　*　　　*

The night nurse injected a steroid into Reggie's chest making it feel as if a three-hundred-pound man were standing on Reggie's sternum. She asked Reggie to rate his pain on a scale of one to ten. Reggie started at eight but quickly yelled "Eleven, Twelve, Fifteen!" Nurses tried all their tricks to make him comfortable.

"Is the pain going up your arm?"

Reggie had heard nurses ask this constantly. He answered "Yes!" each time. After a harrowing night in which he experienced three more heart attacks, he stabilized and the pain finally got under control. He was taking it one hour at a time. He focused on the fundraiser and what a glorious day that had been. He learned that he had value. That, and his promise to his brother, were keeping him going.

For the next two days leading up to his stent surgery, as if by magic, his life turned into a remarkable series of uplifting moments. Jolted by the news of his massive heart attack, many of his family and friends pictured their lives without Reggie. The event would unleash fears and feelings unfairly buried for years.

Anne was in the room when it started. Ben opened up like never before.

"I can't imagine what a gut punch that must have been -- getting lied to by my Mom. For eight years. She knew I wasn't your son, but she... But you didn't leave. You were always there. I had Christmas because of you. I have Samantha because of you. I know how fuckin' lucky I am that you were lookin' out for a punk like me. I just want to... thank you and make you proud."

Ben's older sister Skylar was next. She presented the book *50 American Heroes Every Kid Should Meet*. Hope listened in awe while Reggie, who relished reading to his granddaughter, related the stories of Ben Franklin, Frederick Douglass and John Glenn. Then Skylar made up her own biography about her stepdad:

"He never speaks bad about people. He listens. His jokes will make you laugh, even his dorky ones. If you ever need anything he will help as best he can." She picked up Hope to let her daughter see Reggie up close. She shared a thought she had never spoken before.

"And if it weren't for this loving man, I would not have been strong enough to be a Mom."

His two oldest, Gavin and Grace, were next. They had brought a dozen pictures taken the day after Reggie and Anne's wedding. The entire family had laughed for hours as they foolishly tried to install the harvest gold Honeymoon fridge by themselves. It took hours to get the ice dispenser to work.

Gavin summed up their feelings: "We were just kids. From the very beginning, you were the one who would get down on the floor to play with us."

His sister Ava surprised him the most. Upon reading the heart attack news, she flew in immediately from Seattle. In her mind, the gift of a kidney was so magnanimous it convinced her the family was no longer one to be avoided. In her visit with Reggie she unloaded the turmoil she had kept buried for decades. Her three brothers had always been so close – all three still lived in Illinois. Her one sister, Harper was so much older and had moved to the east coast right out of college and never buddied up to her. She had always felt like the family outcast. Reggie reminded her she ostracized herself. As a child, she would rarely play with them and was inexplicably spiteful. As an adult, she had never once invited any family members to Seattle. Ava admitted her part in the lifelong estrangement. She promised to lighten up on the family -- to be a real sister going forward. It was Reggie's first-ever heart-to-heart talk with her. He thanked her again for her work on the fundraiser.

Reggie got no one-on-one time with his mother, Ruth. She was only in his hospital room when others were present. On her way out, Reggie called to her. "Mom, if for any reason this stent surgery doesn't go as planned, you better make a big fuss over me. I'm worth it." The other visitors sat silent, feeling this a bit morbid to be sharing with his mother but Ruth smiled at the secret coded message. She walked out with a renewed happiness for her son.

Reggie was astounded. This open dialogue continued for two straight days. He felt like one of the most fortunate men on earth. He believed he was hearing feelings, thoughts, and deep emotional revelations that were usually only spoken at funerals.

The morning of the stent surgery, Reggie was sleeping when the sound of Lincoln's walker hitting the door jamb woke him. Reggie was surprised to see him alone. Usually Anne or Zoey hovered nearby.

"Hey Dad. You asleep? OK if I visit?"

"Have a seat."

Lincoln sat on his walker just inside the door. Reggie hit the button that would lift the bed to a sitting position. He noticed Lincoln was in a serious mood so he stopped himself from making a joke.

"You really scared me Dad."

"I'm sorry. I guess I scared a lot of people."

"I don't know what I'd do if you were gone. Who else in this family could ever know what I go through each day? What it's like... to be me?"

Reggie nodded. He knew this was a real moment. He could tell Lincoln had something more, something important he needed to say.

"Sometimes I think that you feel guilty that I have vertical talus. That it pains you to watch me move. And that you somehow gave it to me -- blame yourself for it. I don't want you to feel bad about it. Yes, I'd rather be able-bodied, but... you should know, I would rather be like you than someone with two good legs who couldn't measure up to you."

These words filled Reggie with so much pride he wanted to burst. He realized he was wrong *again*. He didn't *just* have value. In Lincoln's eyes, no one could ever do for him what Reggie could do. He was indispensable. *Irreplaceable!*

He thought about the conversations over the past two days. They had built up his self-esteem into a brick fortress and Lincoln had just sealed it -- made it impenetrable. Reggie now knew what his mother had always been talking about, his *genuine* value. He wished he could jump off the bed, run to Lincoln and hug him.

Lincoln was on the same page. He stood up and pushed his walker aside. Using every ounce of grit and strength he could muster, he inched across the floor toward Reggie with no support at all. He held his arms out to the sides to help with his balance, struggling to stay upright. He felt pain with each small step. His right foot slid more than stepped. He refused to fall as he crossed the short room.

He leaned over the bed and embraced his father.

CHAPTER 39

How Much More Drama

Lucas and Kim inched slowly down the sidewalk. Lucas wore an old, loose-fitting t-shirt, shorts, and flip flops. To reduce incision pain, he pressed a kidney-bean shaped pillow, a gift from the transplant center, against his abdomen. At rest, Lucas felt fine. Walking was getting easier. Getting in and out of bed or a chair was still wicked painful. He hoped to make it all the way to the fire hydrant today.

The fatigue was unlike anything he'd ever lived through. His body gobbled up massive quantities of calories just to heal itself. He still fell asleep a few times a day – twice so far in the middle of a conversation. He was sticking to the prescribed diet -- limited sugars and lots of water, but most of the time he had little energy. So frustrating for a man used to moving about constantly.

He made it to the fire hydrant. Kim, wearing a stylish pant suit, celebrated by jumping up and down and announcing, "He makes it all the way to the corner! The crowd goes wild! Ladies and gentlemen, I present the first ever trophy for the *I-can-walk-a- full-block* challenge!" She raised her arms and danced circles around him in triumph.

He smiled. Her exaggerated enthusiasm was helpful and he appreciated her coming home at lunchtime to check on him. She had gone back to work after a full week of caring for him non-stop. He felt like a three-year-old. He turned around and baby-stepped his way back toward the house.

"Oh my, check it out!"

Kim showed a picture on her phone of Reggie and Anne finally leaving the hospital -- posted an hour ago. They appeared thrilled. She laughed. "Poor Reggie. He ate hospital food for *eleven days.*"

Lucas glanced at the photo. "And somehow hasn't mutated."

They both reflected on the final leg of Reggie's hospital stay. The stent surgery had gone perfectly and to everyone's relief Dr. Conway reported no signs of heart damage. Reggie could now live his life with a renewed, full blast of oxygen getting to his heart and a new kidney filtering out toxins. He was a new man on the inside. The family could finally celebrate.

Lucas and Kim reached their driveway as Reggie and Anne unexpectedly drove up, obviously taking the long way home. Reggie got out slowly. He was dealing with the agony of his own incisions but still moved better than he did a year ago.

"Hey little brother! Got a minute?"

Bali and Fiji welcomed Reggie by licking his toes. Kim had to get back to work. Anne grabbed water bottles out of the fridge to serve the recovering patients on the patio. She pretended she needed to go to the store giving Lucas and Reggie a chance to recap their roller-coaster journey. Reggie asked her to bring out a pair of scissors and Lucas's wallet before she left.

Lucas shook his head in disbelief that Reggie was here sitting on his patio when he certainly should be home resting. He figured Reggie had a solid reason for stopping by. They discussed the list of over-the-counter medicines the doctors told them to avoid for the rest of their lives and what the hell Lucas was going to do with his life now that he was leaving MediaCast.

Reggie took the Blood Donor card out of his wallet and picked up the scissors.

"I don't think blood donation is really *our thing* anymore. We're a bit beyond that, don't you think?"

Reggie sliced up his original card. Lucas could still read, "Issued: 1979" on one of the pieces. Lucas took the scissors and chopped up his own card.

Reggie started a somewhat prepared speech. "Thank you for giving me a kidney. You're going to hear me say it a gazillion times in person, emails, texts, and who knows, maybe I'll sky-write it someday. As long as I'm alive you need to know that every time I say thank you for the kidney, what I really mean is thank you for saving my life three times."

Lucas sat back in his chair and sipped his water, trying to figure out Reggie's math.

"First, you stepped up and sacrificed a kidney for me which saved me from a life on dialysis. I will live healthier and longer because of that – no question. I will take great care of it. And because you stepped up, I was in the hospital when I had a widowmaker -- a ninety-eight percent blockage! There's just no way I survive without medical care thirty feet away. So, you saved my life a second time."

Lucas wanted to contend this was a coincidence and it was truly the skill of the nurses and surgeons who saved him, but he felt it best to just listen.

"And best of all – I got to rekindle all my family relationships. We said things that had never been shared before. I was living in a dark place and didn't even know it. My bonds are stronger – even with Ava, can you believe it? Lincoln and I – we're closer than ever. This whole experience has changed how I see the world and myself in it. So, you saved my life a third time by making it meaningful."

"You're welcome," Lucas said.

Lucas raised his bottle of water. "Here's to family." They toasted.

Reggie expressed concern, "The sad thing is after all that work on the fundraiser and the surgery, you don't get anything for it."

Lucas remembered a line from the very first kidney website he had researched: *There is no benefit to being a kidney donor.* He was sure it was wrong when he first read it and he proved it was incorrect over the past year. He took a long sip, making sure his words came out exactly as he meant them.

"But I did." He paused for only a second. "I got two thousand dollars in free medical testing. I learned I had high blood pressure and how to get it under control. You saved *my* life right back."

Reggie scooped the donor card pieces into a pile. He hadn't thought of that side of Lucas's experience. Hearing it out loud, he sat up taller, prouder.

Lucas continued. "Most importantly, for the rest of my life I get to walk around this earth having heard my brother say *thank you for saving my life*. How priceless is that? No one can ever take that away from me."

He challenged his brother, "Now, I'd really like you to look me in the eye and try to convince me that *I didn't get anything for it*."

Reggie couldn't. He felt something on his arm. A small fly. He brushed it away. It reminded him -- he hadn't felt itchy at all since the surgery.

"That really helps," Reggie said. "Thank you. One question. Some people look into donating an organ but change their mind. Did you ever think about backing out?"

"A little. But you were in trouble." He thought of Molly. "You don't hesitate, you just help."

He paused for a long moment.

"And Reggie, I haven't been outspoken about this but I'm appalled at the numbers. We've got a hundred thousand people in this country who need a kidney *today*. Three hundred million of us, but only seven thousand a year become living donors. Really? I believe society is better than that. The problem is nobody knows how it really works, what a donor goes through. Recovery is a bit rough, but donating is not *that* hard. It's only one month out of a person's life to save another life."

Reggie could see his brother was bothered by the numbers, especially since Reggie was now part of the statistics.

"So -- you believe if more people could understand how rewarding it is, that it's safer than ever and not really that demanding, more people would actually donate?"

Lucas nodded. Reggie knew his brother was the kind of guy that would let this trouble him. Maybe for years. Reggie had an idea that might help.

"Maybe you could do something about it. Have you noticed that when Lucas Nichols tells a story or picks up the microphone, people tune in. You're good with words. You say too many of 'em, but you're good with 'em."

Lucas laughed. And nodded in agreement.

"Maybe you should write a book. You could walk people through the whole transplant process and try to keep 'em entertained the whole time. You should tell our story -- how much more drama would you need?"

They both chuckled. Reggie watched Lucas stare at the plants in his backyard for a long moment. His wheels were spinning, contemplating the idea. *Had he just opened another door for someone?*

Anne was back. She appeared around the corner and announced it was time to get Reggie home. They walked together to the driveway. Anne lifted Reggie's walker into the back of the Enclave while Reggie painfully climbed into the passenger seat. Grateful for his sacrifice, Anne hugged Lucas.

"You are a wonderful brother. Thank you for everything."

Staring at his phone, Reggie slammed his hand against the SUV door and exclaimed, "Oh... my... word! Look at this!"

Lucas baby-stepped to the SUV window and read a text on Reggie's phone. It was from Harry Schott: "Very moved by you and your brother's story. I'm in. Decided to become a kidney donor. I'll keep you in the loop."

Reggie and Lucas wanted to high five but each knew it would be too painful. Their story had inspired another donor! They smiled at each other, ecstatic.

As Anne backed out of the driveway Reggie leaned out his window.

"Hey, this transplant business was a hoot! Let's do it again next year!"

Lucas laughed. If Reggie was making jokes, he must truly be OK.

Lucas gingerly entered the house. The recliner looked welcoming but he elected to move into his office instead. He was officially still a MediaCast employee and wanted to keep up - maybe help his team where possible before his last official day. He opened his work laptop and saw there were 841 unopened emails. Exhausting. He deleted only a few but felt tired. He should probably rest. He closed his laptop wondering where his next job opportunity might take him.

He thought about Harry Schott. Imagine that! His brother's co-worker was so inspired by their story he was going to donate a kidney. Amazing.

He opened a new document on his home computer and typed two words. Only two words. He stared at them. These words were a commitment he wasn't confident he could fulfill. But maybe they could save lives. He thought about deleting them. Something compelled him not to – maybe because the words were inspired by his brother. He read them again:

Chapter One.

He thought of his brother's brave journey, the goodness he had witnessed, and he started typing.

Resources

Please consider saving a life through the
generous gift of organ donation.

It just might save your life at the same time.

National Kidney Foundation
30 East 33rd Street
New York, NY 10016
(800) 622-9010
www.kidney.org

Donate Life America
701 East Byrd Street
Richmond, VA 23219
(804) 377-3580
www.DonateLife.net

UNOS

United Network for Organ Sharing
700 N 4th St
Richmond, VA 23219
(800) 292-9548
www.UNOS.org

PARENTING 101... By Trial and Error!

"Fantastic! A whimsical account with hilarious life lessons."

"From diapers to discipline, a rare look at the family dynamic!"

"The most unusual collection of family anecdotes."

"A great read for new Mom's everywhere!"

Find Us at MojoTen.com

Made in the USA
Monee, IL
28 February 2021